AF490499

# THINGS ARE AS THEY SHOULD BE

## And Other Words To Die For

P.M. Raymond

UNCOMFORTABLY DARK HORROR

Copyright © 2025 by P.M. Raymond

ISBN 9798893990225

All rights reserved. No part of this publication may be reproduced, distributed, or transmitted in any form or by any means, including photocopying, recording, or other electronic or mechanical methods, without the prior written permission of the publisher, except as permitted by U.S. copyright law. For permission requests, contact editor@uncomfortablydark.com.

The story, all names, characters, and incidents portrayed in this production are fictitious. No identification with actual persons (living or deceased), places, buildings, and products is intended or should be inferred.

Book Cover Design and wrap by Christy Aldridge of Grim Poppy Design

First edition 2025

Edited & formatted by 360 Editing, a division of Uncomfortably Dark Horror.

Editors: Candace Nola & Mort Stone

Published by Uncomfortably Dark Horror, owned and operated by Candace Nola. Pittsburgh, PA

Follow us on all social media, our Patreon, or on our website to stay up to date on new releases, appearances, and more!

Committed to *"bringing you the best in horror, one uncomfortably dark page at a time."*

Patreon www.patreon.com/c/u12231330

Website www.uncomfortablydark.com

# Advisory Warnings

Violent scenarios
Sexual harassment
Instances of sexual coercion
Stalking
Animal endangerment
Mental health issues
Child endangerment and death-
(alluded to but not explicitly described on the page)

# Publication and Award History

"The Entitled Life and Untimely Death of King Booker" appeared in Dark Yonder, Issue 1

"Adventures in Babysitting" appeared in The Furious Gazelle and was a 2025 Horror2Comic Quarterfinalist

"The John Hughes Guide to High School Girl Transformations" appeared in Pyre Magazine

"Cinderella at Midnight" appeared in Malice, Matrimony, and Murder anthology

"Rent Party" appeared in Punk Noir

"Gotcha" appeared in Kings River Life Magazine

"Backward and Forwards" appeared in Flash Fiction Magazine

"A Nasty Business" was the 2024 Sisters in Crime Eleanor Taylor Bland Award Winner

"Don't Drink the Water" was a 2025 Killer Shorts Screenplay Competition Semifinalist

"Things Are as They Should Be" (short story) was a 2025 Horror2Comic Semifinalist and 2024 Killer Shorts Screenplay Competition Finalist

THINGS ARE AS THEY SHOULD BE *and other words to die for* (collection) was a 2024 Claymore Finalist

# Early Praise

*"P.M. Raymond is a bright new star in the world of speculative fiction. Not to be missed."* — S.A. Cosby, author of BLACKTOP WASTELAND

*"Creepy, atmospheric, and jam-packed with un-ease, P.M. Raymond has expertly crafted worlds that made me uncomfortable in all the best ways. She had a fresh and unique voice that sings through characters and settings. These stories will haunt me for a very long time."* — Steph Nelson, author of MAKE NO MISTAKE

*"THINGS ARE AS THEY SHOULD BE…is an incisive collection of Southern Gothic stories where inheritance and power often lead to violence. P.M. Raymond blends folklore, social horror and*

*the supernatural, while exploring vengeance and the brutal cost of maintaining order. Justice is rare. Innocence does not always survive, and monsters rarely hide. Sharp and precise."* — Cynthia Pelayo, Bram Stoker Award-winning author of CHILDREN OF CHICAGO

*"The imaginative stories in P.M. Raymond's THINGS ARE AS THEY SHOULD BE And Other Words to Die For slip between Southern Gothic, thriller noir, and atmospheric horror with ease, bending reality till the familiar turns treacherous. Inside these pages lurk meddling ghosts, monstrous humans, and even a Santa gone wicked. Together, these tales guide the reader through a landscape of the strange, the cursed, and the beautifully unsettling."* — Andrew K. Clark, author of WHERE DARK THINGS GROW and WHERE DARK THINGS RISE

*"With nineteen deeply imagined and unsettling tales that showcase immense range and mastery of the genre, P.M. Raymond's THINGS ARE AS THEY SHOULD BE... transports readers to an otherworldly New Orleans, where the thump of Blues and Dirty South Crunk music and the aroma of a bushel of fresh peas are rendered in tandem with demons, spells, curses, and monsters to create a sudden and unforgiving sense of terror. The gothic setting, gorgeous prose, and unforgettable characters make this a powerful must-read collection."*

— Tamika Thompson, author of THE CURSE OF
HESTER GARDENS

# Contents

# Dedication

For all the women of a certain age who look like me.
It's never too late to dream.

"There is something at work in my soul which I do not understand." ~Mary Shelley

# 1

# Society

"I SHOULD'VE DONE THINGS differently," Emily mumbled.

She knelt next to the libation altar, her corset digging deep into her narrow hips. "Crazy coot and her liturgies." Aunt Melinda had constructed the prayer shrine following the tragedy three months ago, but Emily treated it like clutter more than anything else.

Emily crossed her arms and slowly turned to the bowl in the corner. "How do I get that insufferable woman to bend?"

She fingered the bowl's rim, its contents of earth from the backyard garden smudged on the tip of her gloved fingers. She tilted the bowl slightly, the pebbly dry soil rushing to the rim, then released it.

"What's done is what's done."

Emily dusted her hands and retreated to her bed.

She slipped off her gloves and unfastened the series of buttons on her right sleeve as she settled into the mattress. She massaged the arm littered with screaming grapefruit-colored welts and hardened dark bumps then repeated the same on the other arm. Anxious anticipation tingled through her body as she caressed the fresh rashes, the sensation heightened from denying her nails access to the crusted layer of scabs lined like mole holes waiting to be uncovered.

Emily rubbed with increased vigor. Her head flopped back, curls unfurling from the unkempt bun, bouncing down her slim mocha neck. Her fingertips grazed over her arm like skipping stones. Emily was unable to control the sensation building in her core, in her stomach, and between her legs. She gave in, releasing a tremor between her thighs as she picked and scratched at the welts.

As the escalation subsided, Emily finally opened her eyes and stared at her bloody fingertips. It had been weeks since she considered this urge alarming. She had been able to keep the flaky, dry crevices and rouge fissures hidden under cotton crinolines and satin flowing skirts. She even hid the weeping sores forming on her inner thighs by entering and exiting the bath without her housemaid's assistance.

Emily wiped her hands with a handkerchief that she stuffed into her sleeve and slipped a fresh pair of cotton lounging gloves on, tucking the old ones under her mattress to burn later.

COMFORT ENTERED THE ROOM with a bright smile, her one-sided conversation in manic flow. "Mr. Theroux's chickens are producing mighty fine eggs these days." She nodded as if she agreed with her own statement. "Yes ma'am! And what a peculiar gift of a black chicken."

The plainness of her cotton grey day dress offset her healthy chocolate brown skin. Her animated gestures punctuated the conversation.

Emily assessed the naïve country girl and wondered if this maid was more trouble than she was worth. And if Aunt Melinda had hired this skinny little thing only to vex her.

Emily stewed at her aunt's slow pace in securing a suitable partner. With the unexpected death of her mother and father, a marriage shored up her future in more ways than one. *Les gens de couleur libres* may have been born free people, but the government employed a slippery sleight of hand to unravel colored folks' rights, especially the ones reserved for inheritance. This situation could only be squared with a ring. From Mr. Theroux.

Comfort drizzled more words in rapid succession. "Has your aunt secured a visit with Mr. Theroux yet? Your aunt says he is quite a catch from a good family that goes way back." Her heavy skirts grazed the floor as she made her way to the one window in Emily's room. Comfort threw back the closed shutters to let a breeze carry a bit of the Louisiana humidity in.

"And she says—" Comfort turned from the window and stared at the formal sterling silver tray at the end of the bed. With a quizzical raise of her brow, she interrupted herself. "Why haven't you touched your breakfast, Miss Emily? Was it not to your likin'?"

Umber-colored tea, serene as a lake, filled the cup. The intact coddled egg laid by Mr. Theroux's unusual chicken nestled in its ramekin.

Emily adjusted her white-gloved hands in her lap, hiding the pink stains seeping through the no longer pristine fabric. She cocked her head. "I'm not feeling very peckish at the moment. That's all."

Comfort offered a straight-edged smile to her mistress and the blotches upon her face. "As you wish, ma'am." Comfort glanced back at the open door. "It's not my place to ask…" The maid's gaze pierced and grabbed Emily's attention, "but about your condition—"

The sound from Aunt Melinda's cane pounded the floor with a force that tittered the teacup in its saucer. Emily and Comfort halted.

Aunt Melinda's tone was as crisp and cool as winter's frost. "Comfort, take the tray and leave Miss Emily to her thoughts. *Tout suite.*"

Comfort's lightheartedness dimmed slightly under Aunt Melinda's terse remarks. The young maid nodded with deference to each woman and collected the tray, taking care not to touch any other surfaces before offering a stilted curtsy as she left the room.

AUNT MELINDA PACED WITH crossed arms as she chaperoned the examination.

Dr. Albertson's lean fingers shifted Emily's chin in a side-to-side motion like a piece of summertime fruit from the farmer's market. Emily held her posture firm and proper, her back rigid against the vanity. She fixated on the crimson swirls of the velvet Baroque wallpaper lining her room as the doctor poked and prodded.

"Oh, dear, things have progressed since my last visit," he murmured at the fiery polka dots peppering Emily's caramel-colored cheeks. "Should have called on me as soon as you saw the creams weren't behaving as expected."

Emily smoothed the bodice of her bone corset, entombed in its prim ivy-pattern fabric. Her breath whispered out in a lingering exhale. "Aunt Melinda claimed her home remedies would be sufficient."

"They have been for generations, child," Aunt Melinda interjected.

Dr. Albertson eyed the elder woman with a patronizing *tsk-tsk* before responding, "I know your kind rely on roots and whatnot," he motioned to the humble altar assembled in the corner to his left, "but medicine is the civilized remedy this pretty girl needs."

Emily averted her eyes as the doctor invaded her personal space. Her disquietude lay not with the overly ruddy complexion that hid her fine skin or the good doctor's musky breath on her cheeks. But with the herniated dollop over her right brow.

The doctor rummaged and pulled the magnifying glass from his case with a flourish and studied the bulbous hematoma. The doctor's eye appeared distorted in the glass. Emily wondered what distortions met his gaze on the other side.

"I hear there is a Mr. Theroux in your sights?" He sniffed as he leaned in. "I hear he comes well recommended."

Emily couldn't contain her irritation at the presumptuous nature of his prying comment. "Never you mind, Dr. Albertson, what may or may not be happening in my garden." Her caustic tone caught the doctor by surprise.

"Now look here—"

A squawk from Mr. Theroux's chicken floated from the courtyard, cutting through the acrid tones rising in the room like an alligator's snout surfacing from a placid swamp.

Aunt Melinda rescued the conversation. "Mr. Theroux is suitable enough, isn't that so, Emily?"

"Well, given I have never been graced with his presence," she fumed, "I can't rightly know."

Aunt Melinda studied the doctor's scowl. The scowl of a man who only tolerated the *gens de couleur libre* as long as they settled their debts and didn't get too big for their britches.

Tension blanketed the room as thoroughly as the whole cloth quilt covering the bed.

"I trust your temperament will improve as your flawless beauty returns. That is if you are still amenable to my assistance." Dr. Albertson's tone indicated he could giveth of that assistance or taketh it away and teach her a lesson.

Aunt Melinda glared at Emily. Her eyes delivered the message loud and clear. *Tread with utmost care. Your money won't shield you from burning crosses on the front lawn in the middle of the night.*

"Yes, doctor. Beauty that I hope to recapture with your knowledge and expertise," Emily said stiffly, shifting her eyes away. She rubbed her arms, hoping he didn't demand that she roll up her sleeves.

Dr. Albertson nodded at Emily as he carefully tucked the instrument back into his bag. He turned to Aunt Melinda and, with the tilt of his head, wordlessly ushered her out of the room.

Emily sat quietly, patting her face to placate the tingling and tamp down the urge to scratch it raw.

Dr. Albertson and Aunt Melinda returned to deliver a hollow diagnosis packaged as unknowable but treatable.

The doctor pulled a jar from his medical satchel. "Apply this twice daily. I've doubled the curative ingredients in this batch. Should clear up the redness." He pointed at the lump over Emily's eye. "That may be a bite of some sort. Check your bed for spiders before you retire for the night." Before Aunt Melinda escorted Dr. Albertson out the room, he added, "Take some fresh air. That is always helpful."

Emily gently caressed the bump over her eye.

Aunt Melinda watched as the pout on her niece's lips crinkled into a grin.

"Certainly, Dr. Albertson," Emily said, a calculated gleam in her eye. "Aunt Melinda," her voice so sugary sweet even the doctor turned from his notetaking to observe, "Perhaps Mr. Theroux can stop by tomorrow afternoon for some cool sweet tea?"

Aunt Melinda responded with a tight-lipped, "Perhaps," and chafed at the judgmental smirk on Dr. Albertson's face at observing the complex inner workings of the esteemed Brownstone clan. "Perhaps, my dear. I'll send a calling card around this afternoon for a supervised chat tomorrow."

Aunt Melinda remained calm. Now with God and Dr. Albertson as witnesses, she would need to accelerate her plans. She smiled and waved her arm to allow Dr. Albertson to pass.

And with that, the door shut behind them.

THE AIR CIRCULATED IN a whistle and a whine through the open shutters that faced one another on opposite sides of the master suite. On the day of her brother and sister-in-law's funeral, Aunt Melinda had claimed the larger room with the efficient and luxurious feature.

Aunt Melinda slipped her soft-soled shoes from her feet. She leveraged her weight on her cane and knelt at the window next to her vanity. An earthen bowl filled with moist soil sat next to a cut crystal glass and matching pitcher. She blessed herself the Catholic way and began her morning prayers.

Water from the pitcher lapped into the crystal and mixed with the cornmeal in the bottom of the glass. She poured a portion of the murky liquid over the soil with her right hand, offering words of manifestation to the ancestors. She transferred the glass to her left hand and directed prayers to Emily's departed parents for their continued guidance and revelations.

Aunt Melinda rested the half-empty crystal next to the bowl.

"That'll do just fine," she said as she rose to her feet. She settled into the chair at her vanity and tugged the thick braid rope next to it.

Within minutes, Comfort appeared at her door.

Aunt Melinda placed a clear jar packed with a creamy white substance in Comfort's open hand. The maid lifted it to her line of vision like a crown jewel.

"You know what to do," Aunt Melinda said.

"Yes, of course." Comfort curtseyed and scurried, jar in hand, from the room, leaving Aunt Melinda fanning herself at the table.

The maid wandered down the hallway toward her other mistress's chamber.

EMILY HAD NOT TAKEN a respite on the second-floor gallery balcony in days. Not since the rash had blossomed into a full-blown crisis.

But the day following Dr. Albertson's inconclusive diagnosis, Emily did as he suggested. She worried that her absence from the public eye could cause polite society's tongues to wag.

The ornate iron railings surrounding the space accommodated the full crinolines of her skirts and the full institutional gaze of the New Orleans passersby.

The large white sun hat adorned with pink and purple fabric flowers rested in an easy fashion on Emily's head. Its brim leaned enough to cover the swollen knob that had not shrunk from the application of creams and serums offered from the competing cabinets of Dr. Albertson and Aunt Melinda the day before.

Aunt Melinda made her way down the length of the gallery. Without Mr. Theroux.

"Where is *Monsieur* Theroux?" Emily hissed.

Aunt Melinda handed her a small card with bold ink writing scribbled upon it. "I'm afraid he was indisposed today, and anyway," she sighed, "it simply isn't the right time."

"This stalling will not do!"

"It's not stalling. It's preparing you for the right moment."

Emily struck a rigid, long-necked pose, her nose upturned in seething displeasure. She observed her aunt exchange pleasant waves with the other women on Prentiss Street. Emily bristled like a porcupine inside.

Comfort entered the gallery and fussed about, refreshing the sweet tea as rapidly as the women drank it. She offered Emily a refilled glass and said, "Don't worry, Miss Emily, and don't fret about Mr. Theroux. I'm sure it will all work out the way it's supposed to. You'll see."

Emily shot Comfort a look hotter than kettle water.

A leery smile came over Comfort's lips. "Perhaps you can soothe yourself during your morning prayers."

A tight *pfft* exited Emily's lips. "I don't make fanciful wishes over a bowl of cornmeal mush."

"Wake up, girl."

Aunt Melinda stood between the bed and the open window. Comfort positioned herself at the footboard. Both craned their heads and lanterns at the sight before them.

Emily shielded her eyes from the glow that interrupted the nighttime in her room. "What is the meaning—" The gravelly words tangled in Emily's throat.

Bedding swirled around Emily's legs as she kicked, sheets billowing over the wrought iron footboard.

Emily let out a wail as she fell to the floor onto her stomach.

Aunt Melinda shooed Comfort to the right side of the bed, but the maid did not move.

Comfort held the lantern in front of her, sweeping the room with its glow. Searching. She sensed the shadow that hugged the planked floor, its bulk barely registering against the darkness of the room. But she detected it just the same. The wild sight drew her two cautious steps forward.

The starburst of cracks and fissures that Emily had kept at bay on her inner thighs, wrapped in soft cotton and salve, had now networked hard, open caverns all over. The soft fabric of her nightshirt fell away to reveal a chest as dry and barren as a thirsty desert. Only her nipples remained supple. She moved her stiff, splayed fingers over her chest to her face.

Dull screams and cloudy moonlight poured through Emily's room. A lament to a nightmare wrapped in a body that had betrayed her.

Her legs were scaled, the skin as jagged as branches on a dying oak tree. She crawled towards the vanity.

Aunt Melinda and Comfort followed.

Emily grabbed the side of the table and attempted to pull herself to her feet. Her efforts left her flailing as she tumbled over the vanity chair, hitting the floor with a thunk, her back arched like a church woman possessed.

"Get the bowl," Aunt Melinda commanded Comfort.

The incapacitated Emily stretched out spiny fingernails, hooked like scythes, as Comfort ran past.

"What is happening?" escaped from Emily's lips, warbled, and grated like hard stones.

Comfort crept into the dark corner, her skirt's stiff cotton hem shifting like nails on a washboard on the floor. "Hmm." She lifted the ceremonial bowl like the cradle of life in Aunt Melinda's direction, all the while keeping Emily, or whatever she was now, in her line of sight.

Aunt Melinda balanced on her cane. "Let's see what's what." She gestured to Comfort to come closer as she pointed her cane in Emily's direction. "That root woman you called must have worked."

The maid cautiously leveraged the bowl and her lantern. The flame danced like marionette shadows on the wall, illuminating the unthinkable, yet the older woman was neither startled nor scared by the fervent figure before her.

Emily wept softly.

"Save your crocodile tears." Aunt Melinda chuckled. "You didn't have many to shed when you," tears of her own caught in her throat, "—when you decided your dear parents weren't hurrying your matrimony along." The old woman exhaled as if she had held this accusation in her mouth, in her chest, in her soul for too long. "You think I didn't know?"

AUNT MELINDA WINCED AT her own naivete, her easy acceptance of the tragedy of Emily's parents expiring so suddenly. At her own affliction that robbed her of even footing shortly after.

Ideas percolated in Aunt Melinda following the reading of the will and her niece's anger. The disposition of the estate was contingent on the young woman's marriage. Until then, Aunt Melinda would be the executor. She chalked up her niece's behavior to ignorance of the state of things but mostly to Emily's naturally self-centered worldview.

It was Dr. Albertson who casually, or perhaps not so casually, gave voice to more sinister theories over the course of innocuous parlor talk.

*Aggressive mimicry,* he called it.

In the animal kingdom, one being could hide in plain sight as protection from another. Or lie in wait disguised as a friend but secretly inhabiting the trappings of a foe.

The good doctor implied arsenic can aggressively mimic cholera just as easily as a cool breeze off the bayou. The implication was never uttered in polite conversation again, but Aunt Melinda didn't need to hear the foul words repeated to know. Like a flame to a pile of kindling, Dr. Albertson's scandalous words burned through her.

Now it was Emily's turn to feel the heat.

"IT'S A LIE, YOU old hag!" Emily — or the thing that called itself Emily — rasped as she sunk into the recesses between the bed and the vanity. The thick, calloused landscape of cracks and scales grazed against the metal bedpost, the jagged edge slicing along a fissure on her thigh. Blood dripped and spread in a dark mess on her buckled feet.

Comfort shook her head as the flickering light caught a glimpse of her mistress's face. The lump over Emily's right brow was joined by a matching one over the left. Her beady eyes shifted from one fixed point to another. The only semblance of Emily was her lovely mane of brown ringlet curls.

Aunt Melinda leaned closer to the bowl. Her fingers pinched and dug in the dry, crumbly soil. Comfort's hand trembled from suspending it in the air for so long.

"There it is," Aunt Melinda crooned, soiled fingers grasping the dirt's bounty. "The root woman delivered on her promise."

"Yes, promise," Comfort repeated. Then with a quiver, said, "She delivered on that black chicken too."

As Aunt Melinda fished another item from the soil, she turned toward Comfort with a triumphant smile. "Just as you said, child."

Aunt Melinda held in her left hand the two black eggs she mined from the dirt. "See Emily? The dirt can bury all kinds of secrets." She threw the delicate orbs onto the floor. The membranes splintered with moist cracks.

"You should know, *cher*, that Mr. Theroux is never coming for your hand. Not after..."

A faint chatter swelled, like dough rising, in the room. *OHHHH*, or some variation of which neither Aunt Melinda nor Comfort could ever fully explain, flooded their ears.

A blood-red yolk squirmed through the broken exterior, and a faint pinprick as blue as the light from a firefly in the garden followed.

"The truth of your sin shone on the outside of you," she spat. "The acrid dirt, absent of your libations, held your parents until all was uncovered."

The girl, who was a beauty but now a beast, moaned.

Eyes wide, Comfort blurted out in the octave of a high-strung child bursting with wonder, "I ain't never seen a *fifolet* before!"

"That's what you and those Cajuns call them." Aunt Melinda's voice deepened with sorrow as she said to Comfort, "I call them Maxwell and Lucille."

Comfort immediately crossed herself and sighed, "Emily's ma and pa."

The twinkle glided round and round Emily's head as she tried to swipe it away. The lights floated through the shutters and into the moonlit night.

"There they go," a reverent Comfort replied wistfully.

"Home," Aunt Melinda responded.

Comfort stared in rapture at the bewitching events that had unfolded.

Aunt Melinda pounded her cane to bring the maid back to the matter at hand. She wagged her stick at her niece. The creature in the corner bore down with a hiss, and that same stick bopped it on the head. The creature retreated.

"We still have work to do here," Aunt Melinda mumbled. The work of waxing and massaging the changes that are about to come.

Comfort nodded her head as she surveyed the yolky goop on the floor. "The devil and the righteous sure do use eggs every which way."

WINTER HAD COME AND gone. A new springtime social season was dawning, and Aunt Melinda anticipated a full calendar of visiting and oversight of the Brownstone social schedule and financial ventures. After all, everyone would be keen to rally around an elder whose dear niece was sent overseas for an indefinite period under doctor's orders.

The good Dr. Albertson's discretion was purchased through a gift and a threat that certain afflictions can come on as suddenly as cholera. He no longer visited Aunt Melinda for innocuous conversations in her parlor.

The furniture in Emily's room had been covered and left abandoned, a time capsule of the life she used to live.

The creature had been relocated to the attic. Cages with a variety of rats and a selection of edible plants lined the space. Comfort continued to tend to her mistress's needs and occasionally sang *What a Friend We Have in Jesus* with the gusto of a believer.

Talon scratches grazed the floor and mingled with throaty groans above. Aunt Melinda hoped those groans would be mixed with tears.

***END***

## 2

# The Entitled Life and Untimely Death of King Booker

King Booker came for what was his.

The door to Sunnyside Lounge swung open, separating the specks of dust floating in the gray air. King, a lean shadow of a man, glided through. An elderly patron sat on a stool at the end of the bar nursing a whiskey, ice cubes fading into the brown juice. King knew him as a regular. "Hey now, Mr. Caruthers. How you doing?"

"Mama Said" was churning from the jukebox. King didn't picture Mr. Caruthers as The Shirelles type.

"I'm fine as gumbo on rice, young man." Mr. Caruthers shook his glass as he raised it to meet the level of his bespectacled eyes. "Fine, indeed."

15

King extended a respectful hand to his elder. "Good to hear." He glanced at the bartender, a dingy, once-white towel in his hands, buffing a highball glass. The nod from the man gave King his cue to continue through the hallway to the right.

Muffled voices became clearer as he approached. King reached the end of the hall, the door half open. He stepped in where the conversation was in full flow.

"Naw, man, don't tell me Russy can't get you on at the shipyards." Calvin gave his a's a long drawl when the mood struck him, so shipyard sounded like ship-yaaards. "Just ask him. He'll do right by you." Bixby let an annoyed glare connect with Calvin.

Bixby, a young man not old enough to drink at Sunnyside's, but old enough to go to jail for the less-than-legitimate activities that took place behind closed doors, continued counting one-dollar bills. "You don't know what you talkin' about. Russy looks out for Russy."

King made his way to the side of the card table both men used to divide the stacks of currency from the previous night's take. Sunnyside did a brisk business in liquor and an even brisker business in cards and dice. This was one of King's last pick-ups of the morning to collect that weekend's earnings.

"Hey, fella," King coaxed Bixby. "You are mostly a grown man. Need a grown job. Better think about the future. For you and that honey of yours." King and Calvin laughed as Bixby became increasingly uncomfortable.

"Don't you bring Eda Mae into this!" he snapped, but he swiftly changed his demeanor. King was an important man in certain parts of New Orleans. Bixby had seen firsthand how a smart mouth could end poorly for a man who dared to get on King's bad side. "Besides, I might have more than Eda Mae on my dance card. What you know about it?"

King palmed Bixby's short afroed head like a basketball. "Be careful, young man," he said, his banter casually aggressive. "I might mistake you for a wannabe who thinks he's got game." King's eyes focused on Bixby. "Watch your tone with me, son."

"Boy, you stepped right in that one. Say your apologies for disrespecting Mr. Booker," Calvin commanded with a grunt.

"I didn't mean any disrespect." Bixby's cheeks glowed with embarrassment and fury.

"I didn't mean any disrespect, Mr. Booker," King said and punctuated the "B." Bixby, cloaked in humiliation, repeated the apology. More laughter from Calvin followed, and the discussion transitioned to King's business.

"You got my package, Calvin?" King waited, left hand in the pocket of his suit trousers, right hand flipping his car keys. A black rabbit's foot charm dangled on the end of the ring. He leaned against boxes of Cutty Sark piled against the wall as high as his six-foot-four frame, careful not to stain the cardboard with his coal black hair greased with pomade. Calvin rubber-banded the stacks of cash on the table and stuffed the wads into a Winn-Dixie brown paper grocery bag.

Motioning King to the other side of the room, Calvin asked in a hushed voice, "We ready? Good to go, brother man?"

"Yeah." King inched closer. Six months' of planning would come down to tonight. "Now, the old woman got a key on her. Like a skeleton kind. Make sure to get that off her. The room upstairs at the end of the hall on the left. That's the one to go to." King gestured to his ear. He could see Bixby craning his neck like a peacock, trying to catch a few words on the wind.

"Get them empty Crown Royal boxes out to the traaash, Bixby," Calvin yelled in the stock boy's general direction without taking his eyes from King.

"Yes, sir!"

The conversation between the adults continued. "Ooh, wee!" Calvin whispered. "Folks be sayin' your mother-in-law got Fort Knox in her house. You think it's in that room?" With a look of disbelief, he added, "Boy, if that old girl had that kinda dough under her roof, why you never seen it?"

King shrugged. "She been skulking in and out that room as long as I been living there. Always locking the door. If she ain't got nothin in there, then I'm Chuck Berry doin' the duck walk."

Calvin pulled a pack of menthol Kools from his shirt pocket, searched, and found a brass Zippo lighter in his pants pocket. "Also heard Miss Dorothea leans a little too much into the mystical, if you know what I mean. Maaaybe that's why Big Man Horace took a bite off his Smith & Wesson. Or maybe he had some help with a hex from Miss D." Calvin's veiled accusation about King's mother-in-law had made the rounds in their social circles, dying down for a while but, much like a buried casket in St. Louis Cemetery No. 1, popped up from time to time.

King rolled his eyes. Spirit-mindedness was nothing new in this city. He didn't see it as a conversation worth having, but he gave a knowing chuckle anyway. "Time to wrap things up," he concluded, voice stern and weighty. "Tomorrow, a new day will dawn. A new king in town."

With a pep in his well-heeled step, King left Sunnyside and strolled back to his car, a sly smile on his lips. King rolled the paper bag and stuffed it under the passenger seat. Sometimes, he daydreamed of skimming some bills off the top but never worked up the nerve. He sensed that Miss Dorothea would know.

Ducking in and out of betting dens from Uptown to the 9th Ward, King gathered the illicit earnings made possible by the city's uncanny ability to normalize vice. All for the comfort and care of Miss Dorothea.

King snaked his way home. A warm breeze blew through the Crescent City, the ding, ding, ding, of the streetcar coasting down Carrollton Avenue in the air. He took advantage of this late summer rarity, pulling down the soft top of his pale blue 1965 Lincoln Continental and letting the smells of the Mississippi swirl through. King was careful to stick to the Black folks' part of town lest he raise unwanted attention from those who didn't take too kindly to young men like him driving a fine motor vehicle like this.

King's plan to take full control of Miss Dorothea's gambling empire was simple, but it had blind spots. By the time the sun rose in the morning, he would find out what those were.

"AT LEAST YOU DID something right." Miss Dorothea did not mince words. Especially words reserved for King Booker. King breathed, measured in his response. "Them fools know not to short me, Miss Dorothea." The idea that he had to reassure his mother-in-law that the weekly pickups were correct was one more indignity he would not miss. *Soon enough,* floated into his mind.

Miss Dorothea sipped her tea from the fine china cup she used most mornings. Elegant brown skin, legs crossed at the ankles, posture straight like the nuns at St. Aloysius taught her. She sat in her favorite Queen Anne armchair, swaying gently to the sounds of Irma Thomas radiating from the transistor radio. Her aubergine-toned suit jacket hugged the thickness of her waist. Her flared skirt danced close to the tips of her satin heels. In the sitting room filled with chintz, silk, and the finer things in life, Miss Dorothea held court.

During the early days of King and Flora's courtship, he got a narrow lens into the inner workings of the fiefdom. Big Man Horace, now Dead Man Horace, had been committed to the earth two years by the time King made his advances. He aimed to take over as man of the house. He didn't account for Miss Dorothea. But he should have.

Infamous mob boss Carlos Marcello made the usual moves to take the keys to the kingdom after Horace passed on. Then, a closed-door conversation occurred. No one knew the specifics, but it was clear that Miss Dorothea would have no problems moving forward. The community took note.

On those lazy Sunday afternoons during the pretense of romance, King feigned an upstanding reputation, and Flora pretended to not know the truth. King was a small-time hood and full-time ladies' man, but this didn't stop Flora from making her presence known to King. She wanted a husband; he wanted easy street. A match made in transactional heaven.

Flora attempted to advance King fully into the business by offering him as a replacement for Russy on the collection detail. Russy had just gotten on at the shipyard and discovered an untapped potential for five-fingering shipments that could be resold for a profit.

But King never rose above errand boy even after the cake was cut and the rice was thrown. Miss Dorothea preferred to handle the "important" matters herself. Being sidelined nurtured an ill temper in King and fueled an iceberg of anger in him, just like his mother's neglect had done.

His formative years were spent watching the shadows of his mother and her nightly guests beyond the cotton sheet that carved out a space in the single room just for him. She would dance and do other erotic temptations with these men, and sometimes women, that he didn't understand. He would huddle with his hands over his ears and try not to hear. Occasionally, those guests would lay hands on him. Other times, the grumble of hunger in his small belly would go ignored for days. Voicing his needs for food, comfort, or safety was met with an open-handed slap. A hardness had taken root inside King and begun to sprout as a young child. Now that callousness had grown full and strong and there was no sheet big enough to separate it from King.

Flora whisked into the room with an entitlement nurtured under the indulgent eye of Miss Dorothea. "Oh, Mama, it's such a lovely day. Please, no unpleasantries before lunch." Her colorful polka-dot dress skimmed her ample hips. White crepe pumps gave her calves a look that almost made King forget about his irritation with Miss Dorothea.

"Besides," Flora cooed in King's direction, "I don't want my man in a mood before he takes me out tonight."

Yes, tonight, settled into King's mind.

King picked up the morning edition of the Times-Picayune and leafed through the headlines. Lunch counter sit-ins in Birmingham, boys off to Vietnam, wherever that was, and pork chops on sale for 55 cents a pound at the A&P.

Peering over the newspaper, King replied, "That's right, baby. A nice dinner at Dooky Chase." Miss Dorothea would be in the rambling house on her own so King's plan could swerve towards its lethal conclusion.

Flora fiddled with the amber charm dangling from the gold chain around her neck as she settled in the chaise lounge near the radio. In the early planning stages, King had contemplated throwing Flora into the blueprints as well. She had outworn her usefulness at this point, but two bodies might be one too many, encouraging police scrutiny. King didn't need that.

"How was your morning, dear?" asked Flora.

"Fine, I suppose. Calvin tryin' to get Bixby to man up and talk to Russy about the shipyaaards." King mimicked Calvin's signature drawl.

Mother and daughter glanced at each other. Flora responded, "You've gotten awful friendly with that Calvin. He's a good earner, but you need to put some grass between you two. He is an unsavory sort."

*You have no idea.* King nodded and decided to appear agreeable. Miss Dorothea finished her tea and made her way to the kitchen.

The afternoon wore on like one of Reverend Singleton's Sunday sermons. Family business out of the way, King kept himself busy with newspaper reading and listening to the radio. Ernie K. Doe's song "Mother-in-Law" flowed from the speakers of the transistor radio, filling the sitting room with its lyrics of truth, at least in King's opinion. He shook his head in time to the rhythm.

The titular mother-in-law in K. Doe's song was a doppelgänger of King's version. She was Satan's proxy on earth with a sharp tongue. Questioning and belittling without remorse.

The music had a bounce to it, but King listened with a bleak heart. The song of a worn-out fella whose life would be much sweeter if this mother-in-law from hell would leave him alone resonated with King. He heard the words as a call to action.

"Dang right, Mr. K. Doe."

Flora glanced up from her needlepoint. "What you say, sugar?"

"Um, um, just clearing my throat, dear."

King checked the pocket watch in his vest. 5 p.m. Let's see. He went through the plan in his mind. We leave at 8 p.m. for dinner. A little dancing at the Dew Drop Inn. Is Fats Domino playing tonight? I think so.

He tapped his foot as he strung the pieces of the night's forthcoming events together.

Okay, Calvin knows where the key is. Did he tell me who was helping him? No, never mind. I don't need to know. Just need it done.

"Make yourself useful, boy!" Miss Dorothea moved a stepladder through the open sitting room doorway, motioning for King to come over.

King, with a forced grin, answered, "Of course, Miss Dorothea."

"Here." She handed him twine with sachets pinned to it. "Put this up over the door. Here some nails for ya."

King quietly hung a length of garland along the top edge of the frame. A noticeable stench emanated from the cheesecloth packets dangling from the twine. King was accustomed to the unusual odors from the various knicks and knacks this family displayed around the house. Not to mention the peculiar chalky rows that lined the entrance to some of the rooms — including the mystery room on the second floor. Over the years, King wondered why these vestiges of make-believe — Flora called them good luck charms — were entrenched in a family who pride themselves on being so bourgeois and cultured.

"How's that, Miss Dorothea?"

The matriarch visually dissected King's handiwork. "Hmm. It'll do."

King let out an audible breath. "Okay then." Old biddy, that one. Dismisses my help, and she still won't let me call her Mama. He turned and walked through the newly adorned door, then turned to Flora. "I'm going to get ready for our night out."

"Okay, my darling," Flora said, never lifting her head from her needlepoint.

KING TIED THE LONG end of his black silk tie under, then over, and tightened the knot. "You sure are dapper," he said to no one but himself. King glanced at the rectangular Westclox on the nightstand. According to the black hands on its beige face, it was 7:50 p.m. Time to rock and roll.

King opened the door to the bedroom and yelled, "Flora?!" Flora hadn't done her usual primp and prep in their bedroom. Sometimes she used her mother's room, "To preserve some mystery, dear," she would say.

"I hope you're ready already. We're going to be late if you di𝅓"

"I'm in the sitting room, sweetheart," she bellowed from downstairs.

King gave himself a once-over then walked out of the room. He glanced down the length of the hall at the door. The door that held all his dreams of power and control. "Soon enough,

Mama, soon enough." King wondered if he was talking to his own mama or the wretched one waiting downstairs.

He entered the sitting room and immediately noted the redistribution of the furniture. The oak coffee table had a new home under the bay window, and rolled up next to it was the hand-knotted Turkish rug peeking from behind the chintz-covered sofa. King could see a white circle outlined in the lacquered wood floor where the rug used to be.

The stench from the garland draping the entrance swirled into his nostrils and hit him with a dizzying sensation. He unbuttoned his jacket and loosened his tie, which felt like a silk boa constrictor squeezing out all his available air.

Through blurry eyes, King saw Flora and Miss Dorothea standing at the far end of the room. What the hell?

"'What the hell' is right," Miss Dorothea answered smoothly.

"How... what...that was, was...", King's speech drifted off.

"Yes, my dear. That was in your head, but Mama heard it anyways," Flora said with a self-important tone.

King stood in place in front of the door, rocking, eyes wide. Miss Dorothea walked towards him.

"Did you really think you were going to get away with this?" she asked, words brimming with sass and anger. "Did you think I wouldn't know? I got my little ears all over town."

A trickle of urine edged down King's leg. His fear leaked right out of him, leaving a wide damp spot around his crotch.

"Em, em, em, you stupid boy. Well," Miss Dorothea turned to Flora. "This is your mess, so you gonna have to fix it. Told ya not to marry this worthless piece of a man. You old enough to know better."

"Fine, Mama." Flora's voice sounded slightly exasperated but with inflections of anticipation. "It's been decades since I've had the pleasure..."

Wha? Whaaa? Whaaaaa? King's bewildered thoughts were caked with terror.

"I know this is confusing for you, dear," Flora purred. "But you never did know your place in this family. And," she tapped the rabbit's foot that once held King's car keys, "you should never, ever, try to have Mama killed. She gets prickly about that kind of behavior."

Sharp pinches of pain began to seep into King's legs. He stood upright and taut. Blinking ceased as his throat muscles tightened, tongue swollen like a sponge filled with water.

"Just in case you're wondering," Flora murmured, "Calvin has been handled." She clipped the last word for emphasis. "He was a mess, by the way. Begging and pleading. So... unbecoming." Flora sauntered around King, eyeing him with the curiosity of a snake about to strike.

Miss Dorothea joined Flora in her appraisal of the situation. "Here ya go, my daughter." She handed Flora a needle-like dagger with an ornate silver handle of intricate split-tongued gargoyles.

"Ya see this here? This Louisiana toothpick?" Flora asked, knowing that a response would not be forthcoming. "I'm going to use this, and it is going to hurt. Oh, Lord, is it going to sting. But because I once loved you," she blew King a kiss from her crimson lips, "I'll make it quicker than usual. But it won't be less painful."

Miss Dorothea handed Flora a hemp pouch. Balancing the dagger in one hand and the pouch in the other, Flora began shaking out a white chalky substance, tracing the circle with it.

"I bet you're wondering how we knew, aren't you?" Flora asked. She stood up from her semi-bent position, speaking to King but barely looking at him, her head cocked as if it were a two-way conversation.

"Well, you and that smart mouth of yours got you in trouble. You mocked Bixby one too many times. Lucky for Mama and me, he has kin who knows the craft like we do, and he was happy to oblige with the information. Sweet kid, that one."

"Hush, child. This ain't no time for schooling a dead man."

Tears drained from the corner of King's eyes.

"Alright, Mama. Geez. I'll get on with it."

"Let's see..." Flora, thoughtful and proper, began. "If memory serves me correct, oh, it has been a while since I've had to do this." She put her hand on her hips. Flecks of white dust peppered her satin skirt. "Oh, Mama, you go on and start the incantation. I'll be the spirit conduit," Flora said in a quick tone. Then she nodded hesitantly, as if she was trying to remember the last item on a grocery list. "So, that means..."

"Come on, child. We ain't gettin' paid by the minute."

"Mama, please!" Flora composed herself and continued. "Ah, yes, and, King, my no-good King, that makes YOU the subject of this little ritual. So sorry, dear." With a dry stare, she flipped her smooth, fluffed bob and winked. King's hysterical gulping sounds filled the room.

Flora and Miss Dorothea closed their eyes and raised their hands in a V shape. As they lifted their arms, King also began his ascension from the wood floor. The enchantresses levitated his towering frame from the door to the middle of the white encrusted circle and then gradually lowered him to the floor.

The pair, in sequence, confronted King. Through a sheen of escalating horror, he witnessed the impossible.

Flora and Miss Dorothea no longer had eyes. Or human faces.

Flayed skin peeled back from the forehead to their chins. It coursed and contracted like fingers do. The sinewy musculature of their new faces was inky black, pulsing with abandon. In the middle of this cranial nightmare, a round sucking hole appeared. A set of testicle-like inflamed tonsils dangled in the center.

The Miss Dorothea-thing began. The chant started as a low murmur. King could hear but not react. The Flora-thing joined in.

*Trèt. Trayizon. Mantè. Traitor. Betrayer. Liar.* The Haitian Creole words filled the space with their conviction and their damnation.

King's mind broke as the chant gained steam. The crescendo climaxed in a burst of wild energy. With a swift flick of her wrist, Flora — or whatever she was now — flung the dagger directly at King's chest, and it hit its mark: the heart. King writhed and contorted, back arched, slack-jawed, a silent scream of despair lodged in his throat. His last thought was of gratefulness that this ordeal was at an end. His body fell limp to the floor, dispersing waves of chalky dust.

Both creatures fell to their knees, weak, perspiration coating the bulging masses protruding from their heads.

The incantation had two distinct phases. The first concentrated on gathering power. The second on releasing it. King was released, alright.

In an act of hubris and stupidity, in 1965, King Booker lost it all — the only thing that was important anyway — because he got greedy. And his mother-in-law got prickly.

CONDOLENCES FOR THE UNTIMELY death of Flora's beloved husband, King Booker, poured in. The whole of the neighborhood seemed to fill the house on Prentiss Avenue in the Pontchartrain Park neighborhood with warm casseroles and uplifting words.

"Your sympathies soothe my soul, Reverend Singleton," Flora half-moaned into her lace handkerchief. The holy man patted her other hand and said he'd pray for her. Her lashes flickered and spasmed at the thought.

Next-door neighbor Mildred Thibodeaux, a widow herself, tried to make sense of it all. "What is this world coming to? King AND Calvin Bouchard in the same week? King stabbed over a car? No Lincoln is worth anyone's life."

Miss Dorothea excused herself. "Overcome with grief," she said.

Climbing the stairs, the voices of her house guests faded. Miss Dorothea reached for the skeleton key in her freshly-pressed black suit. She approached the door at the end of the second-floor hall and paused. She slid the key into the lock. A neat click sounded as she turned it clockwise. Miss Dorothea stepped in, careful not to disturb the chalky row of powder lining the entrance. She closed the door and headed up the stairs to the attic.

There were no jewels, or gold, or cash stashed in the room. Just a large wooden bed chest with leather straps across it. She opened it. A collection of trinkets was inside. Miss Dorothea took the rabbit's foot from her jacket pocket and tossed it in. It lay there among other knicks and knacks, including a brass Zippo, a clean Smith & Wesson, an old blues album... and an amber pendant dangling from a gold chain.

"Don't need money when you got souls to trade." Miss Dorothea closed the chest. The lid hit with a dull thud. A chorus of guttural moans responded.

*END*

# 3

# Pied Piper of Présage

MELVIN BOOKER SLID THE stiff black disc from its worn cover featuring a grizzled black man holding a guitar like his life depended on it.

"Go on now. Get to it, Mr. Booker," a voice urged from the back of the stilted shack on the edge of the Louisiana swamp. Uneasy murmurs mixed with an undercurrent of ginned-up whoops ricocheted through the tiny space.

The blues were no laughing matter, and neither was the chain of events Melvin had set in motion. *Get to it, indeed,* he reckoned.

THE SHACK WHERE MELVIN rested his weary bones for the better part of sixty years was simple, but it was his. The unit had running water on most days (*glory be to God*) but always looked like a stilt or two was fixing to break away, giving those worn planks up to the brackish wetland below.

The late Mrs. Myrtle Bonneterre bequeathed Melvin an old record player he'd been tinkering with off and on. Figured he could bring its innards back to life, maybe sell it for a few dollars.

Melvin found the gift to be a curious gesture. He, like many others with brown skin and country ways, was still subject to the unequalness of their circumstances regardless of what the Johnson administration laws proclaimed. But Melvin had to admit that Mrs. Bonneterre treated him marginally better.

She'd even give Melvin a $20 bonus every Christmas along with a lecture on saving his soul, which she added as a little lagniappe for free. More than most received, Melvin knew this, but not nearly enough to balance a lifetime of assaults on his dignity and his value on this earth.

It was curious, Melvin would later recall, that a broken record player and a gravelly-voiced musician would be the spark to a powder keg of destruction for him and the town of Présage.

HE FOUND THE ALBUM in a *2 for $5* bin at the farmers' market over in Calcasieu Parish while on his search for a few knick-knacks he could resell at the flea market. That day's haul was decent - a piglet salt and pepper shaker and the singular work of Josephus Brownstone called *I See You.*

The first time Melvin played the album, he was busying himself with shelling a bushel of fresh peas to bag and sell the next day. A calm rhythm had set in between Melvin's fingers, his mind, and the motion of his body.

Succulent heat buoyed by the soft humidity crawled off the bayou. The metal fan on the kitchen table whirred and spun, purposeful and steady, yet it did nothing more than swish the heat about the room.

Melvin brushed a trickle of perspiration from his brow without missing a beat. His fingers slid down each pod, over the seam, releasing the peas into an old clay bowl. The music of woe in a twelve-bar chord progression lingered in one ear and out the other for Melvin.

He heard the refrain of the title song, and it was solemn enough.

*Catch you on the old train*
*Makin' you feel no pain*
*I think you need to begin again*
*I see you*

Salt of the earth guitar licks came next, and Melvin let the rhythm take him on a winding journey, just him and his fingers pulling at snap peas. He expected the refrain to repeat. It did not.

*Shakers, money makers*
*Lucky, are there any takers*
*Be careful what you wish for*
*I see you*

Melvin chalked up the unusual lack of repetition to the blues being the blues. The following day he accidentally dropped the ceramic piglet shakers as he transferred them from the counter to his box of sellable wares for the market. He found a shiny surprise inside the cracked pieces. A gold coin.

Making ends meet was a battle, uphill, both ways, that Melvin lost most weeks. That beauty of a coin changed things, at least for a little while.

Chappy's Pawn Shop paid $250 for it and, with money to burn, he celebrated with a trip to the liquor store. Snatched up a bottle of Johnny Walker, which raised some eyebrows with the clerk who knew old Melvin was more of a plastic bottle whisky drinker. Had himself a quiet party back home on the front porch overlooking the placid swamp, a warmth in his throat and joy in his heart. When Melvin listened to Josephus Brownstone again, he realized the words in the song had come true.

He got a kick out of the coincidence but didn't pay it much mind. Until the refrain did another refresher for his ears.

*Fire on the water*
*Should have been smarter*
*All's well that ends well*
*I see you*

Melvin didn't know what to make of it, but a crisp shiver coursed through him just the same. The anomaly stirred him so much that he invited his nephew, Obadiah, over to have a listen.

"Uncle, you been on your own too long." Obadiah flipped the vinyl over in his hands, touching the edges like it was a slim waist. He put the record down on the kitchen counter and picked up the album cover, pushing in at the corner to expand the cover like a wide mouth. "Didn't it come with one of those sleeves with the lyrics on it?"

"No, no, it didn't." Melvin pulled the chair opposite Obadiah, the wooden legs scraping against the floor. As he sat down, he said, "Put it on the turntable. See for yourself."

"Don't mind if I do." It took Obadiah a handful of steps to enter the living room, where the worn player sat on an end table. He settled the needle onto the grooves.

Uncle and nephew drank in the sound, humming along once they got the hang of the tune. Melvin's eyes widened halfway through the song. The refrain did a switcheroo yet again.

*Snatch that witch*
*Cause she snitched*
*Life is for the rich*
*I see you*

Melvin's old finger wagged in the direction of the record. Obadiah ignored him, still listening intently.

"There, right there! The song before talked about ah, ah, shakers and fire and water. Now it's goin' on about snitches and riches." He sank back in his chair, his hand covering his mouth as if to keep the surprise from escaping.

"Naw, Uncle. That right there," he nodded towards the spinning vinyl, "is an old blues man's look at love gone wrong with an upside. That's what you heard." Obadiah tacked on a chuckle directed at Melvin for emphasis.

Melvin's confusion was lost on his nephew. Where did his cryptic prophecies blow away to? Obadiah chided his uncle once more before heading back home.

A week later, Obadiah's common-law wife caught a bullet from a local two-bit hustler for her ill-placed phone call to Sheriff Knox. Obadiah's grief was more bearable when he got word of a little nest egg in a safe deposit box left for him upon her passing. Obadiah recognized the coincidence, and now he was a believer. Like a locomotive gaining steam, he started spinning tales about the record that captured the town's imagination. Soon, folks began asking to hear the vinyl oracle.

As more coincidences stacked up, more travelers made the pilgrimage to Melvin's abode. The omens became more precise as the record seemed to learn from each Présage resident who stepped foot in the hut at the edge of the swamp. *I See You* became a savage crystal ball, seeing the worst outcomes delivered with a silver lining in the ever-changing refrain.

"Come on, Booker. Get to it." Anxious listeners squirmed in their seats, hands clenched or in prayer, waiting for the needle to touch down. The music spoke to each listener with a distinct message of misery and miracles. They all left Melvin's shack, hopeful that Josephus Brownstone's favor would be worth the asking price.

Melvin tried to curb the almost daily vigils to his home but was unsuccessful in his measures. Local authorities paid a visit or two to inquire about the gatherings but were mostly looking for a shakedown to keep the spigot of looky-loos flowing. The unwanted attention, oddly, gave Melvin a sense of importance that had eluded him as an invisible part of the tapestry of Présage.

Believers came from all walks of life.

Black and white folks sat in one room together, an unheard-of occurrence in Présage. Josephus Brownstone brought the races together like nothing else in this area could.

So, Melvin charged by the head and figured it made no sense to not get a little something out of it. The pilgrims knew the fate held in the grooves of the vinyl was a give and take, but that did not deter them.

A deviant element would loiter in the back of Melvin's turntable sermons and plot how to take the Josephus record and make their own sideshow out of it. A few times he'd been held at gunpoint, pistol-whipped, or tied up, and the thieves would just ransack the place and take the earnings he stored in an old coffee tin.

Melvin was scared out of his wits the first few times this happened. Then the record started making things right.

Ruffians from Melvin's side of town burgled the shack, taking the money and Josephus with them. The following day the record, the money, and a scrawled note sat neatly on his porch. Presumably, the bandits thought it best to restore order. Because the record told them what consequences would befall them if they didn't. After that, there was no more trouble from his people.

However, the other side of town hadn't gotten the message.

Foolish high school students thought Melvin was getting above his station, and they sought to remedy that. With bats in their hands and vinegar in their step, the pair menaced Melvin into a corner, used their whiteness to demean his blackness, and took the record and what cash he had stored in the coffee tin. The two young men, in the prime of their hate-filled lives, were found a few hours later impaled on a barbed wire fence surrounding the Prater farm on the outskirts of Route 16.

Melvin heard through the grapevine their skin was flayed, exposing rib cages snacked on by vultures before they were discovered. He knew when the boys did what they had done, the record and the money would find their way back, which they did. When he got word of the vicious condition of the bodies, he knew to keep his mouth shut. Never mind he was an old laborer who could barely labor these days, he would be the main culprit for this. Présage would see to that.

It took one more month of Sundays before damnation finally landed at Melvin's doorstep.

The banging at the door riled Melvin out of a deep sleep. He rolled over in his boxer shorts and white tank top and rested his thin legs on the floor. The pounding was accompanied by a familiar voice.

"Uncle, open up!"

"Child, why are you at my door this late?" he groused. Melvin's tired eyes focused on the clock next to the bed. It read 2:22 am.

Melvin pulled on his bathrobe and padded to the door. "Stop your walloping before you knock the damn thing off its hinges." He opened the door and Obadiah spilled into Melvin's inner sanctum, nearly tripping over his own two feet. His breathing was heavy, like his lungs had made room for an anvil inside his ribcage. A sheen of sweat slicked the young man's face.

"What's gotten into you? Did you run all the way here?"

The disheveled person in front of Melvin was a far cry from the Obadiah he knew. Hell, from the Obadiah he saw a month ago at Rev. Wilson's sermon on reaping what you sow.

"Why didn't you warn me?" Obadiah mumbled, running his hands over his tight afro. "I mean, I can see not telling all those other greedy fools, but me?" His voice rose, "We're family, man, we're family!" He took Melvin by the shoulders, his stale breath invading Melvin's space.

"Slow down, slow down." He steered his nephew to the kitchen. Obadiah quivered like the North Pole had sunk into his bones despite his long-sleeved shirt and worn denim. "Let me get you something cool to drink, and you can explain all this."

Obadiah waved his hands. "No. I'll take that." He pointed to the jug on the counter as he slid into a chair at the kitchen table.

It was Melvin's homemade moonshine. He nipped on the mediocre liquor when he wanted to save the good stuff for a special occasion, and he was fine sharing it with Obadiah.

Obadiah accepted the jelly jar filled with his drink on the rocks. His hand trembled as he gulped the beverage in a continuous swig, draining the glass. Only the slick cubes remained, clinking as he sat the glass on the table.

Melvin stared down at his nephew, perplexed. The overhead lightbulb dangled precariously over the table, casting elongated shadows of the men underneath it. Melvin stared intently at the dark shapes that morphed as his nephew's frantic breathing increased. The shapes began to meld together. Melvin thought it looked like two young men flayed on a fence. He suddenly raised his eyes.

As much to himself as to his nephew, he asked, "What's gotten into you?"

Obadiah wiped his mouth with the back of his hand and took in a trembling breath. "I thought it was strange when Hank Halpern started stepping out with Eva Murphy. She'd never given him notice. Now sunlight can't get between them."

"Well, young love is fickle. Off and on," Melvin said slowly. "Sometimes it takes a while for things to spark." He realized he didn't believe that.

"What about Big Fred and all his new cars? Mrs. Carlton from church losing all that weight in the blink of an eye? Now, Uncle, listen to me. I have seen everyone who came here getting what they wanted. What they thought they wanted." Obadiah enunciated each syllable to within an inch of its life as if it would help Melvin better understand.

Melvin understood, all right. Something had vexed his nephew's mind. The kind of thing that sent folks to Louisiana Psychiatric Hospital in Jackson.

"But they — those people who heard Josephus — are starting to..." Obadiah glared up at Melvin. The stare alone caused him to take two steps backward.

"You mean to tell me you have no idea what happens with that record?" The words shrieked out of Obadiah like an owl's squawk. Then his eyes went unresponsive like a ragdoll.

Melvin watched Obadiah turn his head as if a string were gently pulling it. He followed the young man's gaze.

The album.

Propped against the record player, the jacket cover was visible by a sliver of moonlight through the window hitting half of the cover like a radiant saber. Melvin could have sworn it appeared as if Josephus were winking or grinning. Maybe howling.

Obadiah shook his finger at the album, agitation in each motion. "This place is changing. Changing real bad." The whine in Obadiah's voice frightened Melvin to the quick.

"People do change when they get what they want, don't they?" Melvin asked, even though he knew the answer.

Obadiah's eyes welled with tears. His mouth contorted in a moan. Melvin stepped forward, but the young man put his hands up. "Don't come any closer."

"Let me help ya, son."

Obadiah abruptly stood up, the chair falling on its side. Shadows danced on the floor, disconnected from both of them.

Melvin froze.

As fear swam through Obadiah's eyes, Melvin knew he was drowning, too, in whatever this was.

He watched as Obadiah unbuttoned the cuff of his shirt. Streaks of wetness cut through the Louisiana dirt on his face as his eyes pierced into him. Obadiah continued to stare as he rolled the sleeve's fabric back and over itself.

Some of the pustules dotting Obadiah's arm were not ruptured. Yet. The lesions could be mistaken for a large, opaque blister. But it was the broken ones that caused Melvin to wish he'd paid closer attention in Sunday school. It was times like this he could have used a good Bible verse to cling to.

The popped pustules seeped with a sticky ooze. A crust formed around the outer edges, and small bubbles squirmed from the pus. Melvin couldn't tell for sure what was crawling from the sore, but whatever it was, he wanted to unsee it.

"This is how it crops up! This is how it starts," Obadiah cried. "This whole place is diseased…" His voice mutated from a cry into a sour, rumbling laugh.

Melvin covered his pinched mouth to stifle a shriek. He closed his robe tight as if that could keep the sickness off of him. "What does Dr. Willard say? He got to have a shot or pills for this, don't he?"

Obadiah staggered past Melvin.

Melvin clasped his chest in an exaggerated hug that Fred Sanford would be proud of and lunged backward away from the walking contamination.

Obadiah paid no mind to Melvin. He lumbered to the door and mumbled, "Everyone is sick. We're all sick." He turned his head to look back at Melvin. "But you aren't. Why?"

"I don't know." He stammered, "Could be the water, you know."

After the incident with the boys on Route 16, Melvin couldn't be sure he wasn't on the radar of local law enforcement. He dared not venture too far from home. Melvin had wondered why no one had knocked on his door begging to know the unknowable for more than a week.

Obadiah shushed and flapped his hand in Melvin's direction as if to say, *please stop talking nonsense.* The floorboards creaked with each step. Obadiah opened the door and said, not to Melvin but to the world, "What is going to happen to me?" He walked into the night.

He sat at the table with a highball and a fresh bottle of whisky. Melvin twisted the cap and silently reveled in the snap, then poured a full glass. Drank it as fast as Obadiah drank the moonshine.

This was a special occasion, after all.

He refilled the glass. The heat from the alcohol soothed his racing thoughts but didn't tamp down the visceral images enough. Melvin downed a second drink and hoped it would obliterate whatever thoughts remained as he sat in the quiet.

Melvin raised his head, not sure if he dozed off or passed out. His stupor blew away as he noticed the open front door. A burning smell floated by. The misty smoke crumbled Melvin's senses from the inside, its tendrils clawing at him to join it outside.

Melvin obliged.

His cotton robe brushed his calves as he stepped from the shack. Slender branches and brittle leaves crunched under his feet, but he barely noticed. He was fixed on the tangerine glow about 10 miles from where he stood.

A chorus of voices, high-pitched but indiscernible, wafted along with the smoke toward him. Melvin felt the stickiness of the Louisiana heat on his skin, sweat dampening his forehead. He wiped it away with the back of his hand. A residue of wiggling pus smeared his fingers.

Melvin retched. A flush of bile and whisky-infused vomit gushed from his mouth and tumbled at his bare feet.

He hopscotched over the puddles of purged fluid to stumble further into the night. A dark mass careened toward him. A month ago, he would have described it as an angry mob. Now it was indescribable.

A chorus of tones and sounds like nothing ever heard from the living filled the air.

The spectacle that walked, jumped, and trudged toward Melvin didn't register as people to him, even from a few miles away.

It was a carnival of beastly apparitions. Some crawled, and others swung from trees and buildings along the way. Their shadows leaped from the ground, undulating against the moonlight. He wondered if Obadiah was among the madness.

Melvin scurried into his shack, wet vomit footprints in his wake, and locked the door. He dragged a chair from the kitchen and cocked it under the doorknob. The equivalent of a Band-Aid on a sucking wound, but he figured something was better than nothing.

"Oh, no, oh, no, oh on," he whimpered.

The blisters began popping up like whack-a-moles that never retreated all over his chest. He whipped off his robe to find more pustules sprouting on his arms.

The cries thickened as the merchants of death grew closer.

After careful, adrenaline-fueled consideration, Melvin decided the best way to put a stop to this was to simply destroy the record.

He dragged the toolbox from under the sink with one hand, his whiskey in the other, and settled near the record player. He flipped through the metal chest searching for tools of destruction. A ball peen hammer, a pair of pliers, a flathead screwdriver.

His hands wavered as he removed the vinyl prophet from its sleeve. Melvin found out quickly that the vinyl, made of sturdier stock, bound by threads of darkness, was unbreakable.

None of the implements dented what Josephus had created.

Josephus would not be silenced.

Melvin slumped to the ground. High on whiskey and low on resolve, he gave in. Melvin drank the last drink he was ever going to have, then put the record on.

And waited.

The lyrics filled the shack like a hollow wind. Glass shattered from the windowpanes like tubular bells. Flames licked at the vegetation outside the shack. A precursor to the biblical level of brimstone that would infiltrate these four walls.

*Doesn't God speak, chastise, punish with fire?*

"The Bible tells me so."

As Josephus spun and spun on the turntable, Melvin sat paralyzed by the refrain, *fire on the water, should have been smarter.*

The warbly graininess of each guitar riff fused with Melvin's remaining chaotic thoughts, but Josephus would get the last word.

*Ready to fight for your life*
*Forgot to do what's right*
*Fire on the water*
*Get ready to hollerrrrrr*

A ghastly grin spread across Melvin's face. He hugged his bony legs to his chest and rocked, his grin breaking into an uproarious cackle. Melvin turned his head to see Josephus on the album cover, weeping. But his mouth was clearly laughing with him.

Evil like this doesn't politely excuse itself; it asks for a second helping. Melvin hoped for the salvation Mrs. Bonneterre told him about.

Waves of heat streamed in under the old wooden planks.

Melvin steadied himself against the wall. His flesh cratered with the moist network of strange vermin, awakened from the cloudy abscesses that dotted his body.

The bill had come due for Présage and its Pied Piper.

Screams swelled just beyond the wooden door. The chair shook, its legs grinding into the floorboards under the weight of what was outside that wanted in.


*END*

# 4

# Adventures in Babysitting

2025 Horror2Comic Quarterfinalist

*October 25*

A FIERY RED PINTO Roundabout maneuvers into the driveway across the street. The gleam from its rail bumper refracts the sunlight like the North Star. You watch this new arrival and mentally compare it to Sebastian Stewart's invitation to show you his penis behind the Prentiss High basketball bleachers. Intriguing? Sure. But in the end, nothing to see here.

As the car comes to a stop, the hatchback window reveals the silhouette of a full dome of hair haloing the driver's seat headrest. A shadow of movement flits from the passenger side.

Peeking through a sliver in the curtains, you observe a slender woman slink out of the driver's seat. Her ebony frame is swathed in a paisley halter dress, her thick, jet-black hair styled with voluminous curls that only pink cushiony rollers could create.

The passenger door swings open with flair, and a little girl barrels out. Her hair is parted into two Afro puffs, a staple of most little girls in this neighborhood. The patches on her bell bottoms are placed strategically to cover the telltale signs of roughhousing.

This tiny but mighty storm in a teacup runs across the un-kempt lawn, zigzagging under the late afternoon sun, then stops on a dime. Your grasp on the curtains tightens, your eyes squint in disbelief. Is that cheeky little kid staring at you? Her body squarely faces in your direction; eyes lock. She raises her right index finger towards you with a slow, come closer, wag. You swish the fabric panels shut.

Your mother calls you to dinner and mentions that Mrs. Brownstone and her daughter Lyla just moved in across the street. She states you should go over and inquire about babysit-ting before that Carla Rayford down the street beats you to it. You're intrigued by the pint-sized finger pointer, so you promise to stop by tomorrow.

### October 26

You approach the Brownstone house. You better secure this babysitting gig, or your mother will trip a fit and you'll never be able to get that new Jackson 5 album with your current piggybank savings.

Lyla is jumping rope. The soft thump of her patent leather shoes as they hit the cement driveway is like a metronome. You say hello and introduce yourself. Her charcoal eyes grab you, *(thump, THUMP),* mesmerize you. Without warning, on such a clear, breezy day, a sour tang bubbles from your stomach and fills the back of your throat. You didn't feel nauseous until this very moment. "Is your mother home?" you squeak out.

Lyla declares Penny is inside.

You aren't sure which is more disconcerting. The fading sensation you were on the cusp of vomiting or a child using their mother's first name.

Lyla's lanky legs bip and bop as she lingers on you. Her shadow elongates, and you find it strange that Lyla's jump rope handles cast a shadow that morphs her little hands into claws. You shake your head as the door opens and turn to greet Mrs. Brownstone.

Lyla scrapes past as you complete your due diligence on the babysitting front. Mrs. Brownstone desperately needs after-school care, and she was not at all impressed with the Rayford girl's attitude. You negotiate $3 an hour. Just as you are counting your babysitting chickens before they hatch, you hear the commotion of movement in the background. With one hand, Lyla is moving a kitchen chair, and with the other, you see furry feet and a plump midsection dangling under the other arm. A greyish brown bunny squirms as she sets it down on the floor. *Oh, great. Pets.*

As you turn to leave, Mrs. Brownstone stops you and asks you if you are free to take Lyla trick or treating later that week ("I know a pretty girl like you has all sorts of trouble to get up to, but it would be a big help"). You wonder if Sebastian will be out trolling with his skateboarder friends that night. Maybe you'll run into him. The bleachers weren't so bad, and Lyla would be a good cover story, so you say yes.

As you turn to leave, you hear Mrs. Brownstone gasp. Lyla stands in the hallway, a mint green Tupperware bowl cradled in her small hands. Whatever is in the bowl sloshes around in a dark ruby liquid. As Lyla moves closer, a stench percolates to the front porch. You reel from the odor, a mix of spoiled chicken and cough syrup, burying your face in the armpit of your tie-dye t-shirt. Mild cramps jumble in your stomach. *Not this again.*

Mrs. Brownstone shrugs her shoulders in embarrassment, the universal gesture of *kids get up to the darndest things,* then sternly rebukes her daughter ("Lyla Dorothea! Put that back in the kitchen!"). She apologizes for the outburst and offers you an extra $2 an hour for Halloween. You say absolutely. Embarrassment can be lucrative, and who were you to turn it down?

Lost in thoughts of money, money, mon-nay, you cross the peculiar neighbors' lawn, which has browned quite a bit since yesterday. As you step off the curb, you hear the squeal before you see the thick smoke from burning rubber. Mr. Cochrane's wood-paneled station wagon rocks to a standstill, his cursing continuing after the car stops. You nearly walk straight into his front bumper and an early grave.

"You better take care of yourself so you can take care of me," Lyla murmurs seemingly in your ear.

You heave in a gush of air, the shock widening your eyes. You whip around to see the little girl skip across the parched grass to Mrs. Brownstone, erect like a centurion at the front door.


### October 27


You try not to judge. What do you know about kids? Teenager or not, you're still too young to cast aspersions, but you sense Mrs. Brownstone must have her hands full, especially with a strange child like Lyla.

In fact, on your first day of child-minding, Lyla begs you to watch a magic trick she'd been working on for years. *Years? Hmm.* Her soft, cool hands take yours. In her cotton candy pink bedroom filled with porcelain dolls that sport an eternal scream in their eyes, she murmurs indistinct syllables and vowels, a secret language presumably shared by first graders and their clans. Lyla demands you close your eyes as she tugs your hand forward.

A sudden rush of wind swirls and encompasses your palm, prickling your skin. No other part of your body is subjected to the tactile gust. "What are you doing?" Your eyelids flutter but remain clamped shut like a superglued blindfold. Panic explodes in every nerve, nourishing your body with spiraling alarm.

Your eyes finally open just as a saucer-sized black portal sucks Lyla's Madame Alexander Little Red Riding Hood doll straight into it and then closes like the shutter of an old camera. Your panic goes next level.

"You're stronger than I thought," Lyla says with a satisfied yet blank stare.

You run from the house, but as you cross the weedy, tangling lawn, and reach the street, (no Mr. Cochrane in sight) your pace slows to a strut. By the time you walk through your front door, the afterbirth of recent events is expunged, and you can't quite remember what it is you are supposed to forget.

### *October 28*

You're afraid of Lyla, but you're not sure why.

You can feel her psychic thumbprints milling around in the card catalog of your brain – curating, rearranging, erasing – while you push her tiny rump higher and higher on the swings in the backyard.

The two afternoons you've spent guarding (*that's what it is, right?*) six-year-old Lyla, she confirmed her age using finger arithmetic, has bundled your nerves like a nightmare origami.

An idea flashes through your head (*Hang yourself before it's too late*) as you see the rabbit near the fence. Lyla jumps from the swing, arms waving in a wild and choppy motion. If her shoulders unhinge from her body, you will call it a day without one glimmer of shock because this is starting to seem normal (*no, it's not*).

Lyla abruptly stops and stares at you, eyes vacant to the core but dancing around the edges. Her face is placid, except for the slight crescent smile.

The look dares you to comment. But what can you say? Lyla just made that rabbit disappear into a warping hole. Then she made it reappear, but now the feet are where the ears should be, and the ears are coming out of its mouth like tonsils (*OH MY GODDD!*). The atrocity screeches with an otherworldly fervor. You join in.

### *October 29*

Your mother won't entertain any "crazy talk" about that sweet little girl. Her fear washes over you. She knows more than she's telling you.

You reflect on what love means and when love means absolutely nothing. Somehow you know love won't be enough to save your mother, not when Lyla needs you unencumbered and beholden only to her. Lyla housed that in your head yesterday. That and the blurred image of your mother (*Mama!!!*) in that dark portal.

This is okay with you. The knowing part. Can't stop a Lyla train that's already left the station. It gives you time for extra hugs, a few *I'm sorry's* that make your mother question your non-moody disposition ("Are you okay?"). Lyla terrifies you so much, but you know, somehow, that even though Lyla is going to banish your mother to that grim place, she has grace somewhere inside her because you will barely remember her or recollect what happens to her when she's gone.

Love isn't enough to save Mrs. Brownstone, not that Lyla ever really liked or loved the woman. Lyla's mother isn't her real mother but more like a caretaker. And things are not working out to Lyla's satisfaction, so... In today's very special episode of "Svengoolie – Lyla's edition," the little tike combusts her substitute mother in a horrific blaze in the barrel can in the backyard. Even made her climb right into the can and douse herself good and plenty with the gasoline.

Lyla disappears the charred wriggling mass to the same plane your hand must have dipped in that first day you sat with her, the place where the rabbit most definitely went, the place where your mother will eventually...

For some reason, no one else in the neighborhood notices the piercing cries, the vines becoming one with the Brownstone house, the utter darkness and despair starting to coat this street. You suspect Lyla has been working her magic from the day her patent leather shoes touched the ground.

### *October 30*

You consider killing Lyla while you both cross over Prentiss Avenue, a nice shove in front of the midtown express, but you're not sure she can be killed. You try to veil this thought from Lyla but wonder if it matters. She's probably wise to every machination you have.

Your memory is not Mr. Cleaned as diligently as it had been days before. But why? Why would Lyla allow the breadcrumbs of terror to linger, swimming around in your head? Lyla is planning something. But what?

### *October 31*

Choices. Such a funny word. It implies that you have agency in this world. Lyla's world. You stand at the curb, your thoughts mired in the quicksand of what's to come and wait for Lyla (*and death and destruction*) to appear at the front door. When it swings open, you see Mrs. Brownstone standing there, cloaked in woolen darkness. You could have sworn she had gone somewhere (*burn, baby, burn*). The inkiness shimmers in the background.

Mrs. Brownstone, or whoever she was before Lyla crossed her path, stares at you, a hole where her right eye should be, her left eye milky and seeping. She gives you a faint sneer and tells you not to let Lyla eat any candy along the way ("Those fun-size packages of nougat will need a safety check, young lady!"). You think this is absurd since nothing can hurt a monster. ("Have her home by 9 pm, would ya?") The interloper, Mrs. Brownstone, whom you realize you will never see again, practically shoves Lyla across the threshold and recedes into the darkness.

So, you head out amongst the ghouls and goblins, real and imagined, resigning yourself to walking hand in hand with Lyla and a jack-o'-lantern bucket into the valley of darkness.

You don't know what the neighbors see (*yes, you do*). They back away from you and Lyla. You see the O shape form, first in their wide eyes, then in their shrieks (*What's the matter? Isn't it wonderful in hell?*).

You catch a glimpse of Sebastian. His limp penis flopping where his ear should be. You did run into him after all!

When you see the shadow *(Lyla, beautiful, Lyla)* gliding down Prentiss Avenue, taking and inflicting, you want to dance with it, twirl with it, and cry with it because...

You are the new caretaker.

***END***

# 5

# The John Hughes Guide to High School Girl Transformations

Lyla's sleepover was supposed to secure her place in the pantheon of Rosemount High's 'in crowd'. She'd studied the John Hughes Guide to High School Girl Transformations—*Sixteen Candles*, *Pretty in Pink*, and *The Breakfast Club*. Lyla dissected every pout, every *bitchin'*, to solve the Rubik's cube of teenage angst. But there was one move left. Shannon.

Shannon was the gatekeeper of coolness. Lyla tried desperately to flip her afro-curled outsider status, but little digs from her nemesis kept her off-kilter. The worst was at lunchtime. Shannon would pull Lyla's ringlets, orange pizza grease still under her nails, and howl "boing". The entire table would laugh. The message was clear. Shannon had control, and Lyla had to endure it until the gate opened.

Lyla's mother would say, "If all else fails, just be yourself." But Lyla didn't want to be herself; she wanted to be one of *them*.

That fateful night, five pajama-clad girls wiggled in anticipation. The VCR whirred as it sucked the black cartridge inside. Instead of Ferris Bueller's mug filling the screen, grainy footage glared from the television.

"What the hell?" Shannon grumbled with low-key indignation, arms crossed, ponytail swinging. "Food stamps don't cover VCRs?"

"What's your damage, Shannon?!" Lyla blurted out, frantically pushing the eject button.

The moment Shannon rolled her eyes, Lyla realized her mother was right.

Lyla's gaze turned dark like marbles. Claws tore through her nail beds, facial bones cracked as her snout elongated. Lyla reached for Shannon like a hideous Elasta Man. Lyla's hooked fingers grabbed Shannon's golden ponytail and yanked. A bloody chunk of scalp rested in Lyla's hands. Teenage voices shrieked and cried, but it was Shannon's screams that gave Lyla life.

"Boing!" Lyla yelled from the top of her guttural lungs. *It feels so good to be myself.*


**END**

# 6

## Too Late to Turn Back Now - I

THE BOTTLE BLONDE STANDING between Delphine, and eminent destruction, spoke with a nasally whine. "Who's in charge here?" The woman slammed her oversized handbag onto the counter. The large barrel curls that cascaded down her back bounced in sync with each syllable.

A thought treaded just below the surface inside Delphine—*Is this a bad idea for a good reason or am I just...*—as she tucked her hands into her cardigan pockets and rocked on her feet to calm her nerves and avoid finishing the thought.

"Welcome to the Far Burger Bar. How can I help you, baby?" The cashier's words that greeted the blonde were friendly enough, but the worker's posture indicated the total opposite. Her arm lazily draped the register, slick red bedazzled nails rap, tap, tapping on the register.

Delphine appreciated the bun of micro braids affixed to the top of the cashier's head and the baby hairs slicked into submission around her forehead. The woman's brown-sugar complexion was similar to hers, so she wondered if she could pull that same style off.

"I need to talk to someone," the blonde said with an attitude the size of Montana. She shuffled through her handbag, the contents smacking together before pulling a torn red envelope and a vial half-filled with crimson granules from its depths. "About this!" She waved the ripped paper and the glass tube in the woman's face.

"I'll get the manager for ya, boo," the cashier declared as she aggressively popped her bubblegum. She pressed an intercom on the wall next to the register. "Customer up front," the cashier said, offering the woman a counterfeit smile. Delphine wondered how many orders got a little lagniappe of spit or hair when the customers got bossy.

The blonde leaned over the counter in an effort to leverage her body as a tool of intimidation in a way her shrill voice could not. "Best believe I got my lawyer on speed dial for this!"

The cashier cocked her head to the side. "Ma'am, we are not liable for your misuse of our products. It's covered in the terms and conditions." Her words were as bland as dry toast.

"Just get the manager," the blonde's voice screeched. "And I want my money back." Delphine watched as the woman's back heaved up and down, both hands planted on the counter, as if expelling the words was a Herculean feat.

The heavy scent of smoky grease and beef fat bombarded the cramped space. Two short-order cooks, both stocky men, slapped flat metal spatulas on the rows of seared patties. They moved with muscle-memory precision. One whistled a jaunty tune.

The cashier cleared her throat and pressed on. "But you know the spell is non-refundable if it's been opened?"

"Get your boss out here," she growled, her voice rumbling an octave lower. Delphine wondered if the baby voice was an act, something she'd learned in her younger years as a manipulation tactic. Unfortunately, no one had told her that she'd aged out of it the way she probably aged out of getting carded or having drinks she didn't order magically appear in front of her at a bar.

The cashier shrugged and filled a large plastic cup with ice from the beverage station to her left. "Something to drink while you wait?" The woman requested sweet tea on the rocks and sucked it down in a few deep sips. The cashier sighed and motioned her to move to the side.

"Fine," the woman huffed. She replaced bits and bobs that had been strewn on the counter during her deep purse exploration but left the empty cup. The woman slung the massive tote over her shoulder and stepped to the end of the counter. As she turned, she flipped her blonde curls and said, "All yours."

Delphine covered her mouth as she gasped, then over-corrected with a weak smile and stumbled into the counter.

The right side of the woman's face, from the hairline to her chin, was enveloped in a blistered, slick, lumpy growth. It reminded Delphine of a relief map constructed from greasy pepperoni. Her brown eye played peek-a-boo with the extra folds of skin, sliding in and out of view from behind the crease at its leisure.

The canyons and crevices that covered the woman's face would forever live rent-free in Delphine's mind.

"Welcome to the Far Burger Bar. Can I take your order, boo?" The cashier's voice gut-punched Delphine back into the reality of her surroundings. She wheezed and held her stomach.

*It's too late to turn back now.*

The menu suspended behind the counter, above the grilling station, was the most significant ambient light source in this steeple roof outpost of mass-produced, nutritionally questionable food. The building could have been a renovated one-bedroom mother-in-law suite. A series of dull red and yellow rectangular tables were situated along the walls, square versions down the middle. Delphine imagined that the manager must be in the master bedroom behind the door marked "Back Office–Employees Only".

Delphine studied the backlit Plexi set of options. Hunger had left her days ago, but she would have to order something. This was not an establishment that adhered to *no purchase required*.

"Now, who needs my attention?" A booming voice reverberated against the worn white walls as a man strolled through the employee door and planted himself across from Delphine.

He was a striking figure in a grey three-piece pinstripe suit, his two right-hand fingers snug in a watch pocket in his vest. His stare took Delphine's breath away.

The owner of the startling voice possessed a sun-worn face, as if island vacations were his business, and coiffed silver hair with a grizzled, yet impeccably roguish, beard to match. She was taken aback at the lush softness of his grey. Nothing like the coarse, brassy texture her mother's had been.

Delphine was pleasantly surprised by how fit and trim the man, who must be late 40s or early 50s, appeared to be.

The pleasantness evaporated quickly.

The man flashed Delphine a slight grin that slid into a hearty laugh. Her stomach dipped like a 747 abruptly losing altitude. She could see an endless black hole just beyond his impeccable teeth.

It scared the shit out of her.

"Ah, yoo hoo!" The blonde fluttered a handkerchief at the manager; her red lips curled in annoyance. "I'm the one who needs assistance." He strode purposefully to the end of the counter to meet the blonde with the blob as a second face.

"Mizz? Can I take your order?" The cashier stared blank as cardboard at Delphine. The gaze was generic; her eyes void of the spark that connects living humans to one another. A ripple of unease swelled through Delphine.

"If you need more time, you can stand to the side," she said, her fingernails skimming her braids. "If you want, I can catch you after the next customer?"

Delphine glanced over her shoulder. Eager patrons squeezed in a line that stretched to the back of the restaurant.

"I do need a moment after all," Delphine whispered as she shuffled to her left, the worn soles of her dingy knockoff Keds squeaking under her gait. She shook her head to clear it of–what had her mother always said–cobwebs? *Clear your fucking head of cobwebs and stop livin' in the clouds!* Her mother said that as well.

The negotiations between the blonde and the GQ manager had stalled.

"Well, well," the manager said as he contemplated the items the blonde had thrust into his hand. He turned the torn paper scraps over. Then he shook the vial, the ruby grains flying from one end to the other.

Delphine detected a tremor in the blonde's clasped hands.

"I hear you want a refund on the ineffective spell." He bobbed and weaved in front of the blonde, assessing the look of her. The woman shrank back. "Seems to me that the *'Eye for an Eye'* spell worked just fine. Maybe not on the target you intended, but," he licked his lips, "sure was effective in my estimation."

The blonde let out a *pfft* and stammered, "The instructions were too fucking cryptic! What in the beer and Skittles does *'mix with the light and darkness of your heart before serving'* mean, anyway?"

The man raised an eyebrow at the woman's outburst. He held up a finger to shush any further complaints. His attention shifted like a camera coming into focus. On Delphine.

"Can I help you, Miss?"

The direct attention unnerved Delphine. She offered a milquetoast smile as she tugged the sleeves of her threadbare sweater, stumbling over her feet near the Formica counter. Delphine's habit of encroaching on conversations not meant for her ears was a compulsion that was as ingrained in her as breathing air or adhering to the New Orleans tradition of eating red beans and rice every Monday evening.

It was her FOMO that had her here in the first place.

Delphine watched as the manager waved the blond past the waiting line and through the hinged countertop swung open as he said, "Let's see what we can do." He ushered the woman through the Employee door.

"I'm ready," Delphine blurted out. Her heart pounded like fists into kneaded dough.

"Excuse me, lady. No cutting." The curt voice of the man with his hands buried in his denim pockets edged in front of Delphine. Two children boxed him in on either side, bickering like alley cats.

"Scooter, stop picking at your sister, for Christ's sake!" the man barked. Delphine could only imagine how thin this man's thread must be.

A young boy's feral shout of "She started it!" bounced through the restaurant, answered by the younger girl's belliger-ent, "You're a stupid head!"

The man addressed the chaos that flanked him. "Don't make me turn around and bring you both back home!"

*He's bluffing his way through this.* Delphine could hear the theatrics in his delivery. Heavy blustering like he had a full house, but he only held a pair of twos. *There's no way he's turning back now.* In retrospect, Delphine recognized it was how her mother would often talk to her.

The threat, implied or otherwise, conned the two youngsters into silent compliance.

"Uh, yeah, we want three large fries, three Hot Damn burgers, and I want those burgers dressed, you got that? With the lettuce and the pickles and everything."

The cashier nodded.

The man paused for a moment to review his options. The cashier exhaled with exasperation.

The spells on the menu did not have a list price. Although this was Delphine's first visit to the Far Burger Bar, she knew the man and his brood were not considering cost at this point. She recognized the deliberations boiled down to two inextricable truths—retaliation is wonderfully satisfying, until it's not, AND by the time the giver of such retaliation understands this, will they care? Whatever menu option led to a 'no' was the one the customer generally went with. Delphine's observations from the sidelines seemed to support this.

"Yeah, um, I need...two *Tit for Tat* spells." The man let out a cavernous breath. "From the kid's menu."

*This is for the two bickering...?* Delphine knew it wasn't polite to judge, but judge she did.

"Care to supersize that? Maybe a *Hula Hoop Ring of Fire* spell that they can grow into?"

"Nah, I'm good."

*Thank goodness that man has a dime size of common sense.*
"That'll be $14.28."

The children mended fences for at least a few minutes as they carried on a vibrant whisper conversation behind the man. Delphine's nosiness got the better of her (again). She angled her body to give her ears a better position.

"That booger face Kitty Linton is going to get it good," the boy said, arrogant and unapologetic as he fidgeted with a slingshot stashed in his front jeans pocket. "Teach her to show me up at dodgeball." Then he shook his head, ginger-red hair flopping like a guitar god. The boy appeared to be about twelve years old and bitter beyond his years.

The little girl slumped her shoulders forward. "Maybe I don't want mine after all," she sulked, stroking her mousy blonde ponytail like a security blanket.

"You're such a chicken! Bawk, bawk, bawk!" The boy teased gleefully. Their tenuous truce was effectively over. The girl crossed her arms and stomped her feet, glistening tears pooling at the edge of her almond-shaped eyes.

The man handed the cashier a twenty and tucked the change in the top pocket of his denim jacket.

He corralled the children to the side of the register near Delphine as he motioned for Delphine to take his place.

As he scooted past her, Delphine's eyes fixated on the man's fingers. Or lack thereof. He was missing digits to varying degrees. Some to the base, some to the first knuckle. Except for his thumbs. Those were fully intact.

Whispers of Far Burger Bar slipped as easy as bites of pecan pie and sips of café au lait into the regular Sunday lunch conversation between her mother and the ladies of the church. The legend twisted its way into every conversation that Delphine could remember growing up. Except it was called Stinky Joe's Juke Joint at that time. Before it opened its doors beyond just Black folks to attract more business and spread more misery.

Delphine would listen, crouched near the kitchen door, her Sunday dress covering her knees but not long enough to touch her Buster Brown shoes. The hushed conversations of the elders were like catnip to Delphine's ears. As teacups clinked in saucers, the gaggle of silver-haired afros did not mince words. After a certain age, elders rarely do. The rumors spun off their tongues with delight and a swirl of fear. Before Delphine would see firsthand missing fingers and missing faces, she remembered her elders' words about Stinky's:

*An unholy place that messes with things that shouldn't be messed with.*

Delphine was schooled in the ways of the juke joint turned Far Burger Bar, its menu, and the toll to be exacted as a ghoulish bedtime story to keep her in line.

The man's missing digits confirmed to Delphine he had messed with things he ought not to on more than one occasion. And had no plans of stopping, by the looks of it.

The man knelt in front of the little girl, took her by the shoulders, and said, "I already ordered it, Sarah. I didn't come all this way for you to change your mind." His pep talk was part saccharine, part manipulative. "You said you wanted it. Now you got it." The words penetrated the little girl. A fresh spring of tears streamed from her blue eyes.

Delphine closed off her mind to the images of what the spells, even schoolyard versions, could extract from such young children.

The cashier reached below the counter for one of the toys that usually accompany a kid's meal. "Hey, would you like one of these, sugar?" It was a miniature puzzle of a Lament Configuration box, her attempt at cheering up the little girl. Instead, the boy snatched the wooden pieces.

"Mine!" The boy's body language practically dared anyone in the vicinity to dislodge it from his hand.

The cashier prepared to offer another toy when the man glanced at her with eyes that said, *stay out of this*. Ignoring the boy, the man reached over and took the girl's hand in his nubs. He murmured gently, "Honey, there's no rule that says you have to use it, but since we're here, might as well..."

"Fine, Dad," she said without meeting his stare. "I'll get it. Just leave me alone."

The boy called Scooter wagged his finger at the girl called Sarah.

The man boxed the boy's ears between his stubby nubs, resulting in a squeal followed by a sulky scowl.

Delphine stepped to the counter, her fingers skimming the cold counter.

"Order up," blared from one of the cooks. Delphine couldn't tell which one with their backs turned.

"Excuse me, sugar." The cashier held up her finger in a 'wait a minute' motion to Delphine. She grabbed the tray of food and the chosen spells of impending schoolyard terror from the cook and handed it to the man.

Delphine observed Scooter balance the platter of food handed to him by his father and scurry to a table near the window. Wrappers flew away as the kids chomped down and wiped beef juice from their lips. Delphine glimpsed the man unwrapping his sandwich with stubs for fingers, and her gut acids bubbled.

"Okay, where were we?" The cashier's brown eyes bore into her as she cocked her head and waited.

"Oh," Delphine hesitated, "I'll, um, take a burger, fries, and a *Playground Retaliation* spell."

"From the kid's menu?" The cashier squeaked out her question, dumbfounded but curious. "Are you sure?"

She nodded her head slowly, then with conviction, as if she were satisfied with her final answer on a quiz show. "Yes. Thanks."

"Supersize that?"

"Nope."

Delphine chuckled inside. She'd done it. The weeks of stewing in her own aggravated juices came down to a burger and fries, a pittance for the reclamation of her life.

Then her stomach sank.

The clink of spatulas against the metal grill was the building blocks of a terrible thing that was going to happen. But then again, it was a terrible thing that had happened to her.

Delphine observed the huddle of customers as she waited. The cashier had already informed Delphine that her spell would be 'made to order'. This spell wouldn't sit under a heat lamp losing its potency. It would be as fresh as milk straight out of a cow's udder. But it also meant witnessing a cavalcade of customers come through. Seeing so many people with spite in their veins made Delphine sad for the world.

But not sad enough to give up her place in line.

"Order up!" The declaration jolted Delphine. The cashier slid the bag with hot, fresh, made-to-order revenge across the counter. A grease patch soaked through the brown paper and, for a second, Delphine was hyperaware of how normal this all appeared.

"Enjoy!" the cashier said with a singsong lilt.

Delphine wasn't sure if her words were a sick joke or part of the customer service training manual. '*Welcome to the Far Burger Bar, may I take your order*' floated in the air behind her as she cupped her wicked package, and exited the restaurant.

Delphine fished in her bag, careful not to disturb the vial inside the red box. She retrieved the matching ruby-red envelope, pulsating and warm to the touch, as she walked to her car. She studied the embossed black letters. A wax seal secured the flap.

The starless night was clear with only a crescent moon dangling in the sky. Delphine stood outside her late-model Plymouth Colt, running her fingers over the seal. Each groove in the hard wax awakened under her touch. Delphine placed the thick paper stock in front of her nose with both hands, the bag crinkling against her small-breasted frame, and inhaled. The world spun softly and slowly as she closed her eyes and said, "You belong to—"

The Far Burger Bar's door flung open with a raucous bang, jerking her from the intoxicating trance. A horde of pattering feet burst through and out into the parking lot. Customers galloped across the pavement in a frantic bid for survival.

Delphine couldn't tell if the patron's bodies were exploding or being torn apart as the walls and windows of the restaurant filled with blood splatter, dripping like ganache down the side of a beautifully frosted cake. A sheet of red viscousness obscured the terror inside, but the glass wasn't soundproof. Muffled pleas for mercy and exclamations to God buffered through the windows.

The man with his two kids barreled through the glass doors and straight into Delphine, knocking her to the ground. Blood coated the man. Delphine assumed he was covered in a mix of several unlucky customers. The kids screamed; their faces streaked with pinkish-red tears.

"Ah, sorry 'bout that, lady," he shrieked. "I'd help you up, but I gotta get the kids home," he declared as if this was the most pressing issue he would deal with all day. He sprinted through the parking lot, the kids trailing hopelessly behind.

Delphine lay on the ground. Gravel, shards of glass bottles, and all forms of spit dug into her palms. Her floral prairie skirt, reddish crimson splatter down the front, was bunched up to her waist, white cotton panties exposed against her brown skin. Delphine stood up, dusting herself and fumbling for her car keys that had fallen out of her cardigan pocket.

"Butter my butt and call me a biscuit! Where are those keys?" she whined. The moonlight caught a glimpse of metal, and Delphine exhaled in terrified relief.

No sooner than she snatched the keys from the pavement, a crashing thud came from behind her. Glass and plastic exploded in red and yellow pieces so close to Delphine that shards peppered her right hand. A dribble of blood seeped from the wound when she pulled the pieces out of her skin. A few more bits clung to her coiled hair.

A shower of sparks like a Fourth of July sizzler sprayed from The Far Burger Bar sign that landed near Delphine. Neon letters flickered, and live wires sparked and wheezed. The sign had fallen from the top of the restaurant structure and blocked one of the roads out of the parking lot.

A raw scream belted out into the night. The blonde, bloody and hysterical, stumbled out of the ruins. Her dank, mangy eye glistened. The good eye was wide and frightened. She ran full tilt toward Delphine, a red envelope in her hand.

Delphine darted into the driver's seat of her car; the bag of warm food stuffed between her legs.

The blonde jumped uninvited into the passenger seat.

"What are you doing?" Delphine yelled. "Get out of my—" Delphine could see the manager's face hovering outside the hatchback window. He clinched the bumper in a vise grip and stared through the dirty window. Delphine turned her head to verify the lunacy; to bear witness in her mind should she escape this. She turned back to her steering wheel, both hands clenched in a white-knuckle embrace around the wheel. Maniacal laughter consumed her lungs.

"You have to drive!" The blonde cried.

Delphine shook her head. "Nope, no. Get the fuck out of my car," her broad smile like a clown about to add to its body count in the basement. The laughter bubbled up again from a place so steeped in fear that Delphine couldn't process this spectacle any other way.

The back of the car rose higher, its rear wheels no longer touching the ground. Gravity slanted Delphine forward. It was only now that she realized the radio had been blaring the entire time. The last song she may ever hear was "What a Friend I Have in Jesus" from the AM gospel station 70 miles away.

The blonde screamed in panic. Through gasps, she wailed, "I said I'd settle for a replacement!" She squeezed her eye shut. "Rat bastard said 'no'!" Her mouth curved in a grimace. The blonde braced her hands on the dashboard as the car lifted higher.

"Wait, what? You stole the spell?" Delphine bellowed; laughter replaced by abject anger.

"How was I to know he would go nuclear to get it back?" she roared. All pretense of her whiny voice dropped like marbles on the floor.

Delphine started the car and reversed with a rip roar out of her parking space. A thunk under her back wheels jostled both the driver and the unwanted passenger. Delphine shifted into drive as she squinted through the cascade of sweat off her brow into the rearview mirror. The wheels began to spin. "For heaven's sake!" In her rectangular view, the man with the silver hair and the expensive suit grasped the bumper and held on like glue.

The blonde began to sob. Delphine was thankful that the good eye was the only one visible to her. She realized the manager was not opposed to collateral damage in retrieving what belonged to him, so this crazy white woman in her car needed to go.

As the back end tilted in the air, Delphine pressed harder on the gas, the arches of her feet knotted and cramped. The man hugged the car, his arms creeping in a taffy stretch toward Delphine and the blonde. The fingers and nails scratched a trail of lands and grooves along the side of the car. Crushing pain racked Delphine's chest as the sturdy seatbelt restraints that kept her body from slamming into the windshield cut into her abdomen. The blonde teetered headfirst, and sandwiched, into the tempered glass.

'*Objects are closer than they appear*' spiraled in Delphine's head as her eyes shifted from the side window to the gear selector.

The Silver-Haired Man heaved as he clung to the trunk. "No refunds, no replacements, ma'am," he hollered. "You knew the rules!" His right fist crashed through the tempered glass of the passenger window. He grabbed the blonde by the neck and yanked her out of the car.

Delphine gasped as she shifted from drive to reverse. The ghastly figure behind her fell backward, and the car's rear fell to the ground and bounced like a lowrider. She shifted back to drive and punched the gas, fishtailed, then skidded away.

In Delphine's rearview mirror, the man and the blonde danced a macabre tango as he swung her around. She saw the blonde's neck loll and fall to the side. With a dramatic swoop, the man snapped the woman's head clean off its shoulders, her curls of hair flying like a shooting star's tail. The last thing she saw was the head rolling on the ground as she raced toward the road to freedom.


*END*

# 7

# Cinderella at Midnight

***11:05 PM***

THE PROBLEM WASN'T A wedding under the cover of night. Lyla knew starry evenings of celebration were a nice problem for mortals to have. No, this problem was much bigger. Walter was missing, and only Lyla, a little pint-sized demon with all the cunning and cleverness of a regular-sized demon, could solve it. At least that's how she saw things as she peered through the crack in the door.

***11:07 PM***

Lyla grabbed the doorknob and leaned stealthily just inside the bridal suite, watching the drama play out like a bad community theatre production. Her normally squeaky patent leather shoes were library quiet as she stood still, absorbing the unfolding confusion.

Blooming roses on scrolling vines accented the wallpaper that covered every wall of the room. The décor was a controlled chaos of heavy wood and overstuffed furniture. It gave Lyla the feeling of being suffocated by a Victorian grandmother's pillows.

The weeping bride was huddled by a curvaceous older woman in a subdued pink two-piece satin suit with a matching veiled hat and a pair of white gloves in her hand, a step beyond her Sunday best. Another woman closer in age to the bride hovered next to her in a pale blue flowing halter dress, presumably the bridesmaid.

Lyla observed varying degrees of panic around the room. This was fertile ground for her to do what she does best.

"Who would want to snatch a defenseless miniature pinscher?" Andrina Brownstone, socialite and bride-to-be, examined the note. The felt-tip block letters expanded, soaking up her tears. She fluffed the crinolines of her wedding gown with her free hand as she dipped to retrieve the red and green plaid blanket that Walter used as his resting pallet. The tartan-style fabric dangled in her shaking hands.

The groom, Vincent Booker, leaned against the armoire near the sliding glass door. "This is a joke, right? Only a psycho would hurt a dog." He strode over to the cluster of frantic women and eased the note from Andrina's hand. Vincent attempted to comfort her.

Andrina gave her well-meaning but socially brash husband-to-be a slight frown. What Andrina had in New Orleans' pedigree, Vincent matched in wealth, but his money wasn't spent on etiquette lessons.

"My Cinderella fairytale is practically sliding into the Mississippi," she sniffed.

Her eyes glistened with a fresh trickle of tears as she pressed the blanket to her cheeks like soft weave harbored clues.

Andrina's midnight nuptials, an elaborate spectacle that spent the last twenty years gestating in her mind, would commence in just under an hour. Guests bustled just beyond the suite's glass sliding door, none of them aware that a precarious situation was unfolding.

Wagging the cloth in Vincent's face, Andrina bawled, "I can still smell the lavender shampoo from his special bridal bubble bath! For heaven's sake, where is *he!*"

Walter's disappearance could very well bring this wedding to a screeching halt, but before Lyla could intervene, she wanted to hear more.

Vincent massaged Andrina's back as the wails leaped and dipped like a rollercoaster of grief. "Walter probably got lost," he said anxiously. "He's pretty resourceful, though. Remember the time he got stuck in the fence at Mama Garrett's house? He wiggled out of that just fine."

Andrina was having none of Vincent's Pollyanna nonsense.

"Don't you get it?" she snapped, stomping her satin heels. "The rings? They were around his collar!" She snatched the paper from Vincent's hand. "Whoever has him doesn't *need* him anymore. They have the..." Andrina pointed to a still-trembling ring finger.

Vincent swallowed hard to steady his nerves. He assessed where on the spectrum Andrina's emotional state might lie at that moment—anywhere from fragile to homicidal. "The note doesn't exactly say he was taken. He still could have wandered off."

Lyla was so laser-focused on the verbal tussle inside the room that she did not detect a pair of soft orthopedic shoes approaching. The booming voice that accompanied the footwear made up for that.

"What in the world are you doing?" Lyla jumped at the accusing voice. Aunt Sylvie observed Lyla with a stern stare. "Get out of grown folks' business," she barked.

"I wasn't in anybody's business," Lyla mumbled. "I can't help it if they're carrying on so loud." She swayed her neck with the response. The coiled Afro puffs on each side of her head bounced outrageously.

Aunt Sylvie didn't appreciate what old-timers would refer to as "back talk" from a sassy six-year-old. "Hmm." She crossed her arms and pursed her lips. "Go find your...I thought this was a child-free wedding. Who's supposed to be minding you tonight?"

Lyla's face pinched in protest at the question. "But I wasn't doing anything," she asserted, fists clenched at the sides of her white cotton dress.

Aunt Sylvie settled a perplexed glance on Lyla. "Go find your family, please." The elder sashayed into the room, the sleeve of her crepe ensemble grazing Lyla's cheek. The woman promptly got to work providing her matriarchal version of comfort. "Oh, sweet Andrina, you mustn't worry. Everyone is searching. Marion, be a dear and grab her a Kleenex."

Before the door could close, Lyla slipped in.


### *11:12 PM*


She made her way to the other side of the bridal suite. The open sliding glass door invited the humid night air to waft in and mingle in the air-conditioned space. Lyla stared out at the manicured grounds of St. Edgewood Country Club, one of New Orleans's most exclusive playgrounds of the rich and richest in the area.

"Just under an hour to find this scrappy little hound," she murmured. The heirloom rings that adorn Walter's collar were as important as the sun rising in the East. *Le Conseil des Dé-mons* tapped her as a background observer, demon eyes on the ground, to confirm this union took place. She was one of their most senior operatives with extensive knowledge of human behavior, having over 200 years of experience. The world would change in the most unholy way, and it was Lyla's mission to preserve humanity until *Le Conseil des Démons* was ready to take control 32 years from now.

Lyla noticed Bea sitting on the edge of a puffed armchair near her destination. As Lyla walked up, Bea placed an empty champagne glass on the tray next to the sliding door.

"Where've you been? You were supposed to relieve me 30 minutes ago," she huffed in a low tone. "I'm on my third champagne, holding down the fort here."

The young woman looked impossibly fresh and cool in a teal shimmery slip dress with sheer sleeves that maximized her athletic brown frame. Bea was Lyla's mortal guide assigned to her late last year.

"Haven't you noticed we have a problem?" Lyla tilted her head toward Andrina and the gaggle of fixers talking but not personally doing anything to find Walter.

"A problem? I thought you said this was an 'easy peasy' walk down the aisle," Bea whispered.

Lyla grew restless with the young woman's unhelpful observation. "Walter is missing, along with the rings. Those rings are everything, so we need to find that scrappy dog."

Lyla let out a hiss that turned into a sneeze. Lyla wiped her nose with the back of her hand. There were still aspects of humanity that irritated her. One of them was pollen. Lavender and hibiscus were in full bloom in the Louisiana nighttime heat and doing a number on Lyla's nose. Bea pulled a tissue from her small clutch purse and handed it to the little girl.

The Brownstone rings, engraved with 'things are as they should be', were the key to the power that the Brownstone women would manifest in the future, not that Andrina or any newlywed before her was aware of. An unbroken line of inheritance to each eligible bride, one per generation, was the Lego block to the plans the *Démons* had set in motion.

"Can't you use your power to open a black portal and find the dog that way?" Bea casually patted her tight curls pushed back with a pearl headband.

Lyla wondered if Bea, with her unbothered attitude and killer fashion sense, was the real demon.

"The portal isn't a party trick," Lyla grumbled. "It can find people most of the time, but not animals. Not reliably anyway."

Bea tightened her lips in recognition of the implication of the hole but remained unfazed by the current events. "Okay, where do we start?"

Lyla waved her hands in a hush motion and said, "I need quiet so I can think."

She glanced outside as guests and waitstaff wove in and around the ceremonial area located about half a football field away. Lyla had to admit the setup was quite a sight. Poles lined the length of the perimeter on each side with lights draped and crisscrossed everywhere, forming a twinkling canopy.

The sounds of "Waterfalls" by TLC began on the heels of "Gin and Juice," ending Snoop Dogg's reign over the DJ's speakers. Lyla shimmied to the musical earworm floating her way, the fabric of her dress airy like cotton candy on her honey-colored skin. Over the decades, Lyla had done the bidding for the *Démons* organization, she enjoyed the 1990s the most.

Early arrivals were beginning to occupy ivory satin-covered chairs fitted with lush aubergine-colored bows. Champagne, poured and served by wordless servers in white jackets, lubricated their idle hands. Lyla wondered which guests would be bold enough to snatch their gift back from the table inside if this wedding didn't come to fruition.

### *11:17 PM*

Lyla felt a tap on her shoulder. It was Aunt Sylvie. "Excuse me, little biscuit, if you insist on being in this room, you should stay out of the way. Us old gals need some fresh air." Lyla politely retreated to allow the women to exit through the sliding glass door. Aunt Sylvie slid the door closed and, with a darting glance, dared Lyla to open the door again.

Didn't matter. Lyla had the ability to rummage through any human for words spoken and unspoken. This, combined with her ability to mesmerize entire rooms of people into a shared reality, made her a legend in the halls of the *Démons*. She had a 90% successful conversion rate, after all. What Lyla did back in 1969 with the moon landing was basically a game-changer.

She watched as the women walked over the freshly cut grass to a bush at the side of the clubhouse. The exterior lights at the corner where they convened shone down like an interrogation spotlight.

"That silly girl wanting a dog in her wedding. Absurd. Just one more thing that can go wrong if you ask me," Aunt Sylvie said.

Lyla closed her eyes. Prisms of color floated inside her lids as words tend to do when she tapped into conversations or crawled through other minds.

"I warned Andrina against marrying into the Booker family. They are just terrible luck." Aunt Sylvie shook her head in dis-approval as she said the words. "But she is set on it, so I am going to support it." She kneaded the back of her neck as if a tight crook was forming at the base of it. "He'll certainly keep Andrina in the style of living she's accustomed to, and she does seem to be sweet on him."

Miss Marion, a woman known for her silver hair and salty tongue, responded, "Hmm, hmm, hmm," and nodded in the negative, "But if you think it's worth it...remember the last time the Brownstones and the Bookers joined together?" The woman rolled her eyes. "Even a snake has enough common sense to avoid this union."

As the matriarchs of their respective families, Aunt Sylvie and Miss Marion had seen a thing or two over the years. So had Lyla, and she knew exactly what they were referring to.

Miss Marion confided as she removed a white glove, "Andrina has lived such a charmed life so far, maybe a little adversity would do her some good." She scratched her hand furiously. "Well, Corky had her chance to make some magic with Vincent," she said with resignation.

Aunt Sylvie paused, then gave her old friend a wicked look. "If I didn't know you any better, I'd think you were stirring something up by recommending Corky to Andrina."

"Oh, now that is foolish talk, Sylvie. Foolish. If Vincent was thinking twice about options, we'd all know it. He can't hide much of anything he's thinking." A fresh round of scratching overtook Miss Marion.

"You okay, cher?" Aunt Sylvie asked as she pulled a small bottle of Gold's Bond from her pocketbook.

Her friend kindly waved it away, then concluded her musings with a chuckle, "Who'd a thought one missing dog could bring the whole house of cards tumbling down? Besides, Walter is the only one coming between those two, right?" The silence from Aunt Sylvie caused Miss Marion to look away.

### *11:17 PM*

Within minutes of the older women reentering the room to begin their subtle coercion to get Andrina down the aisle, the bridal suite door swung open with a flourish.

A blunt twenty-something in a vivid yellow suit and black sensible flat shoes burst through the suite door, barking orders. "Okay, everyone! Small hiccup in the run of the show, but we are staying the course. Chop, chop!" She swung her planning notebook in her right hand like an axe.

"The bumblebee? That's Corky," Lyla whispered to her companion. "The wedding planner."

Corky swung her head toward the fair-haired, gangly man, about the same age, who entered with her. An errant box braid flew within an inch of his face, nearly taking his eye out. His reflexes were quick, avoiding the braided missile.

Lyla sighed and informed Bea, "And that's her lackey, Braden."

Aunt Sylvie held up her hand in an effort to slow Corky's roll. "Corky, I know you have a job to do, but there is a pressing matter of finding those rings."

"And Walter!" Andrina howled.

"Yes, and Walter," Aunt Sylvie said as she stroked Andrina's back. Vincent took a few steps back, as if distancing himself from his bride's emotions would inoculate him from catching any feelings about the situation.

Lyla took in this latest dramatic scene.

"What are you thinking?" Bea asked.

"Not sure yet, but..." Lyla ceased talking in order to concentrate on Corky. The planner's expression intrigued her. Lyla inhaled deeply, absorbing the vibes Corky was emitting. Her ears began to tingle. She massaged them like a radio dial.

Corky took Braden's elbow and moved him towards the door to put some space between them and the others in the room.

But Lyla was now tuned into Corky's mental frequency and the words she spoke. The other tidbits inside Corky's mind flowed into Lyla's like a torrent of lava.

She loved it.

"Can you believe this bride is going to allow a non-essential canine to derail her wedding? She really lacks imagination, that one," Corky said softly but with a bite at the end. She gently tilted her head in a slow roll as if to loosen her neck. A slight grimace curled her lips.

Corky's strong personality and heightened anxiety created color swirls streaming before Lyla like a fire hose. Lyla wondered what Corky was anxious about.

"Walter is so cute," a fidgety Braden commented. His personality was the equivalent of human tapioca, his words like drying paint to Lyla's senses. His fingers bounced between straightening his tie knot and tugging the collar of his shirt.

"Besides," Braden continued, "the rings are sort of important, don't you—"

"But she doesn't need the rings to seal the deal with Vincent." Corky slapped her notebook in her hand as if this were the definitive word in the discussion. She stepped over to Andrina, muscling in between Aunt Sylvie and Miss Marion. The women did not appreciate the interruption.

"All right, let's divide and conquer," Corky announced to the room. "Braden will search the ceremony area." She turned to the older women. "And maybe you two can check the common areas? Vincent and I will check the —"

"Umm, not so fast." Lyla breezed into the center of the bridal suite.

"Can I help you?" Andrina's voice rose in a singsong, confused pitch.

Andrina was being very resistant to Lyla's mesmerizing and mind-trolling techniques. What Lyla would call a 10-percenter, given that 10 percent of humans take a bit longer to be swayed by her tactics. The fact that Andrina would challenge Lyla troubled her, but she brushed it off.

*Fake it till you make it, girl. You got this.*

Bea hung back as Lyla launched into her interrogation.

"We are just as concerned about Walter as you," Lyla stated with a serious demeanor well beyond what her physical years would suggest. "So, I'm just going to jump in."

Andrina's confused stare worried Lyla, so she strode across the room to put distance between the two of them and mentally regroup.

Andrina trailed behind her.

*Great! This woman is following me around like a stain on my soul. If I had one.*

Lyla climbed into the tufted chair next to the dressing table and faced the bride with her best, mesmerized stare, and continued, "Where did you last see the pup?" She asked.

"What?" Andrina cocked her head as if in disbelief that a child would be bold enough to insert herself into an adult situation and be up past her bedtime.

But Lyla could see the tide shifting. The telltale sign that she was wiggling her way in.

Andrina rubbed her neck.

When mesmerizing takes hold, it pinches the nerves just above the collarbone. Lyla knew she was back in business.

"Where was Walter last seen? Who was tending to him?" Lyla's legs dangled over the chair's edge. She clasped her hands in her lap. "I see the crate in this room, so," she stopped and leaned forward, her hand in front of her nose, a sneeze coming but then retreating. She shook her head and continued, "Why wasn't he in it?"

Corky slouched on the sofa, sucking her teeth and checking her nails like this was none of her business.

Andrina said, "Well, for your information, little girl, that is what everyone is trying to find out." She stopped and tilted her head to the left in a good stretch.

Lyla could feel a previously suppressed memory of Andrina's barrel to the forefront. Or that could be wishful thinking on her part. She wasn't entirely sure.

"Walter was supposed to be on his potty run with Vincent, yes." Andrina's eyes cast a dark look at Vincent as he idled by the sofa, a little too close to Corky.

"Vincent," Andrina pointed her French manicured finger in his direction, "said he put him back in the room, but..." She was about to zero in on Vincent just as her bridesmaid, Emily, spoke up from the other side of the room.

"I didn't see Vincent. And I was here the whole time." The bridesmaid with short natural hair, colored an unnatural platinum blonde, fidgeted with her dress as she took up space on the loveseat.

"Ugghh, Vincent, where did you—" Andrina spun to her left as if her eyes needed her body to be in motion to see better.

"Where is Vincent?" she exclaimed.

Everyone gazed around at each other in bewilderment. While everyone was distracted by the Emily and Andrina show, Vincent had quietly exited the room without anyone noticing.

Lyla could kick herself. She hadn't planned on Andrina's mind being Teflon to her mental coercion. Or on Vincent being a runner.

Lyla cleared her throat to grab everyone's attention and get things back on track. "So, there is a gap in the time between Vincent picking Walter up for his poop run and when he should have been returned when no one saw either of them."

"Yeah, that's right, Tiny Sherlock." Andrina planted herself at the dressing table. Lyla slid down out of the chair next to the table for her next announcement. "Talk amongst yourselves. We'll," she pointed to herself and Bea, "get Vincent and bring him back."


### *11:30 PM*


Lyla crossed her arms and mentally reviewed what she had learned. She hesitated to share her investigative breadcrumbs with Bea lest she have to divulge how powerful her mesmerizing really was. But after careful consideration of what was at stake, she decided to give Bea the Cliff Notes version of the older women's conversation.

"If Aunt Sylvie is second-guessing Miss Marion's motives, maybe we should?" Bea squinted as if an original thought was coming to her. "I've been wondering...why does that Council need Andrina and Vincent to get married?" Bea was full of questions tonight, which was unusual for her.

Lyla decided she would answer this one. "Simple. Andrina and Vincent will have a daughter whom they'll name Lucille. Lucille needs to be born so that she can inherit the rings. If Walter isn't found in the next," she looked at her Tweety Bird watch, "the next 15 minutes, give or take, it will shift things. That could be very bad."

"How bad?"

"Black portal goes berserk bad." Lyla waved her hand like a magician's assistant.

Bea raised an eyebrow. "That bad?" She had an idea of what the portal was capable of. "Let's find Vincent."

### *11:33 PM*

The duo found him alone in the groom's suite. It was a mirror image of the bridal version with a few exceptions–the sofa along the wall to the left, the love seat placed to form an L shape, and the end table between them remained the same. But instead of a heavy armoire, there was a substantial credenza near the sliding glass door, and the dressing table was replaced with a fully stocked wet bar with a box of cigars for good measure. Because gender roles were reinforced like prison barbed wire in the South.

He faced the sliding glass doors, peering out at the twinkling canopy that may or may not host a wedding, the dog strap meant for Walter in his hands.

Vincent waved in a 'don't come closer' motion. "This is a private area. You can't be in here." He looked from Bea back to Lyla. "Aren't you a little young to be up this late?"

Lyla was beginning to see that Brownstones and Bookers, Andrina and Vincent, in particular, had slippery minds that did not take well to mesmerizing.

She shook it off and continued her advance toward Vincent until she climbed into the chaise lounge next to the bar across from him. With tiny fingers steepled under her chin, she started her questioning.

"Thank you for your concern about my bedtime." Lyla nodded. Before Vincent could respond, she launched in with, "Where is Walter? Really."

Vincent threw the leash to the ground. Frustration flashed in his eyes but flamed out when he realized it was only a child sitting in front of him. A child who could take care of herself just fine, but he didn't know that. Vincent put his head in his hands. "I wish I knew. I swear I opened Andrina's door and dropped him off in there."

Lyla looked Vincent up and down, way down to his shoes. Things looked suspicious.

"If you walked him for poo time, then why don't your shoes have dirt on them?"

Vincent took a few steps back, bumping the credenza next to the glass door behind him. Just as Lyla was about to go trolling in Vincent's head, he said, "Okay, I didn't walk Walter." He crumbled under Lyla's discerning gaze like a schoolyard snitch.

"Ah, ha! I knew it!" Lyla yelled as if she was destined to wear a deerstalker hat and a pipe cocked between her lips. Or an oversized trench coat.

Lyla puffed her pom-pom hair in delight and satisfaction that she didn't have to crawl inside his head, not that she would find much.

Bea sighed under her breath and smiled.

"I asked Braden, Corky's assistant, to take care of walking him for his, you know, business." 'Business' was in air quotes. Vincent clasped his hands and scrunched his face. "I didn't want to pick up after Walter and get my suit messy." He shrugged and concluded, "There. I said it." He sat against the credenza, hands in his pockets, eyes practically boring a hole in the carpet. "What's it to you anyway, little slice?" His voice was soft with shame.

"It matters a whole lot to me that you make it down the aisle. On time." She tapped her watch. "Don't you think it matters?"

"Yeah, of course, I do. More than you know." Vincent's tone was contemplative and somber.

Lyla felt for the man. "Save the 'I do' for your bride." She slipped down from the chair. "We're all going back to the bridal suite. And you need to face Andrina."

Vincent looked as if he would rather swallow thumbtacks, but he agreed.

As the group made their way down the corridor, Lyla exercised her considerable gifts to reach Corky and Braden and send them back to the suite as well.

Lyla's little face was stone cold as she anticipated her confrontation with Braden. She was curious to pick through his mind to determine why she didn't see this turn of events shuffling around in his pudding brain. *Is Braden a 10 per-center*, she wondered.

### 11:45 PM

Vincent walked in as Corky and Andrina kicked off their dueling accusations. Bea and Lyla were right on his heels.

"How could you lose the dog *aaaannd* the rings? You had one job!" Andrina seethed.

"I beg to differ with you, Andrina. This isn't on me. Vincent was responsible for Walter when he went missing."

"That's not exactly true." Vincent's interjection startled everyone in the room.

"That's one way to make an entrance," Lyla whispered to Bea with more than a bit of joviality in her voice.

Vincent craned his head to look around and spotted Braden.

Braden attempted to fade into the background. His knees buckled as he crouched behind Emily's statuesque frame near the loveseat and end table.

Andrina gave Vincent a glare that could melt stone. "Really? Then tell us all what happened, Houdini!" She sat at the dressing table, arms crossed, legs crossed, complementing her cross attitude. Vincent drew in a deep breath and stood next to her. He rested his hand on her bare shoulder and, surprisingly, she didn't push it away.

"Okay, I deserved that," Vincent said sheepishly. With the requisite amount of guilt, he recounted handing off Walter to Braden for the tiny pup's call of nature.

Andrina nearly shoved Vincent out of the way to get to Braden, who, in turn, slinked even closer to the back wall. "What did you do with him!" she yelled; arms outstretched in Braden's direction as Vincent held her at the waist.

"Okay, fine! I should have said something before," he exclaimed. "I took him for the potty run," he finally admitted.

Lyla slowed down to respond, "You still didn't answer the question."

Everyone turned to gawk at Lyla.

Although she appeared like a spunky child, Lyla was far older than human form would suggest but still young enough in demon years to still be fascinated by making adults uncomfortable.

"Can you stop asking me questions?" Braden raised his hands in an exasperated motion and addressed Bea. "Can you get her to stop it? It's freaking me out, man!"

Bea answered succinctly, "No."

A bit annoyed, Lyla said, "You've been all over the venue this evening, privy to all the comings and goings. It's not so far-fetched that you could put Walter in a service vehicle and ship him off. He'd fit pretty nicely in a box." She waved her arms in an upward motion, the signal for Bea to come over and lift her up. Bea set her on the end table. Lyla felt that being closer to eye level with a suspect gave her leverage given the nature of her size.

With a confused look, Braden finished with, "That's your opinion. Which, I have to say, it's pretty dark for a kid."

"Not so much." Lyla cocked her head and leaned in. "I am a demon," she mouthed.

"Ohhhkayy??" Braden's sideways glance at Bea broke into a crooked smile.

Lyla's surprise at Braden's sudden cheekiness discombobulated her balance. She listed like a Regency heroine in the midst of a fainting spell and plopped into Bea's waiting arms. A few murmurs of "My goodness" peppered the room. Bea softly settled Lyla on the floor.

"I'm fine, nothing to see here." Lyla smoothed out her dress all the while peering at Braden.

He ignored Lyla's impenetrable stare and answered, "Well, for the record, I cracked the door open, and he scooted inside but didn't put him in the crate. I didn't even open the door wide enough to see if anyone was in the room."

In an effort to deflect any culpability by proxy to Braden, Corky added, "I had no idea about this," she scowled at her second in command who immediately found his shoes and the floor more interesting, and finished with, "Anyways, that doesn't explain the note at all."

Andrina slumped cross-legged onto the floor, blankets of satin spilling from her waist all around her. She pulled the folded piece of paper from her décolletage, her off-shoulder neckline dipping dangerously low. "I know," she said dimly. "But why," Andrina kept repeating. She uncrumpled the note, portions of it still damp from her tears, to reveal its vile words and read it aloud. *"Bookers and Brownstones will be the death of the world. Walk away from this marriage, or Walter will not."*

Lyla climbed back into the same tufted chair from the previous detecting session and continued to hold court by turning her attention to Corky. And a side-eye to Braden. "Did you have a bone to pick with the bride?"

Corky gasped with indignant fury. "Whatever do you mean?"

"You know what I mean. You have a history with Vincent, do you not?"

Now it was Andrina's turn to gasp. "What?" Her eyes squinted in anger at Corky. "Is that why Miss Marion lobbied for you as my wedding planner? So, you could muck about with *my* big day?"

"Night, actually," Lyla piped in.

Andrina slowly rose to her feet, silent like a Trappist monk, ready to remove her satin pumps. That could only mean one thing in New Orleans. Andrina was preparing to go medieval on her wedding planner nemesis.

As much as Lyla delighted in Andrina getting flat-footed and ready for a fight, she intervened. "Corky, you tried to date Vincent in the past, but he was never interested, right?"

Corky lashed out, defending her good name for what it was worth. "Truth be told, I never had designs on Vincent. I'm a friend of Miss Marion's family," she said smugly. "That's how I made his acquaintance." She turned her high cheekbones upward and looked at the ceiling, "And he, yes, may have escorted me to a few debutante soirees during carnival season, back," Corky did her internal math, "in 1993 or 1994 when we were at university."

Then Corky pivoted to face Andrina. "It's been three years since that happened. I would hardly say I had *designs* on him at this point." She fidgeted with her black velvet choker, diverting her eyes again. "Besides, he made his choice when he met you," and added, "Obviously."

Lyla noticed that the onlookers in the room rubbernecking during this exchange were highly engaged in the outcome. Except one.

Emily, the bridesmaid.

Lyla observed the young woman, distracted and agitated, but not by the bickering. Then she saw it like a homing beacon, clear as day. Dark, damp stains clung to the blue satin fishtail hem of this fishy bridesmaid.

"Emily—" Lyla began. Her small voice drew everyone's attention away from Andrina and Corky to the new matter at hand.

"That's Miss Emily, young lady," Andrina interrupted in a chastising tone.

Lyla folded her arms indignantly and then did as she pleased.

"Emily...why is your dress hem so filthy?" Lyla hurled the question like an accusation.

Before she could whip the fishtail behind her, everyone got an unobstructed view of the dirty hem. Andrina's eyes flashed hot with displeasure. "Your dress is ruined! This is yet ANOTHER disaster! How could you?"

Corky flew into wedding planner mode. "I'll find some club soda. It'll be fine." She sprinted from the room in search of carbonated sanctuary, nearly pushing Braden onto the loveseat.

"I guess you're in the frying pan now." Lyla tapped her tiny fingers on the winged chair's arms, her stony glare on Emily. "Well? What were you doing out in the dirt? Pushing Walter out into the wild?"

"Who is this kid?" Emily spat. "I went outside..." She paused.

Lyla crawled around in Emily's mind seeking answers.

Emily rubbed her temples and moved downward, right above her collarbone. "Fine," she blurted out. "I was chatting up Rev. Howard by the reception site. That's probably how my dress got dirty." Taken aback by her own outburst, she rushed to her friend. She stuttered, "You were getting poured into your dress in the bedroom, so I thought I had a few minutes." The look on Emily's face was hesitant.

Andrina looked her friend squarely in the eyes and demanded, "Did you see Walter come back into the room?"

Emily sighed, still massaging her neck. "Okay, yes and no."

A collective gasp reverberated off the rosy walls and chintz furniture.

"No, I did not see Walter walk back into the room. Yes, I did see Walter. Out in the ceremony area." She moved over to the sofa and flopped into the same spot Corky had vacated.

"Who was he with?" Andrina and Lyla asked at the same time.

"Well, no one. He was wandering by himself, and, at the time, I didn't know there was anything wrong with that." Emily's eyes pleaded, "Please don't be mad. I didn't know!" She snapped her fingers as she remembered one more thing and followed up with, "But guests were feeding him. That, I know. Saw one of them give Walter some water. Poured it into a cup and laid it on the ground for him. I thought he was fine."

Braden crossed his arms and walked to face Andrina, his expression growing haughty. "See? Based on what I just heard, someone took him when the room was empty for those few minutes when Ms. Lovesick was talking to the reverend."

Emily, ready to storm into Braden, took two steps in his direction, but Lyla intervened.

"Emily, make yourself useful and ask the guests what they know, and meet back here. You have 10 minutes." Lyla said.

Emily stomped her foot and waved a fist at Braden, lips curled, ready to speak her mind. The words bursting into Emily's mind made even a demon like Lyla blush. Lyla quieted the angry woman's thoughts.

Emily lowered her arm, and a faint smile came across her lips. "Yes, I'll go talk to the guests."

As the door shut behind Emily, Lyla turned to Aunt Sylvie and Miss Marion and stated, "Something has been eating at me."

*11:50 PM*

Lyla's ears prickled with the sensation of veiled emotions throughout the room.

Miss Marion was a tougher nut to crack. Her strong will made it difficult to keep her mesmerized over a long period of time. Right about now, Miss Marion was getting annoyed with Lyla, and that could cause a metric ton more problems for the pint-size detective.

"You sure are a busybody, little girl," Miss Marion said with a frown on her face. She winced as she rubbed her right hand. Her white-gloved hand.

"Am I?" Lyla asked.

"Why I never!" Miss Marion bent over to get nose level with Lyla. The stretch of the woman's crepe jacket over her ample hips flattered the older woman's figure, but the stare in her eyes was most unbecoming, Lyla had to admit.

"You listen here, you little rascal." Miss Marion rubbed her temples. "Keep your little heinie out of this!" Miss Marion grabbed Lyla by the arm and began to scoot her toward the door.

"Let go of me!" Lyla protested. The woman released her little arm. "I think I know what happened to Walter," Lyla replied as she rubbed the place where Miss Marion's fingers had grabbed her.

"What is wrong with all of you?!" Andrina shouted. "You should all be out searching high and low for Walter, but yet," she threw up her arms, "I have a carnival happening in here with a six-year-old ringleader."

Lyla sneezed. Her eyes widened, and a cheeky grin came over her lips. "I know what happened to Walter. Most of it anyway."

Stares circled the room.

"Why are you itching?" Lyla squinched her eyes and pointed to Miss Marion's gloved hands. "Are you allergic to something?"

Miss Marion straightened up and smoothed her pink jacket out with a tug at the hem. "I don't have to answer you!"

Aunt Sylvie crossed her arms and took two steps towards the door where Lyla stood. Her bottom lip turned into a frown, and the words that followed matched. "This is not a game for your amusement. This is a serious matter." She clapped her hands once to signal this charade was done. "Go on now. Get to the garden so things can get started." Aunt Sylvie turned her attention to Andrina. "And you, young lady, are going to grab your bouquet and start walking down the aisle. Dog or no dog."

"I will do no such thing," Andrina shouted, tears spilling down her cheeks. "Where is my Walter??!!"

Lyla tilted her head and cleared her throat. "I know how and why it happened," Then she paused for maximum effect. "But there is only ONE of you who knows exactly where he is."

Silence coated the room like a parishioner about to give confession.

Lyla walked through the room, her arms parting the adults like Moses parting the Red Sea and climbed into the same wingback chair where the investigation started and now will end.

With her hands gently placed on the armrest, she began. "Andrina, the note stated you had to choose between Walter or a wedding, correct?"

The bride with her swollen, curious eyes nodded her head. "Yes, I guess that is correct."

"So, who had skin in the game for this wedding TO happen?" Lyla points to Aunt Sylvie.

The room turned to Aunt Sylvie with suspicion.

"Vincent might not be your first choice for Andrina as a partner, but you support Andrina. And Vincent's bank account."

"How dare you!" Aunt Sylvie squawked.

"Be that as it may but it is true." Lyla countered.

Andrina held her hand to stop Aunt Sylvie from taking a closer step toward the little girl. "Aunt Sylvie, you know it's true. But I love Vincent, and those things don't matter to me as much as they do to you." She turned to Corky. "This must be your doing. Where is my dog?" She asked with a growl.

Corky flushed with anger. "You're pointing in the wrong direction, Miss I-Have-It-All," her words a tightrope of tension.

"Ha, you've never gotten over not getting Vincent!" Andrina slid out of her pumps, easy as you please. Vincent noticed this and darted between the two.

"Sweetheart," he said to Andrina, "you know I belong only to you." He pulled her in for a hug. She accepted it, limp and exhausted.

Lyla watched as this all unfolded, hoping for a bigger showdown, but when Vincent diffused it pretty quickly, she continued. "No, it was not Corky, although I can see why you would think so."

Corky shot Lyla a nasty look. Lyla shot Corky a look that made goosebumps rise on her skin.

"The real culprit here is...Miss Marion!" Lyla stated emphatically.

Andrina extricated herself from Vincent and stormed to the older woman and demanded, "Why would you do this? Why are you trying to ruin my big day?"

"YOUR big day? Isn't EVERY day, your big day?" Miss Marion sat in the chair adjacent to the dressing table, a shimmer of fury illuminating her face. "You never get tired of being the queen bee, do ya?"

Aunt Sylvie stared at her old friend with sadness and resentment. "Why would you begrudge young love like this? In such a hateful manner?" Her scorn hit each syllable.

"How did you know?" Andrina asked Lyla.

"The lavender. See how Miss Marion is scratching her hands? How she wears gloves on such a hot evening? She's breaking out in hives from the lavender. She's allergic."

"I don't get it," Vincent said.

"Of course, you don't. Let me break it down. Walter had a lavender bath to start the day. When Miss Marion handled him, the contact with the flower residue triggered the reaction."

"But that doesn't explain why she did it," stated Aunt Sylvie.

"The reason is Corky. Because Corky is like family to her. Miss Marion always wanted Corky to 'do well for herself" by marrying upward," Lyla directed the next statement to Corky, "without realizing that the successful wedding planning business Corky nurtured is, in fact, 'doing well for herself'."

Corky nodded as she walked to Miss Marion and took her gloved hand. "I'm doing fine. And Vincent and I," she looked at him and acknowledged, "were never going to be more than friends."

Lyla climbed out of the chair and stood next to Miss Marion. She said, "Why don't you show us where Walter is?"

Miss Marion pointed to the armoire in the corner.

"I saw Walter with the guest right after Emily probably did. He must have left through the sliding glass door after Braden brought him back." Miss Marion said.

"It was like a freezer in here, so I kept the door open. I forgot to make sure it was closed again," Andrina realized.

"I scooped him up," Miss Marion explained, "and I thought, let's make lemonade out of lemons for Corky. So, I hid him away." Awkwardly, she looked at Corky. "I only wanted you to have what I thought you deserved. Turns out you do."

Andrina had already swung the armoire doors open and squealed with delight.

Walter lay curled up on a tuft of white towels, sleeping. Pebbles of dry dog food rolled on the floor of the cabinet. Water from a plastic bowl sloshed onto the floor as Andrina retrieved him.

"Walter!" Andrina lifted the sleepy dog into her arms. "I missed you so much."

"Are the rings still on his collar?" Vincent asked. Andrina gave him an exasperated glance.

"Oh, okay, I see them." Vincent's inquiry was ill-timed, but Andrina quickly forgave him with a hug.

"You're so tired, my little guy." Andrina stroked his sleek black coat.

Emily ran into the room, winded, but excited. "The guest, the one who gave him water, said a woman—," she stopped as soon as she saw Walter in Andrina's arms. Once she assessed the situation, she responded a bit deflated, "Oh, I guess you found him."

"You've had a long day. And night." Andrina raised Walter's little head and kissed him. "That's okay. We'll carry you down the aisle, won't we?"

Vincent smiled. "Of course."

Lyla clapped her hands, and everyone turned. "Isn't it time for a wedding?" She pointed to the sliding glass door. "Out there?" She gave the adults a look of 'duh' and then the commotion began.

## 12 Midnight

Andrina's Cinderella at Midnight wedding was happening on time, just like it was supposed to.

As Lyla and Bea stood at the back of the garden watching Andrina glide down the aisle toward the man of her dreams, Lyla wondered. Could the bride ever fathom the nightmare that will be made possible, all because this wedding, this union, has come to pass?

"Beautiful ceremony," Lyla mused.

Bea asked, "How does that thing you do in their heads work?"

Any truthful explanation would open an endless cyclone of more fantastical questions that would eventually break Bea's brain. Even Lyla didn't want to purposefully wreak that kind of havoc.

She skirted the question by responding, "I guess I didn't really *need* to go on a fishing expedition in their heads, but sometimes it's fun to do it just for kicks."

"Hmm, interesting." Bea gave Lyla an unsettled smile. "Guess we should skedaddle." She took Lyla's hand and walked away from the ceremony and out to the immaculate grounds surrounding the club. In the darkness, a black hole opened.

Braden yelled out, "Lyla!"

She turned around to see him strolling up behind her and Bea.

Lyla turned to look at the black hole and then back at Braden. "You can see that?" She asked.

"Yes, actually, I can," he said with a tinge of fear in his voice. "You know that's not a party trick."

Lyla rolled her eyes.

Braden extended his hand. "You did good, kid. Well, maybe not 'kid' but you get it."

Lyla shook his hand. "Yeah, I get it, and thanks. But who are you anyway?"

Braden rubbed his chin like he was weighing his options, then spoke. "I'm just like Bea, a mortal guide." He chuckled, "I gotta tell ya, seeing your work in action was a real treat. The legend about 1969, whew, you are a hero."

"Thanks, I guess."

"Sure, well, I have to get back to the reception." With a tip of his head, he offered a short salute and said, "Maybe we'll run into each other again."

With that, Braden grinned and shuffled off.

Lyla, with a startled expression on her face, said, "That was a first. A mortal guide observing me."

"I wonder whom he guides," Bea said.

Lyla had a few ideas but answered, "Who knows?"

The little girl shook her head, Afro puffs bouncing with the weight of a job well done.


*END*

# 8

# A Pretty Smile

Dr. Colburn stared from above, his face half-masked from the nose down, his eyes dark and flat. He pointed the sharp periodontal probe at Lottie's gum line.

"One," Dr. Colburn called out. Susan, the hygienist, typed the number into the electronic chart. If she noticed Lottie's discomfort, she didn't acknowledge it.

Another poke, another yelp from Lottie.

The words spewed out of Lottie's mouth, splayed open by a silicon mouth prop stretching at the corners of her lips like the Joker's smile. "Ahh, aat urtz!"

Lottie tried to repeat herself, but it came out all wrong again. "Awo, aat urtz!"

*Ouch, that hurts!*

"Three. Five. One." Dr. Colburn said. He leaned closer to Lottie's mouth. She wondered if he could smell the remnants of the cappuccino she tried to brush from her teeth before the visit.

It was supposed to be a simple conversation—ask Dr. Colburn for her dental records so she could discreetly move on to a new provider.

"Why do you need them?" Lottie recalled Dr. Colburn's push-back on the request. His tone had morphed from pleasant to a disquieting baritone of suspicion. "Do you doubt the level of care you've been receiving?"

"I'm moving soon," Lottie had muttered. Dr. Colburn accepted her excuse without further questioning.

Besides, his dental care wasn't the specific problem. He had seen her through a painful wisdom teeth removal, an emergency root canal, the odd cavity filling, and veneers. The care was fine...it was his penchant for randomly showing up in her day-to-day life that gave her pause.

At first, Lottie thought seeing her dentist in the wild was a funny coincidence. The first time was in a grocery store's cereal aisle—right after the root canal. She almost didn't recognize him without a face mask.

"Sugary cereals are terrible for your teeth. I hope you're not derailing the hard work we've done."

Lottie bristled at Dr. Colburn's audacity to probe her eating habits. It was annoying but not notable.

Two weeks later, she pulled into a gas station. Dr. Colburn slid into the pump on the other side. "Wow, this is weird seeing you here," he had said, then frowned at the half-eaten chocolate bar in her hand. Lottie tried to ignore his judgment. But the vibes were still low-key—*no problems here*.

And so, it began for the better part of a year—run-ins at a music festival, the multiplex, a concert in the park. Dr. Colburn's 'hello' came with a side eye on whatever Lottie ate and 'helpful' advice on gum disease and daily flossing. It was always borderline intrusive, but then the relentless email reminders from Susan to schedule an appointment began. Lottie wasn't sure if it coincided with seeing Dr. Colburn outside of JJ's Candy Emporium three weeks ago, but she couldn't rule it out. Lottie decided today's annual checkup would be the last.

Susan removed the mouth prop, cascaded a spout of water inside Lottie's mouth, and suctioned the water out. "Veneers still look beautiful," Dr. Colburn said as he leaned over Susan's shoulder. Lottie nodded and closed her mouth to swallow.

"All done." Susan's definitive statement relieved Lottie.

*Thank goodness. Now I can get the fuck out of here.*

"I'll be back with your records." Susan left the room with Dr. Colburn. Lottie sat awkwardly in the reclined chair that Susan failed to put upright.

Susan returned and handed Lottie a manila envelope. "Here you go." The bulkiness took Lottie by surprise. She hadn't realized she'd amassed such a large trove of documentation during her treatment. Lottie thanked Susan and headed to the parking garage.

The click of Lottie's heels filled the concrete structure. Her car was the only one left on the floor. "That's what I get for making a late appointment," she murmured as her fingers tugged at the yellow-brown flap.

Lottie slid a few pages out of the packet. She expected to see billing invoices marked PAID or copies of her treatment outcomes. What she saw stopped her in her tracks.

Printed photos of her eating lunch in the park, mid-bite into a cupcake that she thought she was devouring in the privacy of her car, drinking a soda after a run. All taken from a lurking distance. Based on the stack inside the envelope, there must be hundreds of photos.

Of her eating.

Lotties tucked the packet under her arm and moved swiftly toward her car.

"Ms. Booker!"

Lottie squealed as she turned around. Her heart pounded so hard it ached. "Jesus," she sputtered.

Susan was nearly upon her, waving a manila envelope in the air. As she stepped closer, Lottie tensed.

"Ms. Booker. These are your records." Susan extended the envelope. "Sorry for the confusion." Her manner was casual and calm. Lottie was anything but.

Lottie took the new parcel. She alternated her gaze between what Susan handed her and the alarming envelope in the other hand.

"I'll take that one." Susan reached out, but Lottie took a step back, keeping it out of her reach.

"What is this?" Lottie shook the thick envelope frantically in front of her. "How long has Dr. Colburn been..." At that moment, the good doctor appeared around the corner. Lottie stumbled backward as Susan slipped a latex glove on her hand and a rag out of her medical smock.

"Oh my God!" Lottie turned to run, but her heels impeded her progress. She felt the cloth as it covered her nose and mouth. Susan's arms squeezed around her.

Lottie tried to scream in the deserted garage, but the white cotton absorbed her shriek. As she lost consciousness, Susan hissed in her ear, "After all the work Dr. Colburn put into you, and you go and waste it on junk food and sugar." Susan lowered Lottie to the garage floor. Dr. Colburn's squeaky dress shoes echoed as he approached. He knelt next to Lottie. The last thing she heard was, "You don't deserve that pretty smile."


*END*

# 9

# The Other Me

A CO-WORKER IN SALES, named Justin, although he goes by JD for some reason, was the canary that notified me that I would soon be suffocating in the coal mine of my life. For months, JD had engaged in nitpicking designed to pop a squat in my brain and niggle at me like a tick under the skin.

Ever since I took over the Colter account, his account, his wounded pride needed a target. In the world according to JD, he was robbed of a client and his rightful commission. In the real world, the client decided JD had outlived his usefulness after shipping their order to the wrong warehouse for the third time. Selective amnesia set in, leaving JD with a revisionist history on the matter. Now he spent his days inventing subtle ways to flaunt his disdain and contaminate the well of my success.

JD stepped inside my walled-off cubicle and plopped some loose pages in front of me. "How you like them apples?" he sputtered out, slowly licking his thin upper lip. My stare was cold and dismissive, but it didn't form the boundaries I needed with JD. He continued.

"Read 'em and weep, sista!"

I could have challenged his appropriation of vernacular slang, but that was the catnip he was looking for.

*Fuck you, Slim Shady.*

"So?" I muttered coarsely under my breath.

I scanned the pages, flipping over each one until I turned to the final printed truth. Consolidated Paper Mart's logo was top and center. JD's signature scribbled at the bottom. A new account in the Southwest territory, my territory, belonged to him.

My back was killing me when I turned sideways from my laptop and directly into JD's smugness. The pit grew in my stomach. The 4 pm meeting with my boss, Denny McCallister, VP of Sales, popped up on my screen a few minutes ago. JD's appearance in my cubicle, waving his contractual prize, was beginning to make sense.

I gently tipped my head. Until I could figure out what this turn of events meant, it was better to let him think his provocateur exuberance had not made a dent.

"Calm down, JD. Denny mentioned a few realignments in yesterday's meeting." I could be overthinking this, right? Just last week, Denny mentioned a new account in JD's territory to me. That sounded a lot like realignment talk in my book. Still, I had to wonder if Denny was treating us both like suckers.

In an effort to get my co-worker out of my hair, I dismissed JD with, "I am busy right now; can I ignore you some other time?"

JD stared at me intently. "Funny," he said dryly.

This comment must have hit him a certain way. The tension in the air thickened, evidenced in his smarmy, malicious gaze coated with gross lust that I hadn't encountered from him before. I tugged my nubby sweater hanging on my shoulders closer. Air-conditioned coolness circulated in the office. I guarded my chest, but not from the chill. Before I could demand JD cut it out, he said something so strange it fractured my intense thoughts.

"Come and get me," he whispered.

"What?"

JD rested his hands on my desk and leaned forward. "You heard me."

A wave of disgust doused me. I swiveled to stand up from my desk. HR was definitely going to hear about this, and so would Denny.

"What the fuck is wrong with you?" I asked.

With an air of contempt in his faded blue eyes, JD challenged me.

"Huh, you can play innocent all you want, but I know," he huffed. "We all know."

He stepped toe to toe with me and smacked his lips. A mess of dusty blonde hair flopped over his forehead.

"That same choc-o-latte skin? Wild curly hair? I know what I saw."

JD's proximity caused a wave of bile to screech to the top of my throat. His soggy breath lingered, hinting at the previous night's beer bong and school fight songs.

I closed the distance between us. Our noses were aligned almost evenly. I noted a slight flinch in his posture. The power shift gave me a rise.

I whispered, "Be on your way before I make that decision for you."

Maybe it was something in my eyes that caused JD to take a few steps backward. With a *psst,* he turned and left.

*Damn nut*, I thought. *Come and get me? What the hell does that even mean?*

"Ain't that some foolishness?" I said.

It didn't take long for JD's absurd rant to poke at me.

*What a weird come on.*

I flopped into my chair. The glare from the monitor vexed my eyes. The details of spreadsheets and emails were slightly blurred. I propped my lower back against the lumbar bump in the computer chair and rested my neck along the top.

As I took a deep breath in, my lids fluttered to a close. Random voices floated by while I retreated into my mind's shadows. This job was rough enough without passive-aggressive workplace antics  — emphasis on aggressive.

My aching fingers rubbed in a clockwise motion around my temples. Feeling a little more soothed, I stretched my arms above me in a Zen manner. Denny's chattering voice in the distance pricked my ears. I forced my eyes open and took a deep, re-energizing breath.

"Hey, Gwen?" I called out over the wall. Gwen was the only other person of color and one of three women on the team. Our rarity in this office should have made us kindred spirits. Alas, we were more like circling tigers most of the time.

The slap of Gwen's floppy loafers against her bare feet signaled her impending entrance. "Hey, girl?" She stepped sheepishly into my cubicle, peeking over her shoulder like she was scanning for prying eyes.

"What's up?" she asked in a subdued tone.

"JD was in here talking crap about, *Come and get me?*" I gathered from Gwen's expression that I sounded nonsensical. "Oh, never mind. It's nothing."

Gwen reached into the back pocket of her snug jeans, a frizzy poof of chestnut hair fanning her eyes as she tugged her phone loose. "I heard old boy giving you a hard time, but you should have expected it?"

My blood boiled slightly as the words landed. "What? You think I deserve JD's disgusting snark?" I huffed. "He is a walking HR infraction 90 percent of the time."

Gwen cocked her head and sighed. "I'm not here to tell you how to run your life, but you need to be more..." she lingered for a second, then finished, "discreet." She said it like a disapproving Auntie.

"Fine. You can get the fuck outta my off—" I said, but the image on her phone stifled the command. No, more like shoved it down my throat, never to see the light of day.

Gwen extended the unlocked phone, revealing a video. The sound was silent, but the woman gyrating on the screen had a lot to say to the camera in front of her. A woman with choc-o-latte skin and wild curly hair in a spectacle of lingerie that hung on her every hip swivel.

I snatched the phone, startling Gwen.

*No, it couldn't be…it's not possible.*

The Fan Girl account belonged to the *Other Me.*

"This isn't what you think, Gwen," I said, my response breathless and weak.

"Well, you could have fooled me," she said, followed by a *tsk tsk.* "What you do with your time is on you, but you know what they say? Things done in the dark always come to the light."

Gwen's retort reeked of puritanical judgment and made me seethe. A knock on the cubicle wall made us both jump.

Denny stood behind Gwen. Next to him was a thin woman wearing an ill-fitting pantsuit with a lanyard around her neck.

"Marissa, I need a word."

"Sure, but I thought we were meeting at 4 pm."

Denny and his female sidekick exchanged rigid glances. Pantsuit lady stepped forward and shooed Gwen out of the cubicle.

My stomach churned, and my heart raced.

*This can't be good.*

"I've got month-end reports due, so I hope this won't take long," I said, followed by a nervous laugh.

And then the pieces fell like a locked safe opening. Gwen's accusation. JD's words.

Pantsuit breathed in deep and exhaled like she was about to throw the world's heaviest stone off a cliff.

"Marissa Booker, your employment is terminated effective immediately."

I blinked wordlessly, staring between Denny and the HR hatchet master. I trembled as the woman continued.

"A complaint was lodged and investigated. It has come to our attention that you have violated company policies and the code of conduct." The woman tapped her left palm with a folder in her right hand.

I glanced at the dossier. I could ask *what violation, what policy, what asshole snitched.* But I decided I didn't want my employer to pull out an 8x11 color printout of a Fan Girl page with someone bearing a striking resemblance, almost identical, sticking her fingers down her crotch to prove their case.

A skinny white guy in a security uniform materialized at that moment. He handed me a small cardboard box. The next few minutes were like walking through taffy, slow and arduous.

"Personal effects only, no corporate laptop, and you need to hand in your phone," the talking pantsuit demanded.

"The phone is MINE," I yelled. My voice wavered and cracked like a lunatic on the verge of tears. Which I was.

Denny nodded. "She wasn't here long enough to have a company phone issued."

"You can't prove whatever it is you think you proved," I said, pleading my case.

"Actually," Pantsuit said, "we can. And we did." She followed up with, "You can appeal the decision to the Labor Board, but know the bar will be high," she tapped the folder, "with the evidence we have compiled."

Denny cleared his throat and said, "We don't take these decisions lightly, Marissa. Use this opportunity to get your shit together."

I wanted to disappear as I walked down the hall past the other cubicles. JD and the rest of the sales team gawked from behind the conference room's glass walls, some of them with that ogling stare that made my skin crawl.

The Fan Girl clip had spread like a fungus to all corners of the office as well as my mind.

My coffee cup bounced on the dingy tile floor and split into three clunky pieces. The sound cut the air like the crack of a whip. However, the diner's status quo remained unchanged. A mix of elderly regulars and restless travelers played out their roles without incident. The former nursed their black coffees and cigarettes, trucker hats shielding pale sunspots, and the latter waited for their bill impatiently with red-faced children in tow. As the sound of the splintering ceramic echoed around the room, no one flinched in the aftermath.

Except me.

My hands quivered in rhythm while the vein in my left temple danced a little jig. Exhaustion had been my constant companion, intent on taking the wheel of my sleep-deprived brain. I cagily mulled over the bits and pieces of my quest so far. None of it made sense. Feeling foggy and uneasy, I steadied myself on the red stool, the rubber soles of my Chuck Taylors propped up on the footrest.

A waitress in white orthopedic shoes grimly mopped up the spilled coffee with an apathy usually reserved for teenagers whose parents just don't understand. The stain blended into the tile, a new acidic layer to add to the ongoing masterpiece, marbled into the dull floor. I wondered if this place had ever heard of bleach and Pine-Sol. The waitress replaced the carnage with a fresh cup and uttered a barely audible request to be more careful.

After a slight glance of acknowledgement, I retreated into my layered, complex thoughts.

The road to hell was paved on the phone screen in front of me. If I had doubts before this surreal journey kicked off, I should have heeded them.

The diner door swung open, a high-pitched ding from the bell intruding on the merry-go-round of conspiracies swirling through my brain.

I pressed the sideways triangle in the center of the video. My thumb and finger spread to zoom in on one of the Fan Girl videos linked in the free library. There was no way this cunt was getting me to go behind her paywall.

The woman's face—my face, I guess—was crisp, clear, and not to be fucked with. I studied her with the rigor of a preeminent physicist. Maybe it was the camera angle or the lighting, but the Other Me's skin was smooth, toasty brown, and poreless. Her shape and curves were slick and supple. Were mine as well? I rubbed my hand across my midsection and determined that yes, they were.

Whoever she was, the resemblance was as uncanny as the last time I'd come across her. Back then, two years ago, she wasn't a twerking seductress but an angry woman in my social media feed. Christened "Black Karen", she went viral after an explosive showdown with a fast-food worker regarding missing house sauce.

The argument wouldn't have been so newsworthy if it hadn't been for how the war of words ended. The footage of Black Karen, her mouth open wide, screaming, showed her pulling her arm back, winding up like a baseball pitcher ready to throw a zinger.

And throw she did.

A squared punch to the jaw of the hapless, helpless worker. A spray of blood and specks that must have been incisors and other toothy bits bounced on the counter. A shocked grimace spread over the worker's lips just before her hands covered the destruction.

Black Karen regrouped and secured a metal napkin holder, which she slammed into the head of the cashier before the victim could sufficiently shield herself. The video portion of the worker wilting into a puddle of her own blood was debated and mocked all over social media, as was the custom these days.

The Kerry Company, my employer at the time, seemed suspicious of my involvement, but I persuaded them that the violent incident involved a deepfake, a digital imposter, not me. My explanation held water. I thought. Then, three weeks later, in the latest round of layoffs, I was let go.

"I haven't thought about that in a while," I mumbled, rubbing my knuckles to soothe my building agitation.

My eyes narrowed like almond slivers. I remember even more about that heinous event. It occurred around the corner from my house, which also explained why trips to the neighborhood corner store would yield random people scurrying in the opposite direction. One poor woman dropped a carton of eggs before running out the sliding glass door as an instrumental of Lionel Richie's All Night Long played overhead.

Black Karen disappeared into the wind, never to be heard from again. I eventually moved back to my home state but hadn't given any thought to this until JD and Gwen voiced their conspiratorial accusations.

Now that the memory lane was open, one more bit of nostalgia skidded into my mind.

The internet picked up on a phrase that Black Karen yelled during her fast-food confrontation. The outburst was auto-tuned and memed everywhere for about a week. The gore was stitched into so many commentary (and comical) videos that the initial shock gave way to a *meh* attitude by the time its newsworthiness subsided.

*Come and get me.*

I realized I'd been softly humming the catchy autotune underneath my breath the entire time I sat in the diner.

My stop in Presagé, Louisiana, was meant to be a brief one, so I slid my backpack over my shoulders, paid the bill, and tipped the generic waitress a crinkled twenty. Outside, the sun seared with a disagreeable heat that shimmered the landscape in the distance.

The Other Me's announcement six days ago was why I was lurking in the middle of nowhere.

I settled into the driver's seat of my well-worn Jeep. Gas station junk food littered the passenger seat, archaeological remnants of the journey so far. As the engine turned over, a blast of cool air invaded the vehicle. I flexed my sore fingers, stiff from extended time behind the wheel. But I couldn't rest now. My next stop was four and a half hours away, and I could make it by nightfall.

When I had originally approached my mother about this strange woman, I didn't expect much. Her mind had always had a flimsy relationship with the truth, and her nervous breakdown did little to improve that. The video of the scantily clad woman with her hips that don't lie elicited a glassy stare, a frail, beleaguered smile across her splintered lips. My mother wondered aloud why I would bring such nasty business into her home.

"You come in here getting me all worked up over things I can't help." My mother rang her hands with such vigor as if she were squeezing each syllable to death. "You constantly say one thing and do another. You've always been that sort of child."

All I could do in response was search my mother's eyes for coherence. All I could see was a feeble, brittle-boned woman.

"You need to leave. Leave things alone, doggonit."

Her nonsense words to this most stressful situation left me plummeting back into the desperate crevices of my childhood. My head ached in my hands as the recollections of hoarding, vengeful swings of a leather strap against my young skin, and the many, many men who came and went, flooded over me. I tumbled far into the recesses of those chaotic times.

No, my mother would be no help at all in unfolding the secrets of the Other Me.

The Other Me.

*THE OTHER ME!*

The irrational quest I had chosen to undertake, regardless of the secrets my own mother held (filthy, wretched LIAR!!!), was the kind of thing that could land me in a straitjacket. But I couldn't go back to an ignorant existence. What had been seen could not be unseen. The Other Me had become a virtual shadow over my shoulder.

Dodgy radio reception kept me company along the route as the day drew to a close. At the I-10, I pulled off on the recommendation of a billboard at mile marker 187 and followed the signs to a midrange motel. That would be my home for the night. Moments later, the bored but polite desk clerk clumsily handed me the room key along with a stack of takeout menus.

I double-locked the door behind me and shoved a chair with a red hexagonal seat pattern underneath the doorknob. Traveling alone was a dicey proposition in smaller towns like this one. My brown skin didn't always come with a warm welcome along this stretch of the Deep South.

I tugged at the chain that hung from the bedside lamp. A flat yellow glow washed over the prefabricated nightstand, and I sank into the half-stuffed mattress that passed for a bed. I knew I would not be sleeping under the covers.

As part of my nightly ritual the past six nights, maybe four, deciphering between hours and minutes has been a challenge, but anyway, I prepared to shower the funk of the day away. The hard water exacerbated my skin's ashiness and increased its irritation to the lace panty and bra set I slipped on from my overnight bag.

I parted the jaws of my laptop, spied on the Other Me's videos, and continued my genealogical research. Pinpricks darted down my back, and phantom fingers wrapped around my gut.

Emails to Fan Girl to find out who she was, or where she was, yielded nothing, but a lucky break greeted me a week ago.

The Other Me sauntered across the screen in front of a pink satin backdrop, snug in a black leather corset and thong combo, a cat - o' - nine tails in her bruised right hand. She was casual and comfortable in her soft, creamy skin, a peculiar grin on her slim face.

"Join me, my little doves, as I take this," she waved her hand down the length of her indulgent body, "on the road."

She ended with the words, "Come and...well, you know the rest."

Finding myself driving like a madwoman across state lines to find her, *HER*, was as surprising to me as seeing a donkey clomp down a fashion runway. But here I was rolling, rolling, rolling.

A fuzzy halo glazed over my vision as I continued to stare at the laptop. No new posts today, but fresh details appeared all the time in the background of the Other Me's old videos. It was bizarre, and I couldn't explain it, not that I wanted to.

Fatigue seeped in, and I willingly allowed it to enter. My head jerked in a last-ditch effort to get a little more wakefulness out of the day, but to no avail. So, I drifted off into a fretful sleep, yes, that is what I did, but sometimes it was so hard to know.

As I awoke the following morning, the zigzag of the laptop screensaver danced up and down in front of me. I roused the computer from its slumber. Oh, mercy, it was there!

The Fan Girl account featured a new thumbnail, a coming at-tractions announcement with the words, "8 P.M.! TONIGHT! LA ROUCHE GENTLEMEN'S HEAVEN!"

I knew the bitch was in New Orleans, but now I had a pinpoint location.

A cup of bland coffee, a fried egg, and a dry biscuit were all I had time for before getting back on the road. I cased the Jeep down the I-10. The landscape through my dashboard stretched on into the horizon like a universe waiting to be explored.

The view was unspoiled save for a few ill-placed shrubs that were barely wide enough for a police vehicle to hide in and ruin a driver's day. Miles ticked by. The road ahead was a means to an end.

I approached the outskirts of New Orleans from the east and gradually maneuvered into the mundane hum of late afternoon traffic. My nerves jumped and jigged like the strings of a fiddle.

*Have I lost my mind?*

If my mother was anything to go by, my grip on reality was gradually loosening, one hinge at a time.

The sun was waning. Its unforgiving heat hung in the air as I parked on Burgundy Street, a tucked-away side road in the French Quarter. My phone sat snugly in its holder affixed to the dashboard. I lowered the window a tad to let in the thick, humid air, which was better than nothing inside my stale car.

Giddy couples sauntered past my dashboard window, their laughter contagious only to them. That type of jaunty ease no longer applied to me. Asphalt streets and French-style buildings boxed me in as I scrolled my fingers across the display, reviewing La Rouche's website. My eyes tugged away from the phone with a start, but in all honesty, I sensed her before I saw her.

The Other Me stood at the corner of Burgundy and Toulouse. I peered through the windshield and held my breath. The sky began its brooding transformation to the twilight hour, ushering in an unusually cool breeze on its heels.

Her curls bounced with each step as she passed across my line of sight under the lantern-style streetlamp.

Finally.

The Other Me.

I slid the phone out of the holder, slung my cross-body bag over my shoulder, and stepped outside. As I slammed the door shut, I had no idea what I expected to happen.

I tried to banish any preconceived notions from taking root in my mind. Only later would I discover that the root was an invasive species, like a psychological kudzu, that had already overtaken my ability to think clearly.

Pavement crunched beneath my rubber soles. Hints of jazz trumpet fluttered in the air. Pulling my jacket closer, my sanity moved further away.

There were many adjectives to describe my mother–eccentric, touched, crazy. As I turned the corner of Burgundy to Toulouse, it dawned on me that those same words now described me. A few steps more, and this would all be over, one way or the other.

The Other Me loitered outside of La Rouche, the establishment that served plenty of vices with zero consequences to patrons who were set on having a good old-fashioned, incorrigible time. Intense, metallic brass sounds danced out of the den of iniquity at the corner. The door swung open as a curvy blonde, followed by an older gentleman, exited into the night to continue their mischief. The Other Me entered and took their valued space inside the four debaucherous walls.

As I peered through the crack in the door, the sliver revealed the Other Me, staring back from a wooden bar stool. I stopped dead in my tracks, paralyzed as the door swung shut.

It was now or never, my mind echoed. Nervous electricity coursed through my skin. I grabbed the wrought-iron handle and pulled it towards me, eyes adjusting from the bright streetlight outside to the dim, cavernous glow inside. The Other Me watched casually as I stepped over the threshold and the heavy door closed behind me.

Carl Jung theorized that what we deny or repress doesn't simply go away but hides in our unconscious. The darker side of our psyche, represented by wildness, chaos, and the unknown, persisted in a shadow archetype. When the shadow was unleashed, it signaled that we were ready to start a new cycle in life. Was I ready? Or was it the Other Me who would get to start anew? How would this end?

It wasn't until I reached the stool, when it was already too late, that I realized the Other Me had always known exactly how this would end.

Marissa can be such a wuss sometimes.

She whined and cried and screamed as her skin peeled away in the dingy shower of that dank motel. Look, it was never my intent for the coup of her (MINE, dammit!) body to be so brutal, but at least when her consciousness awoke today, she was none the wiser.

*I* did that.

*I* made that happen.

Please take your judgment of how I deal with my *OWN* blood and shove it straight up your piehole ass.

"Another whiskey, Alfonse." I direct my comments to the bartender, who is quickly becoming my special friend for the evening.

"One more for the *pole*?" He says with air quotes. Geez. I hate it when guys try to be cutesy.

"Yeah, you could say that." I pound the tumbler of alcohol back, the spice from the liquid heating my throat.

I flex my bruised hand. I didn't have the heart to tell Marissa that before she hit the road, JD's face may have run into her fists a few times. Okay, a few dozen times, but seeing JD's fucked up mug was well worth the discomfort.

But I didn't really blame him for his behavior toward Marissa. She could cover her curves behind those frumpy sweaters all she wants, but you can't hide what God gave you in spades.

JD knew it. Gwen hated it. I took care of her, too.

*You're welcome, Marissa!*

All those years of our mother saying, - *Close your legs. Don't be so fast. Don't be so grown. Do as I say, not as I do.*

I didn't take it to heart the way Marissa did. This is where the conflict, the internal struggle, comes in. When I ride that pole tonight, it will be with not an ounce of shame.

Truth be told, I basically liberated Marissa from her subpar existence. I let her have free rein for the most part, the best part of our lives. But when I'm ready, I'm ready. Marissa had her time in the sun.

Now it's my turn to burn.

But, I will say the most appealing thing about Marissa is, *was*, how easily she could delude herself. She takes, *took*, all the work out of this co-share arrangement for me. She did the Sisyphean lifting, putting her back into it.

She also drained it dry of the fun, too.

After the fast-food fiasco, a woman I spooked in the store around the corner from my apartment turned me in to the police. Marissa conveniently allowed me the joy of dealing with that fallout. Granted, I did the crime, so I should do the time, but I sure would have loved for her to carry *that* load. I ended up spending two years in the state hospital.

Oh well.

The therapeutic stay did wonders for my relationship with Marissa, though. My psychiatrist encouraged me to surrender to the softer inclinations of my inner being. Something about incorporating this and internalizing that, and "here are some pills to manage your symptoms".

*Naw, Doc. If it's all the same to you, Marissa's the one who can be managed for a while.*

The doctor's helpful technique for bringing "the good to the forefront", I discovered, was a two-way street. Marissa came through for a while, but I lay in wait, gathering my strength. For all of Marissa's goodness, she was always more powerful.

I needed to get my shit together and find the weak spots. The tender spots. An affront to Marissa's purity culture was the ticket. I managed to sneak in long enough to establish a foothold with the videos. Shake up her existence long enough for her to forget to lock the door behind her. Now that I have the key, I'm locking that son-of-a-bitch tight.

I twist on the stool, my, Marissa's, Chuck Taylors skimming the ledge that runs along the bottom of the bar. I steady myself on the seat. My fingers grasp the empty tumbler. I jiggle it like a dainty bell.

"Filler up, babe. And make it a double." I wink.

Alfonse, all smiles, comes running with a generous refill.

*Wait? What's happening?"*

I gulp the entire glass of whiskey. Alfonse nods in approval. It may not be as easy as I thought to keep Marissa down, but I'm going to try.

It's my turn now.


***END***

# 10

# Somewhere Over New Jersey

SNOWFLAKES DRIFTED AROUND THE sleigh's metal runners, swirling like invisible fingers grasping at the wind.

"The air bites shrewdly; it is very cold," Santa said into the howling wind, a hand raised in a theatric flourish. He turned to face the other direction, the wind to his back. "It is a nipping and an eager air," he proclaimed and chuckled. It was his Christmas Eve tradition to start the night with this quote, an exchange between Hamlet and Horatio.

"The Bard had a way with words, did he not?" Santa murmured, shifting the wide vinyl belt encircling his belly. Frosty vapor floated above his lips as he blew warm breath into his cupped palms.

He paced in the fresh snow. The layer beneath the fluff crunched under Santa's heavy black boots—a snap, crackle, pop underfoot. He slipped on a pair of fingerless leather gloves and slowly, almost absently, grazed his fingertips over the jagged lightning bolt scar down his left cheek. The puffed and fibrous mark where whiskers dare not grow reminded him that things can go off the rails pretty quickly.

Santa massaged his tuft of salt and pepper beard and considered whether he should start dyeing his hair white again. The home fires were burning cold between him and his wife. The point of no return had passed if he were to acknowledge the breakdown of the relationship properly. And with that brutal honesty came the realization that Santa might be seeking companionship soon—at his age. The night's chill pierced his red woolen suit as the truth of his impending new norm also seeped in.

Santa pulled the lip of his knit beanie hat over his ears, then stuffed his hands in his pockets. He breathed in the nighttime coolness, letting it fill his lungs deep with the prickly, comforting sting. It had been one year since the incident and the subsequent investigation. Santa let out a *whew*, releasing the past and embracing the gratefulness for having it all behind him.

The air mixed with the sweet, smoky smell of exhaust fumes rumbling from Santa's late-model sleigh. The chassis shimmied underneath as the engine warmed the vehicle.

Santa closed his lids and rested his eyes for a moment. He needed a second wind. The blustering chill did little to pep his senses, but the primal scream that filled his ears jolted his sensibilities to life. Santa gasped as he turned around, seeking the source of the savage wail.

"Who goes there? Come out," he panted.

Nothing. No one emerged from the veils of snow and gusts.

"No, no, no!" The words flowed in rapid fire from Santa's mouth.

He covered his ears and swayed for a beat. Santa sucked in a deep breath. The cries came again, but this time clearly within the confines of his mind. He closed his eyes again and let the intrusive thought of the sleigh in free-fall play out. His therapist encouraged him to let these thoughts run their course and address the reason behind the heart-pounding fixations once they concluded.

Santa exhaled as his panic attack subsided. The mental picture of a body — *that body*, plummeting like a man without a wire, screaming into infinity — gradually became less clear, more faint, until it faded into blackness.

One year had passed, yet the memories felt as visceral as the night it happened.

"Will this ever end?" Santa yelled into the darkness.

### 16 Months Ago

A PORTION OF SANTA'S territory was ceded to Papa Noël and his clan generations ago. The niche sector of South Louisiana where the Cajuns laid their heads was a stronghold for Santa's cousin. He could never find that sweet spot to sway hearts and minds to his more popular form of gift distribution. Santa had to admit; the swamp dwellers were a loyal brood.

Santa seethed at the results, placing blame like a branding iron on everyone around him but never himself. His mood had soured considerably since the vote, partly due to the stinging defeat, but also due to restlessness closer to home.

Rudolph had riled the masses to lead a successful unionization effort. Apparently, everyone but Santa was able to sway hearts and minds.

Work slowdowns and strategic call-outs from elves and reindeer during peak delivery schedules led to major disruptions orchestrated by the charismatic, red-nosed Jimmy Hoffa.

Rudolph delivered the gut punch that hurt Santa the most—an infiltration of the official website's chatbot system.

The malfunction resulted in false responses. Graphic descriptions, not fit for children and some adults, littered the FAQ page. An innocent inquiry could elicit a response filled with disturbing acts of sick behavior. The system's architecture was so old that it was like an open door to a bank vault, easily compromised and a ripe target to wreak havoc.

Santa's legacy and life's work were disintegrating before his eyes.

The call from Papa Noël offering his skilled technical department was a bitter pill for Santa to swallow. Another part of his legacy ceded to his rivals.

"It's not like you can post the opening on LinkedIn," his jolly cousin had said. "I can send one of my best to get you through this rough patch."

Years of diverting profits away from upgrades and skills training, a bone of contention in the union negotiations, had come back to roost.

And so, Peter, an up-and-coming talent plucked from Papa Noël's DevOps department, was offered a one-way ticket from the bayou to the snowy tundra of the North Pole.

Over the months, Peter hobbled the systems back together. He was quiet and polite, which didn't sit right with Santa. "Too amenable, too easygoing," was Santa's view.

Santa granted the union concessions in the spring, with adjustments required to be in place by the holiday season. Peter was instrumental in instituting security protocols for all systems and installing a touchscreen interface on the sleigh to manage the reindeer during the ride. Santa knew others would believe his disposition should be one of gratefulness for the clever resources at his disposal. But he simply couldn't allow himself to be charitable about any solution that involved his cousin.

**_One Year Ago_**

SANTA WATCHED AS PETER tinkered with the sleigh's dashboard in preparation for the Christmas Eve flight.

"Where do your people hail from?" Santa asked.

Peter's eyes shifted.

Santa sensed something was..._off_. He didn't like that one bit.

Peter turned toward Santa and answered the question with a question. "My, my people?" He wrinkled his nose, but Santa noted that the inimitable glint remained. "Well, we've been in the Bayou country for generations. We've always been from those parts."

A buzzer sound squeaked from the sleigh's dashboard. Peter went back to work.

An idea came to Santa. "I can make neither head nor tail of this system," he waved his hand over the dash. "Would you be willing to accompany me tonight?"

Peter shrugged and responded, "If you think I could help, then sure. I'll do a ride-along." He hunched over the dashboard once more.

Santa slid across the sleigh's seat. "Then it's settled," he said.

He stroked his beard and tilted his head as he observed Peter completing checks and double-checks of the system. The air swirled around them. Santa tugged his red hat with white fluffy trim over his ears, and it dawned on him.

_Peter._

Subtle inconsistencies existed throughout Peter's appearance. His hands were slightly larger, his height slightly taller, and his voice slightly lower than most elves. Peter's demeanor was also more casual than Santa cared to entertain. He'd seen some of this laid-back attitude infiltrating the warehouse. After the holidays and return season, he would course-correct and whip everyone back into line.

"All done," Peter said. He glanced at Santa with a hearty smile that didn't correspond to the dull expression in his eyes.

The smile offered to Santa seemed insincere or bored, as if Peter was trying to appease him. *Your intentions will not remain hidden for long, dear boy.* Santa was determined to use the uninterrupted, escape-proof time in the air to assuage his concerns or confirm them.

"Let's make haste," Santa said, each word forcefully infused with his trademark good cheer. "The children of the world await!"

Deliveries throughout Europe and Africa were uneventful and quite pleasant. The jolly man and the IT elf casually chatted under the cloudless night.

"Where did you learn to be so adept with this technology?" Santa asked.

"Papa Noël. He encourages and values continuous learning. And keeping his team happy." Peter's tone was flat. Santa guided the sleigh over a gust, leaning into the motion. He sniffed and huffed. *Ah, your true colors are revealing themselves.*

"If you have something to say, say it." Santa snapped the reins. A reindeer yelped.

"I'm not trying to say anything you don't already know." Peter crossed his arms and stared straight ahead. "Papa Noël should have your territory. Everyone knows it. Even your team thinks so."

Santa reactively snapped the reins, causing a few more reindeer to squeal. "Oh, is that so?" He wrapped the leather straps around his hands, forcing them to tilt the reindeer's heads back. The sleigh took an upturn in its flight pattern.

"I know the truth hurts, but you need to hear it. You're past your prime."

"Past my prime?" Santa yelled at the top of his lungs. "Like Papa Noël isn't? He rides the river in a boat and aligns himself with alligators, of all creatures, and you think *I'M* past my prime to run this organization!" He released one of the reins and slammed a meaty fist on the control panel. A clean crack fissured through the glass as the dashboard dimmed and the sleigh lost power.

"What have you done!" Peter screamed.

The reindeer's legs scrambled in the air. The change in condition occurred so quickly that they barely had time to catch their bearings. The rapid descent careened the sleigh to the right.

Santa toppled over on Peter. Panicked shrieks filled the sleigh. Santa tried to claw his way back to the other side to weigh it down with his girth, hoping to right-size the magical vehicle. A gust rattled the undercarriage, slamming Santa harder into Peter.

The door hinges gave way.

Both men fell out of the cab through the open door. Santa clung to the carriage. Peter gripped the sleigh's runner bottoms. His legs dangled like balloon strings floating in the sky.

"Hold on!" Santa shouted.

Peter's eyes were full and wide. "Help me!" echoed into the night sky.

Santa shifted his ample weight, took hold of one of the leather reins, and tried to claw his way back into the cab. He slipped backward.

The sleigh coasted over the ocean, a faint saltiness in the breeze burning Santa's eyes, as the reindeer searched for dry land. Peter clung to the runner.

"Agh!" Santa groaned as he flopped back into the cab like a dead fish. He wrapped a rein around his right arm to act as a brace. The wind whipped at his hair, as his hat, buoyed by a gust, floated into the night.

"You can do this," he whispered, leaning over the side. "Give me your hand!" Santa yelled.

The sleigh hiccupped and bounced. "God help me!" Peter screamed.

Santa unwrapped the rein from his wrist twice but left enough slack to secure him to the sleigh. He reached further down, their fingers mere inches from each other's grasp. Santa's hand grabbed Peter.

"I got you, I got y—" The words boomed into the night, but the rash thought that he would succumb too was louder.

*Maybe...just...let him go.*

Santa looked into the terrified eyes of progress. The progress Papa Noël stood for with all of its forward thinking and embracing of the new.

Turbulence jolted the undercarriage once more.

Santa felt his stomach clutch as Peter's hands slipped away. The wails of utter terror were almost inhuman, like no other sounds he had heard before or hoped to hear again. Peter's body arched like a parachute and bent like a pliable branch as he coasted through the onyx sky and landed somewhere in New Jersey.

The cover-up was swift. Santa implied that Peter left voluntarily, "something about wanting more responsibility". Papa Noël couldn't prove otherwise.

The experience still haunted Santa. The way Peter gripped his hand like a vise, when he tried to release him. The way Santa sliced his pointer and middle fingers across the metal runners as a means to release Peter from his grasp and serve him up to the night.

All the sleeping pills in the world couldn't stop the nightmares of Peter sailing through the air, drifting away on clouds of mind-altering screams absorbed into the night.

SANTA'S THERAPIST SAID IT would get easier. That was debatable as far as he was concerned. Could he ever heal if he could never be forthcoming about his role in what really happened? Santa vowed to himself he would go to his grave trying to find out.

He recently took to vexing this poor woman with quotes from his beloved Hamlet. "Thou turn'st mine eyes into my very soul; And there I see such black and grained spots" was a common refrain when she inquired about his journaling.

Santa shook his head to wipe away the memories, or, perhaps, to stuff them back in their box of shame for safekeeping.

He stroked each reindeer's coat as he finalized his inspection. A full moon rose in the black sky. "Let's be on our way," he sighed as he climbed into his seat and took hold of the soft, worn leather handles. Santa shouted, "Aye-ya!" A brisk snap, and the sleigh lifted on the wind. He barked a commanding "HO, HO, HO" to the row of reindeer.

Halfway through his deliveries, Santa found himself at a remote farm on the outskirts of the rural Midwestern countryside. The hydraulics engaged as the sleigh landed silently on the roof.

With an abracadabra wave, a squall of packages appeared at his side as he stepped out of the carriage. The gifts settled next to him, suspended inches above the roof and its blanket of snow. Santa peered down the brick opening. The lack of a smoke signal did not automatically mean no fire, but in this case, the chimney was dormant.

"Excellent," Santa whispered.

In a fluid motion, Santa deflated, for lack of a better term. His extremities dehydrated in a chorus of hissing sounds. His upper arms puckered, lost shape, and compressed. Santa became a walking pancake if pancakes could walk.

The gifts levitated in the air, waiting for Santa to finish his business before adhering to his suit for the trip down the chimney. Santa slung his shapeless carcass over the edge of the opening, and the red blob tumbled to the bottom.

His meaty sack landed with a thump on the hearth. *Well done, if I do say so myself*, he mused. Santa lay flat and still, listening for movement. The gifts burst from his suit like pretty popcorn into the air and tumbled to the wooden floor.

Santa completed the rehydration process and wiped his hands of errant snow and soot on his pant legs. He crept to the tree in the corner while checking his *Nice* list.

Twice.

He arranged the bright, ribboned boxes under the twinkling pine. Satisfied with his handiwork, he set out to dehydrate when a small, round table near the iridescent tree caught his eye.

A plate of fresh, crustless white bread beckoned. Edges of deli ham peeked from beneath the soft slices like a seductress. "What a sight for sore eyes," he said as he subconsciously rubbed his belly. Although he enjoyed the devil out of the standard cookies usually left for him, he appreciated the savory offerings, like mince pies on his stops in Ireland or something a little different like rice pudding when he swung through Denmark. "Keeps my sweet tooth honest," he would say.

Santa dipped his head to peer closer. The sandwich looked safe, but he still approached it with caution. He'd encountered the telltale signs of a dog or a cat having licked *his* cookies before. Santa gently lifted the bread. The sandwich appeared *clean* to the naked eye.

He reached for the triangular half. Santa cocked his head. A floorboard creaked in the back of the house.

*My mind is playing tricks on me.*

Santa emitted a pheromone that induced unconsciousness, so no one should be stirring, not even a mouse. He knew the possibility was remote, but it did exist. A hot poker scar across Santa's cheek, courtesy of a half-awake Alabama homeowner who mistook the jolly man for a burglar, was proof that sometimes not everyone falls under his fugue state.

He grabbed a sandwich half and bit into the corner. The light, airy bread clung to the roof of his mouth. The ham's saltiness mingled with a light coating of creamy mayonnaise—the perfect sandwich.

Santa took another bite with gusto and swallowed. The doughy mass traveled to the back of his throat. He rubbed his neck to give the bite a little nudge down. His brows furrowed. His fingers clutched at his Adam's apple.

The bite had become an immovable lump. The blockage clung to his airway like a suction cup on a window. The uneaten portion crushed through his clenched hands.

Santa's bread-covered fingers dug into his throat. The fading oxygen to his brain made his mind swim. Santa knew he was in serious trouble as he slumped and tumbled to the floor with a soft thud.

He tried to cough to dislodge the obstruction. The sensation of blood rushing to his head was like lava under his skin. Santa's eyes were wide and fixed ahead of him, the veins inside beginning to burst. Santa's legs kicked and flailed as he fought to stay conscious. The tree behind him swayed as his left boot struck a wrapped Chatty Cathy doll for seven-year-old Ruby, pushing it into the tree's base.

Spindles of saliva began to coat his disheveled, crumb-filled beard. His hat flopped over his right eye. Santa's breathing came in wheezing and shallow.

Strands of light played in front of Santa's eyes. One last gasp of air , and it was over. Santa lay motionless, spread-eagled under the tree like a Christmas nightmare.

His glazed eyes stared up at the ceiling. He blinked as his plump body began to shake. The limbs flattened as Santa's belly withdrew, sagged, and compressed. The dehydration process had kicked in. To the casual observer, they would have seen

Santa's deflated body laid out like a steamrolled Saturday morning cartoon character.

"Arghh" A wet cough came from flabby Santa. A soggy mass of dough flew from his deconstructed mouth and landed with a splat. Santa had inadvertently performed a Heimlich maneuver on himself. His flat blob heaved like a damp sheet blowing in the wind. Santa dragged his limp carcass to the chimney, shimmied up, and scaled the bricks back to the roof.

Back to life.

He sat his rehydrated figure into the sleigh, heart palpitations ripping through his chest. "I almost died," he gasped, "in the middle of nowhere." He swallowed mostly to make sure he could. The reindeer were restless to get on with the deliveries, unaware of the life-and-death struggle that had taken place under their hooves.

Santa pushed the engine button and tapped the dashboard. The sleigh hovered and turned. Within seconds, Santa flicked the reins and soared across the milky sky.

RUBY RAN DOWN THE hall, knocking on all the doors. Her voice boomed at rock concert levels, "It's Christmas, it's Christmaaaaas!"

"Someone's awake," Petra said to Sam as she rolled over on her side to face him. "Merry Christmas, babe," she murmured.

Sam kissed her gently on the forehead. "Merry Christmas, my love," he responded with a smile. They sluggishly pulled themselves out of bed and grabbed their robes to meet the rest of the family in the living room.

Petra yawned and smiled as she watched Ruby's wide eyes scavenge the pretty gifts. Ruby plopped cross-legged under the tree and reached for the dented box that held the doll she had prayed for.

"I'll get the coffee started," Petra said. She shuffled to the kitchen as the boys, Robby and Richey, scurried past to join their little sister.

The aroma of Arabica beans was strong. Sam purred like a cat as he entered the kitchen. "Yes, nectar of the Gods. Pour me one?"

Petra nodded. The coffee pot spout clinked against the mug as she poured the hot liquid in.

"What do you think happened to the sandwich? Looks right awful." Sam flashed the hardened dollop on the plate in Petra's direction before dumping the remnants in the trash bin.

She raised an eyebrow and said dryly, "Just teaching someone a lesson."

Sam wrinkled his brow in confusion.

Petra knew there was no feasible way to explain to her husband what had happened a year ago.

*Oh, hey, honey, I'm half-elf, Santa is real and operating behind a shell of greed and corruption, and, by the way, he let my brother fall to his death. Pass the hot sauce.*

She had exiled herself from her people years ago to live a "human life". She underwent surgery to modify her most distinguishing elf feature, and that was that. But she stayed close to her brother, and his demise burned deep inside her.

Peter was one of many apprentices recruited from the Southeast Louisiana region for a career with Papa Noël. The half-elf community was well-respected since arriving in the area, fleeing on French vessels in the 1700s.

Petra begged Peter not to take the position. She'd followed the independence vote and was thrilled that Papa Noël prevailed. But then Peter confided that the union disputes were a guise to further Papa Noël's ambitions of taking over Santa's portion of the Christmas supply chain.

"Think of it as a hostile merger," he'd said.

"Going undercover? It's not safe," she'd said.

But Peter wanted "to be part of something bigger. The North Pole is the biggest thing there is."

So, he left and never returned to his family.

Petra had been scheming for months about the best way to fix the blame where it truly belonged. An undercover informant confirmed her brother's death and the cover-up that followed. Petra would never know the grisly truth, but what she knew was that the liar known as Santa would not get the last word.

The plan was simple. Petra counted on her nemesis to eat in a hurry. She coated the ham sandwich with a layer of marshmallow spread and foam insulation designed to stick in Santa's throat and work quickly. And Petra could beat the pheromones because of her partial elf heritage if the conditions were right.

The sandwich would have been the final nail in a just world, but Petra had a contingency plan. While Santa struggled against the ham sandwich, she climbed to the roof, loosened the hinges on the sleigh door, and cut a hydraulic line.

*Karma can do the rest.*

"How are we doing on wood for the fireplace?" Petra set her coffee cup down.

"Don't know but—"

"Never mind," Petra said. "I'll go get some. Just to be safe."

She slipped on her boots and coat from the mudroom and headed to the shed. Petra stepped inside. She slipped her phone out of her pocket, pulled out a pack of cigarettes, lit one, and dialed the only number in the Contact list.

"Hey, cher." The jolly voice of Papa Noël greeted her.

"It's done," Petra said. She inhaled the tobacco and exhaled the smoke that mixed indistinguishably with the cold weather vapor outside.

"Oh wee, cher, think you right." The voice chuckled deep and merrily, then softened. "Your brother was a good egg. I hope you know that."

"Yes, I know." A tear drizzled down Petra's cheek, icing over before it hit her chin.

"Any idea where we should start looking for old boy?"

Petra knew the Noëls and the Clauses were all about covering things up.

"Yeah. Try starting somewhere over New Jersey."

*END*

# Too Late to Turn Back Now -II

DELPHINE SQUIRMED IN THE rattan-backed chair, many of the synthetic strands gone and lost to the winds of time inside the house on Prentiss Avenue. "Today is the day." She inhaled after the last word.

She stared at the open flap of the ruby-red box, the matching envelope, and the vial of granules sitting in the bottom. "You didn't go through all of this to change your mind."

*It's too late to turn back now.* The song of the same name by Cornelius Brothers & Sister Rose rolled around in her brain. It was always a favorite of hers growing up, and the tune brought her comfort now.

The kettle whistled on the stove. The water boiled for a nice pot of herbal tea. Delphine wrested herself from her seat and finished prepping the serving tray with a filled, steaming teapot, two cups with mismatched saucers, and store-brand short-bread cookies fanned out in a circular pattern on a plate. Her expected guest should be pleased.

Delphine slipped the tea cozy over the ceramic pot just as the knock at the door cut the silence. She smoothed the front of her pink terry cloth tracksuit with white trim and a logo over her heart that she didn't recognize. Her chestnut-brown coily curls were loose and wild, cascading to her shoulders. Delphine felt liberated by dressing as she pleased after forty-odd years of Mama's chaste interventions. She wasn't sure if it was looking the devil in the eyes that night outside of the Far Burger Bar or if the confines of rigidity had finally fallen away, but Mama no longer held the cards. Now Delphine had the freedom to experience the wider world on her own terms and under her own steam, and she would embrace it one tracksuit at a time.

A ding-dong and a knock.

*Anyway, it's too late to turn back now.*

Delphine steadied her nerves and primped one last time in the mirror. She answered the door and invited the guest into the sitting room. She returned with the tray of refreshments.

"Well, your invitation was most unexpected but definitely welcomed." Carlotta Lee Thompson daintily sipped her tea with a slurp. And a grimace.

The grimace was not lost on Delphine.

"Mama passed almost two months ago," Delphine said, filling her own teacup. "Thought it might be time to put this old bag of bones on the market. You came recommended." Delphine's lie slipped through her lips like a cobra into a baby's crib.

"So sorry for your loss." Carlotta Lee did the sign of the cross and confidently cleared her throat. "I'd heard through the grapevine...," she took another sip of tea, "well, it was an awful tragedy. And you finding her..." Carlotta Lee placed her teacup and saucer on the coffee table. She rubbed her hands together. "I mean, it was something awful, but," with a wide faux grin, finished, "you seem to be doing alright for yourself. You look...different. You look...good!"

*Right.* Delphine's eyes narrowed. *You're overselling it, bitch.* But she also knew how to plaster a fake smile on for appearances' sake and did so. For the sake of accelerating this whole affair, Delphine would have done a belly dance or fucked a kangaroo. Anything to get Carlotta Lee drinking the tea.

The freshness of the spell would diminish after 48 hours, so Delphine was sensitive to her time constraints. It could still be usable for up to one week, but the impact diminished with every passing day. The difference between maximum damage and a reaction equivalent to a head cold. A nasty cold, but a cold, nonetheless.

The spell had six hours and 37 minutes of peak carnage power remaining.

Carlotta Lee flipped open her spiral planner and flicked her pen. "Well, let's get started, shall we?" The realtor wore a neat two-piece ensemble of a navy silk shirt with a flouncy bow at the neckline and a red pencil skirt with peep-toe blue and white heels. Carlotta Lee's long, manicured red nails barely wrapped around the pen as she wrote.

"You may need to consider a few coats of paint and a kitchen refresh, but not a full remodel, mind you." She pursed her lips as she finished her generic advice, "If you want to get top dollar, consider the refresh an investment." She tugged a wisp of her relaxed bob behind her right ear.

Delphine answered Carlotta Lee's questions about rooms, square footage, appliances, and other specs about the home.

*If Mama could see me now. In control. I bet she'd have done things differently.*

Carlotta Lee and her tape measure walked the halls of the house with Delphine.

"And where does this door lead?"

*Bingo.*

"It goes to the attic. Mama was using it for storage, but I did a clear-out, and wouldn't you know, it has plenty of space as an extra room. Or an office, I suppose."

The twinkle in Carlotta Lee's eyes went into overdrive. Delphine could practically see the dollar signs spinning inside that woman's head.

"Should we take a look?" Delphine asked.

"Of course!"

With a wave of her hand, Delphine ushered Carlotta Lee up the stairs and followed behind her under the dimness of the single bulb that illuminated the way.

Delphine reasoned Carlotta Lee had to know what she'd done to her. She watched the back of the woman as she yammered all the way up the stairs. Her haughty flourishes and self-important conversation helped Delphine relinquish any doubts about what was to come.

Carlotta Lee had earned this.

Delphine quite frankly didn't give a fuck anymore. Whatever was going to go down would indeed go down.

"Hmm, how is this space wired? Does it have outlets? The space needs some more brightness, and that isn't going to cut it." Carlotta Lee pointed to the four-pane dormer window as she navigated to the top step.

"I think there is," Delphine said. She brushed past Carlotta Lee and into the blackness. A click and then there was light. The bulb hung low in the middle of the attic. So low that the corners were shadowy enclaves with no clear visibility.

"Oh, how lovely," the realtor frowned at the dusty space as she scribbled in her notebook. "This could be a real selling point." She tapped her pen on her notebook. "Except for the pole in the middle of the room. That will absolutely have to go."

Before Delphine's father let the doorknob hit his backside on the way out of their lives, he had called Delphine's mother a 'hoodoo whore'. It didn't take long for Delphine to understand her father didn't leave. He ran. Far, far away from what her mother was capable of.

Her mother had purchased a spell to make the one she loved the most never leave. Her father got out before her mother could use it, but it wouldn't go to waste.

On Delphine.

"You belong with me", her mother always responded to any request to be normal.

*Please let me play hide and seek with the other kids.*

*No. You belong with me.*

*Please let me join the debutante cotillion with the other girls at church.*

*No. You belong with me.*

*Please let me out of this damn crazy house!*

*No. You belong with me.*

If Delphine ever left, her mother swore the spell would corrupt her, twist her into an abomination not fit to lay eyes on.

"You will not be valued in this world," her mother had yelled, whispered, and sneered so often that it became a deranged self-fulfilling loop.

Two weeks before her mother's death, in a jewelry box inside a hope chest in the attic, Delphine found it. The evidence of her mother's lie. Wrapped in a red envelope and a matching box.

Her mother had never used the spell on Delphine as she had claimed.

She had manipulated Delphine into living her worst life possible. Because sometimes, words are just as powerful as any potion when the target *believes* them.

A new truth had dawned on Delphine. The kitchen table confabs weren't gossip sessions for her mother and the elders. They weren't basking in the schadenfreude of rumors or the misfortune of those supposedly affected by the spells.

Their summits were recaps of what they had actually done by way of Stinky's, rebranded for a new generation as Far Burger Bar's toxic menu.

Her mother's kitchen was ground zero. The epicenter for missing husbands, disfigured wives and daughters, and lingering, grotesque illnesses that came out of nowhere before deteriorating their victims in the most ruthless, painful ways imaginable.

Delphine's mother paid for her deception and duplicity. Paid dearly. Delphine made sure of it.

Now it was Carlotta Lee's turn.

MIDDLE SCHOOL WAS NOT fun for the weird girl who lived with the weird mother on Prentiss Avenue. Delphine understood her strangeness was of interest. When other girls were wearing makeup and Daisy Dukes, Delphine was sweating through homemade, cotton, long-sleeved dresses she was forced to wear.

She would linger at aisle 12 in Woolworth's looking at the lipstick packaging with colors like *Cherries in the Snow* or *Pick Me Pink.* She thought how clever all those names were as she swiped the testers on the inside of her wrist where her mother couldn't see them. She gazed at the models on the posters, none of them as bronze as she was, but that didn't dissuade her from wondering what blue eyeliner might look like under her lash line.

But the main sin that she had been guilty of was not of her choosing. Back then, before trickle-down economics and crack obliterated the middle-class black family for years to come, there was a time when having a nuclear family was the norm for black folks. Still was, not that the media ever showed it.

But Delphine and her mother were not the norm. Her father had left, and having no father in the home was tantamount to being a hussy by proxy. Something that could rub off onto so-called "respectable women".

Later in life, Delphine had come to realize it was less about Delphine having contact with her neighbor's impressionable daughters and more about the women in the neighborhood segregating their impressionable husbands away...because if Mama couldn't hold on to her man, she may try to hold on to one of theirs. The ability to judge someone harshly was a sport with winners and losers. Delphine and her mother were the losers.

But it was Carlotta Lee who delivered the final blow, the tipping point to Delphine's pain and isolation.

One spring afternoon on the playground at St. Mary's Academy, Carlotta Lee promised to choose Delphine for her tetherball team.

"I won't pick you first," she had said with a wink and a smile, "but somewhere in the middle."

As they genuflected under the marble statue of Jesus in a prayer before play began, Delphine was over the moon. For once, she wouldn't be the last one selected. But Carlotta Lee was not faithful to her word. Not even the watchful gaze of Jesus smiling down on them could make Carlotta Lee keep her promise.

Maybe Delphine shouldn't have bragged about the arrangement. Maybe this was a doomed pact from the start.

With each seesaw of names called out by Carlotta Lee and the other captain, the crowd thinned, one by one, as girls ran to stand behind the caller of their name. A dam of pride and fear of what would come stifled the tears.

Delphine stood there alone as the inevitable countdown to Loserville played out. The shame eventually burst through and streamed down her full cheeks. Fighting the tiredness of her existence in the same way, the sobs came in the waves of a five-year-old's big emotions at nap time.

Delphine was the laughingstock of the schoolyard. Carlotta Lee wasted no time distancing herself from the promise.

"Why would I ever pick that weirdo?"

She never knew why the offer was so quietly and dramatically rescinded. The taunting and exclusion would become complete social annihilation for the rest of her school years.

Delphine thought of that incident as her Waterloo, her Trojan horse. If not for this incident, things could have been different, better for her.

CARLOTTA LEE FINGERED THE string hanging from the pole. "This sure does remind me of something. But what?" Her nails skimmed the steel pole, faintly scratching against it.

Delphine hung back as her prey assessed the object. And waited.

"Hmm," Carlotta Lee murmured. "Well, it's neither here nor there. It simply has to go..." Her sentence drifted off as she doubled over, her eyes scrunched closed, her lips puckered. "Oh, my." Another wave doubled her again. "Oh, Lord, have mercy," she belched. Carlotta Lee's arm encircled her stomach. "I think something on that sweets tray didn't agree with me."

Delphine stood patiently near the stairs. And continued to wait. "Hmm, maybe you're right." She crossed her arms and didn't move from her spot.

Carlotta Lee moaned and cried out, "What in the world did you serve me?" Her knees buckled as she collapsed to the floor. She crawled into a fetal position and cursed under her breath, "You raving mad cunt! I should have known," grated through her clenched teeth.

The skin on her body began to toughen and harden. Bones cracked as her limbs shrank in on themselves, folding, and snapping in an excruciating chorus.

At least Delphine hoped the agony was unbearable.

The darkness crept closer, its tendrils spilling from the attic corners for a front-row seat. Delphine restrained herself from clapping at the merriment that washed over her.

Carlotta Lee's mouth opened in a silent cry as skin formed over the hole. Her eyes squeezed, melting into and against the transformation as she reshaped herself into a vestige of Delphine's rage. The worst of it was over in a few minutes.

Carlotta Lee Thompson's conversion into a blue, red, and white tetherball was complete.

Delphine picked up the round, somewhat lumpy sphere and tucked it in the crook of her arm. The leathery skin exterior squirmed and rippled under her touch.

She grasped the pole's string and fingered the hook at the end. As she struggled to pinch the metal clasp to secure the tether to the ball, her right index finger snapped. She tugged and pulled the dangling bit from her hand. She flipped the digit in the air like a coin, then placed the nub in her pocket. "It's already beginning, I guess."

She gripped the skin-leathered sphere and connected the ball to the rope. She reached out and slapped the ball as hard as she could, the rope and ball circumnavigating the pole, wrapping around it like a coil.

The ball groaned. "And it is worth it." Delphine's laughter filled the attic room.

*END*

# 12

# Rent Party

THE SOUR TANG AT the back of Ellie's throat had come back from its retreat a few hours ago. Her mouth watered from the acidic notes as crisp dollar bills flicked from the latest guest's fingers into Ellie's hand. "Enjoy," she muttered through a tight, clothesline smile. She sipped ginger ale to calm her stomach as the door closed.

Ellie threw these 'rent parties' to pay for this dump. Not even a fresh coat of paint could hide the mold or deter the rats from sneaking in through holes in the baseboards. But shortly after taking possession of the unit, circumstances made it impossible to leave and make money outside of these walls.

From her apartment on the eighteenth floor, she entertained a sweaty collection of minglers and drinkers. The cover charge granted each guest a red plastic cup with refills on the spiked fruit punch and shots of Popov vodka. The hand-delivered bodega chicken wings sold by the plate for an additional charge disappeared within an hour, but no one seemed to mind. A steady supply of alcohol brought to her doorstep by the new-fangled gig workers of the world was always the most important.

Low thumping bass boomed from the speakers connected to the laptop against the wall. She stared coolly in Davis' direction as he walked over.

"You have my cut?" Davis asked in a low voice. As her building supervisor and part-time fuck, he threatened to shut the parties down if money and other things weren't forthcoming. Not her choice on either count, but soon, it wouldn't matter.

Ellie took another sip of ginger ale to soothe her roiling stomach. "What the fuck do you think?" she said to Davis, avoiding his beady eyes. She sullenly surveyed the room. Choosing who would live or die was also not her choice.

A hard tap on her shoulder, followed by "Hey," startled her. She turned around to find a tall, dark-skinned man with a megawatt smile and a Kangol cap covering his bald head. He launched into a conversation with her as he shooed Davis away.

"See, Ellie, you need to ramp these parties up." He licked his lips as Ellie crossed her arms and leaned against the front door.

"Really, Nils."

Nils Carter from the seventh floor had no shortage of hare-brained schemes. She learned some of them when he started delivering her monthly grocery order five months ago. He'd been delivering a lot more ever since. Ellie figured if any of his ideas were worth a toss, he wouldn't still be on the seventh floor.

"Yeah, girl," Nils swiped a finger down Ellie's bare shoulder. He grinned and said, "Maybe some ladies, the coffee and cream variety, like yourself, to...spice things up. We could make a killing." He licked his lips again as he stared straight down Ellie's tank top, stretched to its limits over her chest. She didn't stop him.

Ellie sighed, but not with annoyance. "You're a real Gordon Gecko, aren't you?"

Nils was handsome. Ellie would give him that. The kind of man she used to run with down at the juke joints and pool halls down in *their* part of town. The side of the tracks where it was safe for them to let loose, where the police came around mostly for a handout to keep trouble at bay.

There was something about Nils, she had to admit. But he was a means to an end. "I'll take your offer under advisement, but until then, enjoy the party." She motioned toward the living room.

Nils shook his head, a Cheshire grin spreading across his face. He glanced over his shoulder at Davis maneuvering through the crowd, his potbelly leading the way. "If you ever get tired of that pasty *Mister Fix It...*" he said, winking, then disappeared into the assorted group around the room.

Ellie's smile faded as the voices swirled around in a drumbeat of deep laughter and chatter. She turned to check her reflection in the mirror next to the door. Her eyes lit upon a framed picture of a young woman sitting in a high-back wicker chair, hair in a beaded braid hairstyle cascading around her brown almond face. Taken at the downtown mall that had died ten years ago, the sepia photo was of her daughter, Dren. Her hopeful smile made Ellie's heart ache. She hadn't seen that smile in almost five months.

Ellie's eyes landed on her own grey coils peeking from behind her ears, then traveled to the sunspots peppering the back of her hand. Her skin still looked moist and dewy, but Ellie knew it was a matter of time before that faded too if things didn't get started soon.

Davis approached, making his way past CeCe from the sixth floor, her butt propped on the edge of the faux leather recliner where Nils created new life inside her. Just as Davis reached Ellie at the front door, she walked briskly away, but not before she saw the flash of anger in his eyes.

She scooted past the folks, standing and seated, acknowledging the ones she knew and nodding at the ones she didn't. She flung the kitchen door open, walked through, and shut it, leaving the world behind.

The kitchen was outdated. The faucet water ran brown as often as it ran clear. Rust stains patterned the sink. Cabinet doors didn't exist, a good thing as far as Ellie was concerned. She wanted a clear line of sight of any rodents that munched on her pasta and bread.

Ellie approached a cupboard located at the end of the row of doorless cabinets next to the wall. The pantry door, sturdy and ornate, wasn't always there. It was NOT there when Ellie moved in.

A carved face in the middle of the door peered back at her; the lips fashioned in a grimace. But...sometimes it was a roar. Sometimes it was a shriek.

A single milky-white bulb dangled from the ceiling. Ellie stepped toward the cabinet. The light was behind her; the darkness in front.

Ellie reached for the etched face's mouth to grab the handle pierced through its nostril. She jerked her hand back as the lips moved. "For Christ's sake," she whispered under her breath. Ellie steadied her stance, breathing deeply before reaching for the handle again, and opening the gorgeous and grotesque pantry door.

A blackness blacker than anything Ellie had ever seen loomed inside the pantry. Music bumped on the other side of the door, but no one ever heard the ravaged grumbling deep inside the hole. The blackness had a way of sound-canceling its appetite. Ellie peered into the blackness, but not too close. "You said I'd get what I wanted," she huffed cautiously. "A deal is a deal." The blackness moaned as a rush of air blew into her face, her wiry curls flying out from behind her ears. "You owe me a new life outside!" Her words were husky and fearful on her lips. "I get to leave here. Still. Young."

Ellie's transformation back into a fuckable state started with a cup of tea five months ago. Back then, she was a lonely 76-year-old, and what family she did have...

"Mama, I got to live, you hear me?" Dren said, arms crossed as she sat next to Eloise, before she became Ellie, in the loveseat near the window.

Eloise's milky brown eyes stared at her daughter. Her frail hands shook as she picked at the tuft sprouting between the cushion's braided seams. "You can't leave me here, girl. This place..." her voice trembled. Dren was her only child; the only kin left in her life. The fear and loneliness that Dren proposed with her departure fell like thick, stifling waves over Eloise, and it angered her just as much. "You gonna, what, fly off to Florida with that lump of a man?" she yelled.

"Ma!" Dren got up and paced across the dingy carpet. "This is a good place." She waved her arms like a *Price is Right* hostess. "You'll be good here." She sat down again and took Eloise's hand. "I'll call all the time."

"Don't lie to me, girl," she spat. Eloise looked away. "You'll be gone like the wind and never come back if you can help it." She sniffed defiantly. "Maybe when I'm dead, you'll pop back in."

Dren offered to make a final cup of tea as if that could heal this wound. Eloise sat on the loveseat, rubbing the arthritis in her joints. When she called out and Dren didn't answer, she slowly walked her brittle bones to the kitchen.

It was that day when Eloise saw the cabinet for the first time.

The blackness inside the cabinet held Dren's body suspended in its grasp. Black fingers formed out of the dark, squeezing her until blood dripped into the blackness, then sucked Dren into its slice of hell.

Eloise covered her mouth, backed out of the kitchen, and ran to the bathroom, gagging the whole way. It was when she relieved her stomach contents in the toilet, splashed her face, and looked in the mirror, that she saw her youth shining through.

She wanted to run screaming from this devil's place, but she couldn't. From that day forward, everyone else could come and go, but for Eloise, the door opened to another dimension—a molten landscape of searing heat.

The blackness called to her from the kitchen.

The murkiness spoke to her; sounded like a perfect conversation to Eloise's ears. The blackness said it wouldn't hurt her; it needed her. It moaned, *Bring us flesh*, and she would. The internet could deliver just about anything. And little by little, the darkness gave her youth in return. Eloise...Ellie demanded a new life. Demanded to never be alone again. That day, Nils delivered her groceries.

That night, for the first time in twenty years, she had an orgasm.

A RAT SCURRIED ACROSS the floor near the stove. With a nimble spin on her heels, Ellie crouched down and snatched the rodent by the tail before it could squeeze between the warming drawer and the fridge. Its body wiggled and jerked in her grasp, moving in stop motion. Ellie dangled the furry rat in front of the moaning door. "A little snack." She threw the rat inside.

The blackness held it suspended, enveloped in its murkiness. The rat's whiskers twitched, staring at Ellie like the betrayer she was. The darkness moaned, transmitting its foul banter to Ellie. She shook her head, translating it to a simple, "Okay." The bleakness behind the kitchen door indicated the sacrifices could begin.

She rubbed her stomach and walked back into the party.

Ellie strolled over to the laptop and closed it shut. "Hey, y'all, I got a few bottles of Crown Royal in the kitchen. Help yourself."

"Hiding the good stuff?" CeCe chided. "Shame on you!" She said from the arm of the leather recliner.

"Check the cabinet with the door."

"Now you're talkin'" Nils said, slapping his knees and standing up.

"I heard that," CeCe seconded. She bounced from the chair and practically skipped to the kitchen door, the remaining handful of guests following close behind.

Davis headed for the front door as Ellie intercepted him.

"You're staying, right?" Ellie grabbed his arm and gave what she hoped was a convincing come-hither stare. She didn't need him trying to escape and raising the alarm.

"Yeah, sure," Davis said slowly, a leering smile crossing his lips. He turned and followed the herd to the kitchen door.

Ellie's breath caught in her throat as she watched CeCe's hand grip the kitchen doorknob and twist. The creak of its hinges sliced through the chatter. The light from the kitchen ceiling glowed as normal. The space was normal. The others trailed into the kitchen behind CeCe. Ellie braced herself, almost squinting.

"What's wrong with you?" David asked. She realized he was watching her.

Cramps began racking her midsection. "Nothing. What are you? WebMD?" she hissed. "Go, go and have a drink." Ellie whooshed Davis away, hoping her shortness would conceal the pain growing in her stomach.

Davis shrugged. "Whatever," he said in a clipped tone and walked into the kitchen.

Ellie stood for a beat, alone in the living room. The intensity in her belly scaled up from her stomach to her chest. She shuffled in quick, stumbling steps toward the bathroom. "Please don't let me lose the baby."

She flipped the switch next to the door, and light shone upon her face. Ellie gasped. Her eyes squeezed shut as another cramp rocketed through her stomach. "Breathe," she mumbled through clenched teeth. Ellie panted through the spasms, leaning on the porcelain sink like a crutch. Her muscles ached as she struggled to stay upright, sweat drenching her forehead and dripping in her eyes. Ellie gasped for air that smelled stale and slightly moldy.

But it was her face that alarmed her the most. Its wrinkles and sagging that came back meant only one thing to Ellie. The blackness lied. "You promised!" she howled. Tears welled – the baby inside her must also be suffering.

A pop and muffled shouts buffered against the other side of the bathroom door. Ellie halted. She cracked the door as smoky tendrils floated past. Her legs were weak, and her muscles throbbed as she struggled to navigate the hallway, her hands acting as her guide through the haze.

Upon entering the living room, the scene was utter carnage of broken furniture and blood-soaked walls. The blackness had never breached beyond the pantry before.

Nils and CeCe, along with three more scared shitless guests, shivered in the corner encircled by the bleak cloud. One by one, the entity sucked them like peppermints into its black lair.

"Why?" Ellie demanded, her voice cracking, weeping. She stopped in front of the ripped recliner as the last body taking shelter in the corner flew past her, the hapless victim ripping the sunflower curtains away as they surfed into the abyss that engulfed the kitchen.

The darkness curled around Ellie's ankles as her legs gave way. She crashed to the floor, the snap of her arm ringing in her ears.

She moaned, "Ohhh," as her limbs lifted into the air and her body followed. The inky blackness stamped out the light inside the dump that was her prison. Ellie could see nothing as she entered the void behind the cupboard door.

THE NURSE HANDED ELLIE the baby and ran away. The darkness kept its promise after all. The soft cooing from the infant's blackened lips soothed Ellie. The pools of darkness in the babe's eyes did too.

Ellie left the eighteenth-floor apartment with a new life, and she would never be alone. Ever. The blackness would always be with her.

*END*

# 13

# Gotcha

THE ORNATE IRON FRAME encased the black-and-white photo like dangerous vines that snaked through a fence. The image itself was a leafless tree with branches spiraling out from its tall base like an ancient goddess. The dusty earth beneath starved for moisture. Katherine rested a confused gaze upon the relic in her hands.

"Why would Aunt Lydia leave me such a thing in her will?" Her grip began to shake. The frame was too substantial for the image beneath its glass.

My fingers skimmed the turquoise and diamond bracelet dangling from my wrist. Our aunt chose to leave me this heirloom. I didn't ask for it. Nonetheless, I whirled the trinket around and around, hoping my fidgeting would wick away my guilt.

"Remember what we talked about? Giving Aunt Lydia a bit of grace on this one?" I took the photo from Katherine to give it a thorough inspection. "Well, Kit Kat, I can see how this might suck. Really suck." Over the years, I managed to understand what pinpricks could upset Katherine. Aunt Lydia seemed to understand them, too.

I drifted to a distant memory of Katherine and me tangled in a tire swing, laughing, inviting the wind to take our ponytails higher, while mosquitoes feasted on our bare ankles. It was the hiatus before tenth grade. The last summer Aunt Lydia's blueberry cheesecake would be the best sweet I ever tasted, the last time Katherine would be a natural blonde, the moment when we blossomed out of Judy Blume and skidded into Jackie Collins. The very summer Aunt Lydia went through...what she went through. Before we knew Katherine would go through her own similar version of purgatory.

"Maybe I'll hang it over here." We stood in her daughter Mariah's bedroom, all pink and glittery, sad and terrible. Katherine motioned above the tufted blush headboard and started to climb on the twin bed. She teared up and whispered, "Maybe this is Aunt Lydia's last Gotcha."

Gotcha. Another childhood memory. It was a game that Aunt Lydia devised to keep us busy out in the middle of nowhere. The rules were pretty loose, but whoever coaxed, i.e., battered, bullied, or frightened the loudest scream out of the other person was the winner. Hide and seek, pinching, or tickling games counted. Anything that caused a heartfelt scream of shock and awe. The only rule, unwritten, of course, was no drawing blood, safety first and all. In retrospect, I think this bloodless competition was a sadistic measure to keep us under control.

I put my hand on Katherine's shoulder to halt her. "Honey, don't hang that right now," I muttered, partly to her, mostly to myself.

"You've got to be kidding me," Katherine said, irritated, stretching her cell phone out as far as her arm would allow. It was our daily check-in call. She was more distracted today than usual, even if I accounted for any side effects from her new medication. Years of depression and anxiety symptoms had ramped up after the birth of her only child and never let go.

"What are you doing?" I asked. The video swooped from left to right and back again, Katherine still in frame but on a diagonal.

"Can't you see the static on the screen?" Her stare seemed to come through the phone and past me.

As Katherine moved the phone to her right, I caught a glimpse of the dining room table. One of Mariah's fabric dolls, with red knitting yarn for hair, sat upright in a chair. The head slumped forward, but not all the way. The doll's exaggerated black almond eyes seemed to peer up from beneath its lashes. At that angle, its thin, curved smile simulated a scowl of disapproval.

"Listen, Kit Kat, we need to talk about Mariah —?"

"Why?" Katherine turned to observe the doll at the table. Just as she turned her head, Katherine's lips parted into a broad grin. An unpleasant cool rush prickled through me.

"I...I guess I thought maybe you needed someone to talk to. It isn't easy to..." My sentence drifted off. Having no children of my own, I didn't quite have the words for this conversation, a much-needed conversation, about someone else's child.

"Children grow up so fast and out of the things they used to love," Katherine stated, without any hints of sentimentality, then returned to our conversation.

Katherine's Mariah was named in honor of Aunt Lydia's Mariah. I never thought this was a good idea, but my sister was rock solid on doing it anyway. Our aunt did not outwardly object, but she didn't give her blessing either. Just kept her thoughts to herself on the matter, and we all went along as if nothing were wrong, so horribly wrong about it.

Katherine lowered her voice. Her eyes were glazed, much like the ragdoll behind her. "Mariah has been, I don't know, kind of off the past few days. I'm not worried...", she lowers her voice even more, "but sometimes I can hear her talking to herself in the middle of the night."

As gently as I could muster, I sighed and asked, "What is she saying?"

"I can't make it out." Her whisper quivered. "I'm just being a worrywart, right?" Katherine smoothed out her chestnut hair and smiled her trademark crooked smile that resembled an emergent giggle swirled into a scream.

The next day, Katherine missed our daily call. She texted vague excuses and promised to catch up on the weekend. I accepted her emoji-filled apology even though the intent behind the smiley faces and hearts seemed hollow. Katherine was prone to bouts of gloominess that could shutter her away from the world from time to time, but would find her way back in a day or two. I decided to let her be.

RAIN PELTED THE ROOF like a hail of marbles thumping against the shingles. I questioned if my Saturday morning errands were worth the trouble in this dodgy weather. However, checking in on Katherine was non-negotiable. That would happen.

Before heading out, I rang Katherine to make sure my trip would be worth it. When she answered, she didn't turn on her camera, which was highly unusual. Katherine never shied away from her reflection. She knew she was a stunner on the outside, even when mired in melancholy on the inside. The world had told her so from the moment she was crowned Miss Corndog Queen freshman year in high school.

"No cameras, Kit Kat? I've seen you with the stomach flu, so I can handle whatever you throw at me!" I shuddered thinking about the chunky brownish globs of vomit I cleaned from Katherine's hair during a particularly brutal bout with the virus a few weeks after Mariah was born.

Katherine's face appeared in the rectangle of my phone. Her luscious locks were matted like a dog that needed a bath, her complexion, drained and splotchy.

I did not recognize the woman who stared back at me.

Through Katherine's screen, I glimpsed a corner of the kitchen. Dirty pots and pans soaked in brown water in the sink. A tsunami of rubbish escaped from the trash bin. Small micro-movements of flies hovered over the discarded beer bottles, fast-food wrappers, and pieces of raw scraps the insects found to feed on.

Aunt Lydia's dubious picture sat on the floor by the bottom row of kitchen cabinet doors.

Whatever hesitations I held before were gone. I was ready, now more than ever, to confront Katherine.

"It's been crazy around here," she said, squirming with combustible nervousness. A tangled chunk of hair fell over Katherine's left cheek. She pushed it away, her fingers crusted with dried mud.  She plopped to the tile floor in a cross-legged fashion and rocked back and forth as if she were on a demonic magic carpet ride. Her phone acted as a steady cam, swaying with every erratic movement.

"Crazy?" I asked. The screen couldn't conceal the dampness of Katherine's black tee shirt, soiled jeans with muddy feet poking out the frayed ends. I couldn't comprehend any of this. "Kit Kat, why do you look like you've been swimming in a mosh pit?"

"Oh, this?" She tugged at the hem of her shirt. "I was just doing a little gardening."

"In the rain?" I shook my head, "I'm on my way over—"

"NO!" Katherine shouted, a hesitant peek over her shoulder. "Um, I mean," half yelling, "I've been meaning to give Aunt Lydia a piece of mind about that picture. Geez! What was that old goat thinking?" The expression on Katherine's face took my breath away. The last time I experienced a sensation like this was plunging five feet into a dunk tank at the county fair.

Katherine processed her guilt about Mariah, Aunt Lydia's Mariah, by losing touch with the world sometimes. Was it 19, 20 years since it happened?

Every visit with Aunt Lydia was a treat, and that was due in no small part to her Mariah. We doted on our cousin like the little sister we knew we would never have. I remembered it clearly. It was late July 1999 on a Tuesday. The year Katherine and I had marked the days as we wondered when everything Prince had sung about would come true.  On that warm and sticky morning, I headed with Aunt Lydia to the library in town. Katherine volunteered to stay with Mariah, but only because she had secret plans. Those plans were named Davey Kirkman, a bright blonde-haired boy who lived near the cabin.

Katherine's 16-year-old hormones made decisions that would come back to haunt her. I don't know the chain of events. Katherine never gave a full accounting of them, only a basic outline, doling out morsels of misery in doses she could stand. What I did know, what was evident by the outcome, was that she allowed a 5-year-old Mariah to play on her own while she and Davey did some dirty dancing in the work shed near the house. Mariah somehow got tangled in the tire swing rope and accidentally hung herself. Her little white sneakers were mere inches from the patch of worn earth beneath. Aunt Lydia's scream was a Gotcha scream that we never forgot.

As I tried to soothe Katherine, I started gathering my keys and pulled my rain slicker from the closet. She went into a fervent ramble about her Mariah. The tension in her voice spiked as she recounted being awoken last night. She assumed it was by the little hands of her Mariah asking for a glass of water.

"It was the hands of a full-grown stranger", she squeaked. "At least that's what I thought. When I rolled over, there was no one there." She took a deep breath. "I called the police."

"Sure, sweetie, that was a smart move. What did they find?", I asked.

"Nothing," her voice wild and breathy, "but they had no idea what to look for. No idea at all. But I do. Boy, do I know it now."

Katherine broke down. "I think..." She paused, wet, bloodshot eyes digging into the camera, "I think that crotchety old bird gave me MORE than a picture in a frame. I swear to God, she gave me something else with it."

The mud, the dirty water, Katherine's wet clothing. A clear realization surfaced that I wished I could shake. She was trying to bury the picture.

EN ROUTE TO KATHERINE'S, her hysterical incoming call animated my dashboard – "It's Mariah! Oh God, MARIAH!!"

I could barely keep my wheels on the road, skidding and hydroplaning, in my desperation to get to her. Thick sheets of rain covered my windshield, metronomic swipes keeping up with the torrent. I treated the 25-mile drive like a NASCAR event that I had not signed up for.

My voice sounded like a lunatic as I yelled into the dash, pleading with the 911 dispatcher. The curt, efficient woman was calm and collected. She'd probably heard worse on any given day, but for me, it couldn't get any worse. I screeched onto Katherine's manicured block, nearly rear-ending a car with blue lights pulsing on its roof.  More cars just like it, lined the street. All were directed toward Katherine's house. The police had arrived in full force.

I drove as close as I could, threw the car in park, and jumped out, the engine running, soft rock playing on the radio. I pushed past nosy neighbors and towards the first uniformed officer I could find. I had to wait outside the house while men in medical blue shoe coverings walked in and out. A woman in a white protective jumpsuit and mask entered. The ambulance on standby was empty. A good sign or a bad sign? I was told to wait as a team of hunkered-down officers searched room by room. For what, I didn't know.

The last vestiges of raindrops dissipated as the sun shooed away the clouds and baked the air. By the time I was ushered into the house, my pulse threatened to burst through my veins. The lead detective steered me into the kitchen. My nose wrinkled. I recognized the sweet chemical smell, its gentle, dizzying properties that made my salvatory glands tingle whenever I filled up at the Kum & Go on Route 54.

The detective began to speak, but I did not hear him. Didn't want to hear him. Katherine had fallen and broken her neck. (*Sorry for your loss. Can you make an identification?*). A freak slip and fall.

"These accidents happen", said the detective with a pockmarked face, his grey overcoat two sizes too big.

My mind raced. Through a sheen of tears, I asked, "Why are all these cars here for a", the words staggered out, "for a slip and fall?"

The detective carried himself with a no-nonsense demeanor. "When there is a child endangerment call," he raised an accusatory eyebrow, "we respond. Given the chaotic nature of the call, quite frankly, we weren't sure what to expect, so we came prepared."

"What to expect?"

He continued, his words strained, carrying a bit of anger, "Ma'am, your sister called 911 and said she was going to burn down the house with her and her daughter in it. That's a pretty serious threat." He retrieved a small notebook from his pocket and flipped a few pages. "Um, Mariah, your niece? We need to locate her."

"What? What are you talking about?" I cried inside but screamed on the outside, "No, no, no!"

The detective's eyes narrowed with frustration. "I know this is a shock, but minutes, seconds", he emphasized, "count when it comes to finding a missing child."

Through gasps of air, I wiped tears from my eyes, black streaks of mascara smudged on my fingertips. I answered the man, the silly man who had no clue. "Detective, Mariah, Katherine's daughter? She died as an infant." I couldn't say that it was due to a strap in the crib bedding getting caught around her...

The detective's previously stoic look contorted into the look of someone who had heard and seen it all. Until now. "Ah, well, the room down the hall—"

"Yeah, she changes it every year. Like it somehow keeps Mariah...I don't know, alive."

"Well, I guess that explains her," he caught himself before saying *crazy*, "behavior." He put the notebook back in his cavernous coat pocket. "The department has grief counselors if you need one."

I sat at the kitchen table while the professionals who dealt with death dealt with this one. Katherine had already been moved to the silent ambulance. I looked around at the dried smears on the floor and took in the absurdity, the eventuality of it all. The wet mud on Katherine's feet caused her to slip, fall backward, and hit her head in the most improbable way. A few inches to the left, she would have landed on the floor with a nice concussion. Unfortunately, her head hit a few inches to the right, and the base of her neck absorbed the full brunt and snapped.

Aunt Lydia's final offering to Katherine, the ornate picture frame covered in clumps of dirt in the scrollwork, lay solemnly on the kitchen table. The picture was gone.

"Excuse me?", I said to one of the white jumpsuited investigators who was packing up her tools. "There was a photo in this frame. A tree," I raised my hands into an opening arch motion, "in black and white? Have you seen it?"

The investigator held up her pointer finger to let me know to sit tight. She returned with a plastic evidence bag marked with a police description of its contents.

"We found this in your sister's hand. It will need to be processed, but call the station in a week or two to see if you can get it back." She agreed to let me look at the bag after handing me two tight latex gloves.

"Why in the world would she be holding—" That was when I saw it.

Katherine was right. The picture Aunt Lydia left her came with something else.  A very specific intent – to crumble a woman who had already crumbled beyond repair. Katherine saw what I couldn't see, didn't want to see.

The tree in the picture. It was where our cousin, Mariah, died two decades ago. The note on the back in Aunt Lydia's elegant cursive read:

*You took my Mariah. I took yours.*
*Gotcha.*
I screamed.

**END**

<h1 style="text-align:center">14</h1>

# Backward and Forwards

I bet you think you know it all. You don't. But you're about to.

I linger inside these four walls. It's cozy. White linens and a single bare window facing the manicured grounds. Idyllic if not for the steel vertical bars that complement the potted fern resting on the windowsill.

My *AIBOHPHOBIA* is stubborn, resistant to pharmaceutical interventions. The anxiety that spirals from it has not abated. Not when the axe deboned my wife's pretty, little ankle like a chicken leg. Not when the axe lopped Dennis's head to the right of his shoulder blades.

Rationally speaking, palindromes and the associated phobia I now suffer from should be easily coaxed from my mind. But I'm irrational. At least by your standards. My funny way of dealing with the mirror images of certain words and phrases is to blow off steam and go a little berserk. Like shooting at (and missing) the *RADAR* delivery guy back in the fall of 2002. Or running down little *IZZI LEMEL* at the bus stop last year. Oh, and there was that nice family, *BOB*, *EMME*, and *PIP* (who names their kid, Pip?) set on fire one block over. They. Needed. To. Go. Again, irrational by your standards, not mine.

A man comes around every Wednesday afternoon in his pressed khakis and white polo, angling to discuss the little matter of my previous behavior. Reeking of department store musk and authority, he calls himself Dr. *RENNER*. I call him a jerk, but not to his face.

"How are you, Ned?" He stares at me. I'm his unblinking fish in a glass bowl. I stare back, fixating on the dull white walls just beyond his slick black hair.

I shift gleefully in my chair. The leather straps that fasten around my back force my arms to secure me in a loathsome hug. Dr. *RENNER* pulls a small spiral notebook from his creased front pocket, a cheap ballpoint pen skewered through the little book's coils. A click of the pen and he begins writing his version of the truth.

The dry fissures on the tops of my feet, the broken edges of my toenails, the ones that aren't blackened, and the stench of fading urine on my pants is politely ignored by Dr. *RENNER*, but it brings me giddiness knowing he is aware of it all.

"*NED, I AM A MAIDEN*," the doctor says, toying with me.

I breathe in a wisp of air. The good doctor mocks me with this particular palindrome under the guise of testing his therapeutic approach.

My vision rapidly cuts between the smug smirk on the man in front of me and the open-mouth scream of a blurry face. My nerves are battle-hardened. There are no discernible cracks in my exterior. Although I sense my anxiety rising, I punch it in the face and keep it moving.

Dr. *RENNER* doesn't understand that the sight of letters and phrases, mirror images backward and forwards, means much more to me. This weird mole on the butt of the English language holds secrets meant only for me. The biggest secret of all...

*DENNIS AND EDNA SINNED.*

Edna, my adoring wife, up until the point she couldn't stand me, spread her legs and opened her heart to our next-door neighbor, Dennis. So naturally, I opened his head, then hobbled her. Naturally.

You must be thinking...*WOW!* The doctor shares your sentiment. The *DEED* I did, bloody as it was, is in direct proportion to the *deed* done to me, I say.

This is some next-level weirdness, you counter. Judge me if you will, but my actions could be considered a *CIVIC* duty to all deceived spouses around the world.

*WON'T LOVERS REVOLT NOW?* I took care of that, obviously. Sure, Edna is still amongst us, but giving Dennis his comeuppance was a thing of beauty. It's still my best *LOL* moment, his head swinging like a *KAYAK* on the rapids.

I'm not mentally ill despite the name on the building that houses me. I am the sum of my parts. Dennis and Edna sure can't say the same! Ha! I digress. I digress because, well...let's jump into the deep end.

I spend my days staring out the single-pane window. Often, shadows emerge in the distance beyond the edge of the cropped grassy hill where the gravel lane meets the promise of escape. *WAS IT A CAR OR A CAT I SAW?*

The moon and the stars are no longer a comfort to me. The brightness of waking hours is not much better. Backward and forwards, the letters rearrange themselves inside my head, on the tip of my tongue, but without a voice. Because I can't give Dr. *RENNER* the satisfaction of slipping even further down his rabbit hole of assumed insanity. I absolutely, without a doubt, can never give voice to the realization that Dennis is watching me.

*DON'T NOD.* Don't you dare nod with that patronizing air of superiority. Like you know something. You don't know anything.

The howling winds that previously shared their piercing cries only at night now drift past my window during the day. The whistling outside my window comes closer, submerging my mind and flooding my psyche.

*LEVEL. CIVIC. DEED. DENNIS AND EDNA SINNED.* Backward and forwards they go.

Dr. *RENNER* will be back soon with his itty-bitty notebook and his nonsense. High and mighty with his diagnosis that doesn't apply to me. But Dennis will be back sooner.

The white linens are cool and refreshing against the unruly tufts of beard on my cheeks. The fabric drapes snugly around my neck while Dennis's ethereal hands tighten the loop. My hands stiffen behind my back as I wait.

*DENNIS AND EDNA SINNED.* The doctors don't think so, but I know it to be true. So, I did what I did. Right? *I DID...DID I?*

***END***

# 15

# A Nasty Business



2024 SISTERS IN CRIME ELEANOR BLAND TAYLOR AWARD

THE SNOW CAME ONLY a few hours ago, just as a starless night blanketed the sky. The Louisiana weather had been temperate and mild for late fall. Prior to the flurries appearing, the farm had been green and lush. The snow tumbled down in wet, soppy flakes. No other part of the state was subjected to this curious weather event. There was no news flash or run for bread and milk at the IGA as the front blew through. That was the way things were in Présage and the swamps surrounding it.

Pops knew the land had a way of changing right before the final test. That was its way. It was as if this patch of earth was numbing itself for the trauma and the triumph.

Pops recalled the year he won, the land did the same.

Galen sniffed as he dug his hands into his jeans' pockets. "This is nuts." He paced near the hearth in the wood-frame house. A sheen of sweat crossed his brow. "We can't both win." He waved a hand at his brother. "Playing against each other will be impossible."

"This is true," Pops whispered.

Jeff chuckled. "You worried, little brother?" The fire crackled and embers sparked in restrained bursts as he pushed the logs around with a copper-handled poker.

"Speak for yourself," Galen barked as he wiped his forehead with the back of his hand.

Pops shook his head, scrunching his fingers through his thinning, grey afro. Pop's heart attack a few months back didn't immediately trigger a *come to Jesus* moment. It should have. The body was always sensitive to timing for the changeover, but like Pops' ancestors before him, it was hard to get his mind right to these sorts of things. Sometimes a push or a shove was required to stop delaying the process of assigning the inheritance. In Pops' case, his shit-or-get-off-the-pot moment came on a dank night two weeks ago.

Sleep was a restless affair most nights for Pops. But that evening, the dark felt different – pulsating and alive. In retrospect, he wondered if that bleakness had poked him like Cecile would do when he snored too loud. Whatever the reason, Pops awoke to the sound of the bedroom window moving on its tracks. Through half-closed lids, he watched as the window nestled upward, the branches of the big cypress just outside doing the lifting. The leaves swished like hair blowing in the wind as Pops' old fingers clutched the sheets up to his chin.

A moan filtered through the open sill, frightening him something terrible. The cool stream that ran down his leg barely registered. With the morning light, Pops tried to fool himself with speculations of liminal spaces or lucid dreams, but hc knew any excuses he conjured were just a placeholder for what needed to be done.

The land was reminding Pops that all good things must come to an end. It was time. And if he wouldn't do it willingly, the land would make it so, on his behalf.

A series of Farm Olympics was how the estate had been handed down since the 1800s, when Pops's kin first bought this parcel as part of the Louisiana Purchase land grab. Eligible, adult male heirs congregated at the property, summoned to compete through a series of tasks. Primed for it once they reached a certain age, they knew the day would come, and they always showed up. Most returned without thinking twice because they didn't know any better. Some, like Pops' sons, returned with gusto despite the unsavory nature of it all. Somehow, they believed this competition was worth winning.

Pops devised each game. Not to assess or compare the competitor's ability, but because folks needed meaning. The collection of obstacles he hobbled together didn't matter in the least. Regardless of what Pops thought, he would hand down the farm as his ancestors did before him, like a moth-eaten quilt. They drew lots to choose participant order and got on with it.

Cousins Rayford and Randy, twins from the Houston, Texas branch of the family, the sons of a second cousin nicknamed *Bootney,* kicked off the games with the tree chop—a deceptively challenging task for the untrained. The twins assumed they were tougher than the backwoods Louisiana clan. They found out differently as they attempted to bring the cypress to its knees with their axe work. With each chop at the trunk, little splinters of bark flew into the air, but it would take hours for their swings to make headway.

"Those pretty boys been raised on concrete too long," Pops teased them due to their soft curly hair and brown sugar skin. "You'll see. They'll get humbled real quick," Pops had said.

The humbling took some time, but it came for them. The brothers forgot their summers on the farm and the technique Pops had taught them so long ago – create a notch in the base of the cypress before cutting. The sharp snap of the trunk separating was a bullhorn to the city slickers because they dashed out of the way of the somersaulting tree with little time to spare. Arms and legs flying through leaves, rolling like stunt doubles in a movie.

But the tree didn't separate, not completely. It leaned cattywampus to the right midfall like a film stopped on the last frame. Randy and Rayford climbed on the split, putting their weight on the fractured trunk, but it didn't budge.

"Damn, it's standing just to spite us," Randy (or Rayford) said, frustrated and angry.

The unsuccessful attempt to complete the task was a ticket out of the race. The brothers hemmed and hawed, but it fell on deaf ears.

"Take your lumps, boys," Pops had declared. *The land is making its choice known, and it's not you*, thought Pops. And he was glad of that godforsaken tree's presence being further away from his bedroom window.

Rayford and Randy made a few more threats before taking off, tires squealing, gravel spraying from underneath the F150 that carried them to the farm. That was late afternoon. As soon as the twins departed, the air turned, the clouds shadowed the sky, and the white powdery flakes started their visitation.

The removal of the lapsed tree left behind by the twins was Von's task.

"You up next," Pops had said gently so as to not spook the young man.

The youngest of the competitors at twenty-nine years old, Von was the only child of Pops' brother Helms. Went West with his mama when things went south on the farm between Pops and Helms, and this was his nephew's first time stepping foot on the stead since he was a Cub Scout. From the moment Von sized up the tractor, befuddled as a toddler with a spoon, Pops knew things would go sideways with or without his tutelage on the machinery.

At first, Von couldn't get the beast started, the motor hiccupping. On his second try, the metal turned over. He gunned the engine and jerked his foot off the clutch. The tractor reacted as Pops knew it would – tumbling to its side like a drunk on a Saturday night. Von lay crushed under the tractor like the wicked witch of the West.

"As much as Helms and I were like oil and water, still glad he wasn't around to see this happen to his son," Pops had said, head bowed in deference to the somber event. "It wasn't my place to put my finger on the scale in that boy's favor."That was the lie he told himself.

It was late evening by the time that incident occurred, and Pops was left alone with the last two contenders – his sons. He watched as Galen and Jeff took up space with their bodies and their silence near the fireplace.

Galen interrupted the quiet. He stood, arms crossed, brow furrowed, in front of Pops' reclining chair, blocking the heat from the fire. Galen said, "The weather is getting rough out there. Maybe we should consider—"

Jeff came up behind Galen. He placed his hands on the back of Galen's shoulders and dug in, shaking his brother. "It's just fine outside. Will be tomorrow morning too." Jeff leaned toward Galen's ear and stage whispered, "Don't get any ideas about backing out. That would be even worse than losing to me." Jeff patted Galen's back. The smack cracked the air like a whip.

Galen winced. By the time he turned to face Jeff, his brother had moved to the other side of the living room. "You're an ass, you know that? It will be a pleasure to beat you senseless!"

Pops held up a hand in an effort to drain the room of its tension. "Quit it. Both of you."

He remembered squaring off against his brother, Helms. They got along even less friendly than Galen and Jeff, so Pops didn't lose any sleep over winning the inheritance. It was right after Pops married Cecile, but before they had thought of having children.

Before he desperately hoped their little sprogs would all be girls because being a boy in this family only brought strife.

Before Cecile had threatened to put a stop to this business.

It was years after Helms had his son and Pops had his two, that he realized...boys run in this family and girls don't come at all.

Pops assessed both his sons as they stood on either side of the hearth like lanky bookends. Only a year apart, Jeff and Galen shared the same warm nut brown complexion, trim, muscular build, Jeff slightly toner, and hazel eyes. The eyes came from their mother. Other than that, they were as different as hot and cold. Up and down. Jeff sported a shaved head, so Galen countered with dark locs. Jeff was as snarky as an insult comic. Galen was prickly and cautious with a bubble wrap sensibility.

"You two need to stop acting like babies and start acting like grown men. That's the only way," Pops chastised.

"Who do you want to win, Pops?" Galen shouted; his anger coated in an undercurrent of alarm. "You putting your eggs in Jeff's basket or..." He paused, his eyes pivoting from Pops to his brother and back again.

Pops lowered his lids. "I've done all I can do to prepare you. Doc says I'm on borrowed time, so" he shrugged, "now it's your turn, or your brother's, to take over."

"You could stop all this and just choose," Galen pleaded.

Pops rested his chin in his hand. Galen's risk aversion was never very far from any situation, and, in some ways, Pops felt his eldest, at this very moment, was the smartest person in the room.

"Nope, not the way it works." Pops watched as his sons exchanged glances but no words. "The business we run here on the side is a delicate one. That's the real inheritance, and this process is the way it needs to be passed on." He watched the snow spiral outside the frosted window.

Jeff sighed. "Whatever. I'm going to bed." He turned to Galen. "See you in the morning, loser," and strolled confidently toward the hallway as if his exit was the definitive word on the conversation. Galen slinked out behind him and left Pops in his chair, staring at the dark vastness of his property.

Pops gulped his watery scotch on the rocks and let the soft leather chair do its job of dulling his body's senses. He also had had enough of talking. He feared his tongue was already too lubricated and might unleash details he did not wish to share.

The wind clapped the unpainted shudders against the centuries-old structure. The click-clack sounded like a riding crop beating the house from outside. The fire in the hearth glowed a dull reddish-orange hue. A log crackled. Most of the flames were gone, but the heat was still plentiful enough.

Pops held a crystal-cut tumbler in his right hand, melting ice cubes swimming in the honey-colored whiskey. "How did we get here, and why can't we stop?"

The Farm Olympics was a nasty business. Pops would admit to that. But he always told his sons that family was family and "It is what it is". *No use fussing about it.* When it was his turn almost 40 years ago, his pap had sat him and Helms down to explain the reasons and the expected results.

The sons of the brothers would participate. The women-folk were never to know about this pact with forces that Pops and everyone before him could not control. Pops made the mistake of confiding in his lovely Cecile. "Now she's gone and never coming back," he said out loud. He pinched his nose and let out a deep breath, then took a large swig of his drink.

The land the pine tree lot sat on was a body farm. Not the research variety, but the freelance burial ground for those who could pay to make a body disappear. Many a corpse rested six feet under a sweet-smelling pine.

Too many to count over the years.

The family farm covered 500 acres, comprising the house and adjacent parcels. The farm had grown sugarcane in the early years, well before Pops was born, but transitioned to sweet potatoes for a long while. By the time Galen and Jeff came along, the farm grew pine trees, the biggest moneymaker out of all of the crops...of the legitimate crops anyway.

The side business started partly by accident around the early 1900s. A great-great-great uncle, a brown man with too many nice things, was the intended target of a lesson in wealth distribution at the end of a noose. Before that could happen, one of the KKKluckers tasked with this learning curve accidentally killed one of his own. The town took a *laissez faire* view of certain deaths, but not when that death was within their ranks. That ancestor offered to bury the body in exchange for amnesia about the farm and the black man who owned it.

Since then, good old boys from all over the state, and some out of Texas, brought their troublesome wives, pilfering business partners, and any other assorted cast of characters they wanted gone. A fair share of what white folks termed 'uppity negros' were brought to the farm too, especially during the marching days. Pops once referred to them as the 'lunch counter kids' and got a smack across the face from his pap with a stern, "Don't ever mention them. Ever." Pops sure hated being around for all that, so he kept that part of the farm's history hidden from his boys.

The ritual choosing of the farm's successor was out of necessity.

"Got to have the right disposition and a strong constitution to carry this business," his pap used to say. Back in the day, Pops had seen how it was. His pap would be willing to take live offerings dropped off with vague instructions like, "Take care of this one," and teenage Pops would see the terrified look in those folks' eyes as they were led off to the shed out back, never to be seen again. He'd kept that hidden from his boys, too.

Under Pops' tenure, he only accepted deceased bodies. "Do your own dirty work somewhere else."

For all his old man's blustering, he never said a word about the markings on the fireplace mantel. Twelve lines etched in the weathered, soft wood, each line a totem to every 100 bodies feeding the soil of the pine farm. His pap never spoke of the mist that covered the acreage at night. The mist that moved about like dancing trolls in the moonlight. Pops could only speculate as to the origins of the hollering that drifted from the pine trees that his pap drowned out with whiskey for years.

Nor was there a reason given for holding the Farm Olympics even though his pap was still relatively healthy at age 65, even with the alcohol. Or what drove the man who raised him to put a bullet in his temple the day after Pops won. Those were so many things that Pops would not receive a rhyme or reason for, but the root of these actions would peel away like an onion once he was in control. Neither Galen nor Jeff had boots-on-the-ground knowledge of what the true nature of this business was.

Over the handful of summers Pops allowed the boys to use their sweat equity around the farm, they matured from lanky, long-legged children into teenage Rubik's cubes. By the time Jeff and Galen were firmly entrenched in the high school experience, a wedge of meanness was developing between them that only their mother was able to putty over.  Even more so, the last month before Galen headed off to LSU. The last month before any vestiges of the tenuous bond Cecile had taken so much care to mend would tear like sutures of a half-healed wound. Because the land, *it was always the land, dammit*, that would weasel its way into the fabric and rip the family apart from the inside.

It was that August when Cecile watched her firstborn pack for a life outside of this "God forsaken filth", that her headstrong nature got the better of her. "I'm tired of waiting for you to do right by me and by *my* boys!" Cecile was determined to break the silence that the property held and free her sons from its misery.  But she was broken first and taken from the farm.

*Dragged* was more appropriate.

But Pops could never, would never verbalize it to his boys. Upon reflection, maybe he should have. They now had wives at home waiting for them to return. Maybe he should have.

Perhaps having this piece of crucial information would have yielded different decisions regarding wives at home.

Over the years, Pops heard the guarded whispers, the shifty communication that flew between Jeff and Galen, the unspoken body language of sons who did not trust their father. He didn't blame them.

Pops didn't trust them either.

Trust them to understand none of this was about them but existed because of them. Never truly trust if "the enemy of my enemy is my friend" was the premise they now operated under. The farm was getting the best of Pops, and he was no longer willing to struggle to keep it under his grip.

"Nasty business," Pops whispered as his eyelids grew heavy and he gave in to the fitful sleep in the arms of the soft leather.

HUMIDITY AND THE LOUISIANA heat melted the fallen snow from the previous evening, but the air remained crisp and cool, weighted by the rays of the sun. Galen and Jeff stood in the field near the line of the tree nursery, both in peacoats and jeans. Jeff huffed warm breath into his cupped hands.

The row of heavy black containers each held the skinny trunk of a pine. This was the seeding area for the trees. The place where they began their life before growing hearty enough for transplantation to a patch of land about a half mile away, the 'body' part of the farm.

Pops surveyed the final competition's setup from his seat in the golf cart that transported them to this spot. Galen and Jeff talked among themselves, although Pops' hearing wasn't what it used to be, so their words were not reaching his ears.

He shuffled himself out of the vehicle and walked toward his sons. "Well, let's get started," Pops said in a reserved tone. He gathered his flannel-lined anorak close and tugged his tattered Saints ball cap over his forehead.

The bullseye score rested on a tripod stand. The alternating red and white rings converged toward the yellow center of the dirt-filled frame. Two metal crossbows sat on the ground near the sons.

Galen picked up a bow and inserted an arrow into the contraption.

Pops positioned himself to the side of the men and said, "You're up first, Galen."

The final contest was straightforward. Each of the men had five arrows to get as close to the bullseye as possible.

"Okay," Galen said, but his body didn't follow his words. The crossbow stayed at his side.

"Get to it, son," Pops said.

Jeff picked up his crossbow and slid an arrow down the flight rail.

Pops removed his hat and scratched his head. "*Wait...*who's goin' first?" he asked Jeff. Pops wrinkled his nose. The air tickled his nostrils and brushed against his cheeks like a firm hand. He watched as both brothers glanced at each other.

*Jesus, Mary, and Joseph.*

They leveled their crossbows to Pops' line of sight. He cocked his head gently to the side. Pops couldn't know what the boys, his sons, his heirs, and the land's new providers, saw as they raised their weapons to him, but he hoped it was rage.

"You think you're so smart, but you can't game this system, sons." Pops took a single step closer.

Galen took a step back, shaking like a virgin in the backseat of his mother's car. His eyes squinted and winked, from tears or sweat, Pops could not say. But Jeff stayed planted in his spot, even leaning in a little. Pops watched him lick his lips, his eyes wide and sharp.

"The land is smarter," Pops whispered. He wasn't sure if his goal was to soothe them out of this decision or to comfort himself. "Always has been y'all. Don't you know that?"

But soon enough, the land would share its bountiful knowledge with one of them. Maybe even reveal how the pines silenced their mother. How the farm no longer gives itself to growing but to the dead. It does as it pleases, and no number of miles between the generations and this patch of land could change that.

The farm didn't give up, didn't let go. Not when it took Helms in the night after his loss, discarding his limp body under the pines. By the time Pops found Helms' broken body, the life draining out of him, and filling the farm's needs, Helms begged to not die on that land. He honored Helms' last request. Pops would weep sometimes because of this. He never hated his brother again, but it was too late. Pops figured maybe the land had given him its one and only gift.

"The land is smarter..." The words barely formed when the ping of their arrows filled the air and entered Pops' chest.

JEFF SAUNTERED THROUGH THE front door, his gait weary and relaxed. Galen fidgeted with a paper napkin at the kitchen table.

"You buried everything?" Galen asked. Jeff figured his brother was stalling, wasting time, because he knew the answer to the mundane question.

"Yep, sure did." Jeff washed up at the sink, the dirt and grit circling the drain. He stared out the window, lingering on thoughts of the holes he had dug. The row of backhoe pits lined up like poke holes in a cake, in anticipation of his cousins' return later today. The local sheriff picked up Randy and Rayford as soon as they skidded out of the driveway, before they could make it out of town properly. The lawman would take care of them before dropping them off to Jeff.

He thought of the holes that currently held his father and Von. Of the strange mist that hung coating the tops of the trees as he dug.

Jeff turned off the tap and wiped his hands dry with a kitchen towel as he pondered the last hole that would hold his brother. He pulled out a chair from the kitchen table and sank into it. "Guess we have the keys to the kingdom." Jeff tapped his fingers on the wooden surface.

Galen had no stomach for the most unsavory bits of running the farm. Jeff was sure of it. *Did I make a miscalculation in killing Pops?* Jeff wondered. Maybe. Probably. He and Galen had always believed Pops murdered their mother. Neither of them had guilt over the drastic measures they felt compelled to take that morning, but now he wasn't sure of anything anymore. Not since he dug the holes. Not since the land and the mist started moaning new truths in his ear.

"The winner takes it all. Everything," Pops had uttered as he expired, one hand wrapped around the arrows protruding from his chest and a ball cap in the other. "The land won't have it any other way," were his last words through a hard grin.

Galen grabbed two beer bottles from the refrigerator. He twisted off the caps and left them on the counter, then joined Jeff at the table. Galen set one bottle in front of Jeff and raised his beer, but his brother gave words to the whole situation. "It is what it is. No use fussing about it."

Jeff peeled the label from the bottle in his hand. The damp sweat of the cold beer bottle made easy work of the paper. He reckoned that the status quo would stay fixed and perfect here on the farm. No one had given a second thought to perpetuating the ritual with their own sons or being part of the body farm. *And neither will I.*

Galen nodded and took another swig.

*Galen*. Jeff caught the slightest tremble in his brother's hand as he drank his beer. "You alright, bro?"

"Yeah," Galen answered, his voice wavering just a little.

Jeff placed the damp, pulpy label on the table. He offered Galen a crooked smile. Pops had warned him of the land's grab of Helms. Jeff wanted better for Galen. *Maybe I can wait an hour or so. Let him savor these moments.*

The brothers drank the rest of their beer in silence.

**END**

16

# Tastes Like Chicken

"Tastes like chicken," Sebastian says about human flesh, like the whole world should already know this. However, I need assurances. A lot of assurances. My humanity is at stake.

The cavernous steepled roof of St. Hubert Library is posh and indulgent, a reminder that I am an outsider in these parts, a black man in this very British countryside. I study the ornate wooden beams along its arched rafters and steel myself for what will come when darkness blankets the pastoral landscape.

A cell phone rings, jerking me from my languid slouch. Sebastian guffaws in a very upper-crust manner and says, "Jacob, what are you scared of?" He reclines back into the buttery soft leather of the club chair that holds his athletic frame, honey-blond hair falling softly over his roguish face. "Look, old chap," arms open in a grand gesture, "We know what you've gone through, and

174

trust me, you'll be stronger for it. I know you will. After all, you're one of us."

THE ATTACK WAS THREE weeks ago, but I continue to have unrelenting nightmares about it. I used to sleep like a baby on Nyquil. Not anymore.

Sebastian is the one who found me unconscious on the bridle path near the cafeteria. He tells me the most absurd story imaginable about my attack. But slowly, I began to believe. The dreams. The cravings. Is paranoia setting in? Sebastian insists I'm "one of" them. But one of what? He won't clarify.

St. Hubert scores an A for opportunities and aesthetics but a D for its aversion to anyone not sporting a sweater vest or a hyphenated last name. I figure there are two distinct possibilities at play. I'm a Carlton Banks proxy or I'm about to get punked, the former being the worst-case scenario. The chess pieces have not yet fallen into place for me, but there is nothing more soul-crushing than knowing you exist to check someone's box.

Either way, I can't break the rules if I don't play the game, and my floppy-haired friend is in control. For now.

Sebastian speaks in hushed tones and half smiles into his cell phone. His head turns away slightly, but more often as the conversation wears on. He shifts restlessly in the chair, the tail of his button shirt coming out of his black dress slacks a bit. He tucks it back in as he says, "Yes, yes, we're all good, mate." Sebastian shakes his head, "No, don't be daft." He gives an OK signal in my direction, "Jacob is ready. But of course, he has concerns. Maybe even fears."

Sebastian's eyes glint at this fact, and I can't help but feel a mixture of irritation and, of course, fear. Fear that I'm submerging the authentic me for a Faustian trade. Chitlins for "cheerio". Sebastian completes his conversation with his conspirator on the other end.

With a sigh and a hearty slap to his thighs, Sebastian turns to me. "Right," he declares. "We'll get you sorted soon."

We vacate the enclave we've occupied for the past hour and proceed past the rows of leather-bound books, the stained-glass windows at our backs, to the front courtyard of St. Hubby's, as the students refer to it. "Okay, I'll be in touch," Sebastian says, then lowers his lids. My insides jump like a hiccup. "There are plenty of men I could have plucked from this campus. But you," he pointed to my chest, "You are the one. Don't make me regret it." His wide, toothy smile is not comforting. "All right?"

"Yeah, sure."

Sebastian bids me a jaunty farewell, and I stand there for a beat. I watch him meander off to parts unknown, and I head back into the confines of the library to find Marta in the third-floor Rare Books and Special Collections Reading Room.

She's standing over a large book, about two feet by three feet, open wide on its spine, her finger gliding over the manuscript. When I walk up behind her, my shoe hits the leg of a spindle chair, scraping the floor. Marta jumps and lets out a yelp. Her eyes are as wide as they are furious once she gets a glimpse of me.

"What in heaven's name are you doing sneaking up on me like that?" Her tone is harsh, but she begins to relax a little as I make my way to stand beside her.

"Sorry, sorry. My bad. That's American for 'I'm a douche'." I smile and Marta finally becomes *Marta* again. She turns back to the book with its old English sentence structure and medieval block letters that start each paragraph. As if she could read my mind, she says, "It's in Latin, but it looks like old English." Marta puts her hands on her tiny waist, her cropped khaki pants and pink polo shirt make her look more like a college student than me, even though she finished her studies six months ago.

Marta stares at me and asks, "Are you okay?" She pauses. "Since the incident? It's been almost a month..."

I shift my gaze away and down to the substantial book in front of us.

Marta must have sensed my hesitancy. She is always pretty good at reading a room, so she says, "Such a dreadful thing to happen here." She flips a page of the manuscript. "I know the vicar in that town, and he knows everyone, sinner and saint. Maybe I can ask around?" As far as Marta knows, I had a run-in with some lads from a few towns over. I leave out the lingering aftermath of the attack, the part about claws, night terrors, and, oh, that Sebastian has me convinced something stunningly wicked is coming my way.

I couldn't let Marta know that I continue to have the same horrific dreams. Poker hot eyes staring through my window, fleeing through the picturesque forest on the outskirts of campus, awaking to find my fingertips caressing the scars on my chest, drenched in sweat, wondering who had just left the room.

"Well, if you want to, Nancy Drew."

"Who's Nancy Drew?" Marta feigns confusion in her expressive hazel eyes.

"Oh, sorry. Should I say, Inspector Morse?"

Marta giggles. A wonderful giggle.

"DCI Barnaby, perhaps?"

She shakes her head, her strawberry blonde ponytail swaying in rhythm. "You really are a nutter sometimes."

I gaze at Marta as she writes in her notebook. "I saw you with that Sebastian down in the stacks." She wrinkles her nose in disapproval. "He's a wealthy wanker who's morally ambiguous if you understand my meaning. Don't lose your soul to him." Marta winks as if her joke is a surface observation rather than a spot-on, accurate, 360-degree view of the situation.

Sebastian Milhouse-Rutherford *IS* stonking rich and *VERY* much a wanker. Campus scuttlebutt says his family acquired its fortune through defense contracts. Marta says it's all blood money and she's "bloody disgusted by it all."

Far be it from me to judge. Besides, he's grown on me.

After a few minutes, Marta and I part ways. She stays with her musty manuscripts; I go back to my restless, unsettled thoughts.

THE CYCLE BEGINS AGAIN.

When my lids close, slumber brings with it a heaviness as if I am buried in sand from my neck to my feet. The dreams are water binding the granules into a cement chamber around me.

I stride up the path, lush fields on either side, the sole of my leather shoes making the faintest contact with the earth below. The sun sets much too fast. A cloudless, dense sky covers me. The details around me are in high definition. A twitchy rabbit in the brush with metallic reflective eyes, suspicious of my journey to nowhere. The patches of brambles with their glistening blueberries that blink as I walk past.

The air. The air doesn't feel like anything. A detail that is a non-detail. My body lumbers along like a stone floating in antigravity but simultaneously moored firmly, not to the earth, but to the anxiety of the landscape.

Twigs snap behind me in the underbrush. I tense into an unsteady halt. I want to run but my legs always keep me planted in the same spot, a betrayal of the highest order.

The battering is tumultuous, aggravated, and sincere in its determination. I feel the thrashing through a black, obscured veil as if the nighttime is interceding with its version of protection.

My eyes cannot see, but the other senses are fully engaged, fully enraptured in the moment. My stomach muscles seize with every lift and push into the ground. The tearing of my skin is a sharp, searing sensation that heightens my physical response. Pleasure pain throbs through my groin as fight or flight runs through my mind.

This thing that is flinging my body, shredding it, grabs the collar of my tattered wool houndstooth blazer. A smell escapes its mouth that I can only explain as dead. I yell out, and it swiftly covers my mouth. A tough paw smothers my lips while claws fan out over the width of my face.

Before I awake, I hear the same words. A series of syllables with the power and weight of ice-cold water to the face. Words that frame the boundaries of this nightly experience with horror and longing.

*I'm here for you.*

I wake night after night to desperate shrieks. I assume they're mine.

THE PUB IS LOUD. The distinctive punch of darts hitting the board and the clicks of snooker balls against one another boomerang around Marta and me. But the sounds recede, and there's only Marta and the animated conversation she is having with me.

"Can you believe that?" Marta asks as she sips her dram of whisky. "I mean, it's absolutely incredible that anyone in this day and age would continue to hang on to such rubbish." She sways on her barstool, her knee knocking mine.

I smile. "Well, that is quite a story, but what I find unbelievable is—," I lift my own nearly empty dram to swallow the last drop, "—that this weird folklore is readily available in the esteemed confines of good ole St. Hubby's."

"Right?" Marta gestures with her hands, her vibrant personality practically flowing from her fingertips. "Apparently, this goes back to the late 1300s or at least that is when it became a *'thing'*." She does air quotes. "The earth magic practiced by the serfs to ward off the plague somehow morphed into the belief that people can be cursed and shapeshift and all kinds of silly nonsense. Even sillier were the men sent to excise the magic from the rural villages and towns."

Marta's voice is illuminated by the whisky. I rest my hand on my chin and give her an, "Oh, really?"

"Are you mocking me, Jacob?"

"Of course not. You're the expert in all things archaic, so continue."

Marta gives me a playful scowl and keeps going. "So, when the plague swept through the countryside, the peasants used whatever they could to ward off the advancing doom, so you have to expect that kind of drama was a breeding ground for myths." She twirls her hair, adding, "Honestly, it boggles the mind that anyone would believe this foolishness."

I raise an eyebrow. "So, what you're implying is that Sebastian is one of these fools?"

"He's a fool regardless of what he believes."

I snicker. "Fair enough. So it's all vague bullshit about me being 'one of us'. You think this might be his bastardization of that folklore designed to put me on? Huh." I sniff. "I'm smarter than that. I'm an American! Four score and seven years ago, baby!" I brace for Marta's response, but she zigs when I zag.

"Oh, here." She unbuckles the messenger bag on the bar next to her and pulls out folded pages. "Made copies of the best bits for you." Marta slides them across to me.

The pages are not the only thing that slips under my fingers. Marta takes my hand.

I'm stunned but ready for anything. "Ah, ha, keep carrying on like that and you'll get a paper cut, young lady."

Marta's loafer grazes my denim jeans, and I wiggle in my seat, then wonder if I look goofy.

"Look, Jacob," Marta slides slightly off her stool, her khaki mini skirt becoming even more mini, "if there is anything I can do," she squeezes my hand, "anything...let me know. I just want to help."

*Help?* My mind swirls. *Help? Like, help me calm the nightmares by tucking me in and reading me a bedtime story?* I feel the intensity in Marta's gaze go through me and right to the bullseye below my belt. Yes, I could use Marta's help.

Our exit from the pub is swift. The walk to my dorm is not so long that the energy between us is dulled, but it gives us plenty of time to let our thoughts stir and wander. As soon as the door slams shut, it closes out the nightmares, Sebastian and his plans for me, and the rest of St. Hubert University.

After hours of exploration and the highest highs, Marta settles into sleep. My rest takes longer, but with Marta lying next to me, I am able to let go and let the stillness wash over me.

But, of course, I am delusional to think Marta's softness could stave off the dream when my eyes close.

The cycle begins again.

I walk the path. The air is displaced in a sensational breeze. Twigs snap behind me, and the attack ensues.

*But wait. What is this?*

I land with a hard thud on my back. The first time in my dream state that I face the originator of my torment.

The blazing amber eyes languish over me. Their slit black irises like a piece of glass, take my breath away. They are beautiful.

A low baritone ruptures in my ear. *I'm here for you.*

I awake with a jolt.

Marta stirs and reaches her hand to my chest. She whispers, "You okay?"

I'm breathless, gasping for air as I try to lower the pounding inside me. "Yeah, yeah." I flop back into my pillow, then turn to face her and say, "Everything's fine. Go back to sleep."

Marta opens her drowsy eyes and kisses my sweaty cheek. She falls back into her restful sleep. I spoon her, the sweet lavender of her shampoo infiltrating my sheets, and lie staring into the darkened room.

"Jacob, it's been decided. Tonight's the night. Meet me at the cathedral at 11 pm." Sebastian's text is as casual as a moth-eaten sweater.

I tense up, shuffling in my chair. The remainder of my lightly seasoned egg salad sandwich will go unfinished upon hearing this news.

Marta is waiting for me outside the library. Her expression tells me everything I need to know. Two months into our relationship, my ability to pick up on her thoughts is laser-focused and precise. And she usually gives me her opinion, so that makes it easy.

"You're not going to this ludicrous meeting, are you?" Marta stands by the stone gargoyle that flanks the entrance. Her linen shorts are paired with a blue and green Fair Isle sweater vest and white loafers, sending a mixed message about how she feels about the weather outside.

"How did you know? I just found out twenty minutes ago."

"I may have a Ph.D. in Medieval history and folklore, but I'm not an idiot about the present day."

"Point well taken." I try to flash her a wonky smile to elicit a lighthearted giggle. Marta remains resolute in her displeasure.

"Fine. But if you turn into one of those insufferable pricks just because you all have some weird, shared experience, I'm going to kill you with my bare hands."

"I'll beg you to kill me if I turn into one of those insufferable pricks. And since I have everything to live for," I reach for

Marta's hand, "Then let's assume I will come out the other end unscathed and still humble."

Marta takes her free hand and gently moves my face towards her. "Be careful. And know thyself. Okay?"

"Okay, Socrates." I kiss her. I live in the moment, knowing that moments are hard to come by, so I kiss her again.

I wrestle with nervous energy throughout the evening. Who am I now, and who will I be after tonight? Marta's cautions weigh like a boulder on my conscience.

THE DOORS OF BROOKMIRE Cathedral are unlocked, and rows of candles flicker on the ledge of the altar. I walk towards them. I hear only my footsteps, the rubber sole of my tennis shoes squeaking on the linoleum floor.

*Something's not right here.*

I quiver, every part of my body prickly with panic.

I hear a creaking sound. But it's not creaking exactly. It's more guttural and unnatural.

The candlelight projects drunken shadows over the pews but stays just clear of giving any illumination to the pillars that flank the walls of the church.

I hear Sebastian's voice come from the darkness. "Welcome, Jacob."

"Hey, where is everyone? I thought there were, you know, others? When do I get to      ?"

Sebastian rises from behind the pulpit. I gasp. He still sounds like Sebastian, but the thing I see is the upper part of a solid and wide fur-covered torso.

But it is the head that makes me shriek inside my mind.

Sebastian's nasally British accent is coming from a snout that protrudes to a rounded point, jagged, triangular teeth inside the jaw. His eyes are black, round nuggets inside a furry head with pointed ears. I can't see his lower body from where I am standing.

"Holy shit! I'm going to look like that?"

"No, Jacob, of course not." Sebastian laughs and spreads his arms open. "No, this is just our way of completing the initiation."

"What? What initiation?" My anxiety is reaching an intensity that feels reckless and dangerous.

More figures come out of the shadows, from behind pillars, up from the pews.

"Welcome to the Order of the Phoenix." The words swell from the darkness.

"Wait, what?" My mind is racing at top speed. It does not compute. "This is a hazing ritual for a fraternity?"

The lights flip on. Sebastian jiggles the snout. I hear a click. He turns the head and lifts it off to reveal his shaggy blonde mane. "Ha, you look like you've had a terrible fright."

The rest of the members circle and begin chanting as they surround me in a stereophonic, "Welcome to the Order."

"Your initiation is complete!" Sebastian says in a booming voice. I'm standing there in disbelief.

"So, the attack on the bridle path?"

"Staged. But it does seem to have gotten out of hand. Only your shirt was to be torn. Sorry, old chap. Don't hold that against us."

"And all that talk about human flesh?" My shoulders slump, and I let out an audible sigh and shake my head. "Yeah, that was part of the joke."

Sebastian smirks. "Another ingenious way to get your goat, my friend."

He pats me on the back. "Just think, Jacob. Being one of us will give you access to the halls of power, not just in Britain but...everywhere. There won't be a room in the corporate or political realm where you don't command authority. Besides, we need more men, you know, like you." Sebastian sizes me up with a glance up and down. "We can work on the wardrobe. The important thing is you've got the brains for it, or you wouldn't be at St. Hubert's."

The gathered men start their own conversations, giving me time to comprehend the sheer awkwardness, then frustration with all of this. I can hear Sebastian's aristocratic tone dishing out instructions for the rest of the evening.

But none of this answers my most pressing question. "Why are my nightmares so vivid, so real?" I mumble to myself. I stare at the stained-glass window behind the altar and see a puffed white moon rise in the night sky.

Sebastian claps to stamp out the side conversations. "Okay, as the head of the reconstituted Order of the Phoenix, I want to say, 'welcome'!"

"Reconstituted?" I parrot.

"Oh, I forgot. You're American," Sebastian says. "The Order of the Phoenix is —"

"An old group of witchfinder generals." Marta stands there. I'm not even sure for how long.

She takes a few steps forward. The men take a few steps back. "They came for my people back then. And they are coming for them again now."

Marta is completely naked as the day she was born. Her skin blushes with heat but not from embarrassment.

The room goes from silence to murmurs, escalating to open chatter.

Sebastian shushes the men with a wave of his hand and addresses Marta with curiosity. "Well, well, Marta. Come to join the fun?"

I can hardly breathe. *What is she doing?*

"Marta," Sebastian pulls off his jacket from under his costume and hands it to her, "maybe you've had a bit of an episode?"

He snickers in the direction of the Order. "Maybe we can call someone on your behalf to help."

She refuses the clothing. "There is nothing wrong with me. You know that, Sebastian."

Marta looks directly at me. "I didn't want you to find out this way. But know this," she hisses to the rest of the room, "I'm here for you."

I look at my hand as coarse hair begins to break through, and my teeth agonizingly grow. My vision starts to take in colors and prisms I have never seen before.

I know it now. *It's not a nightmare, it's real.*

None of the men in the cathedral are prepared for what is to come. The Order of the Phoenix runs like rabbits in the brush toward the door. They pull the wide iron handles but the door sways out and back in like a final breath. Heavy locks secure it, keeping the men inside.

Marta shapes and shifts, the hair rippling up from her pale skin. Her legs bend and crack, hooves emerging from her feet.

I clomp around the side of the pew, a spectator to her transformation, oblivious to my own changes that are underway.

A surge of energy builds like a volcano inside me, the simmer so intense I think I may lose my mind. I hunch forward and see myself for the first time. Part of myself anyway. My arms are bulging masses of musculature, my hands, my paws, are clawed and thick. I inhale and exhale with expanded arms flinging upward out to my side. The pews on either side of me sail through the air like toys and land, one near the altar, the other near the door taking the heads of two of the Order members with it.

Marta's roar is as thunderous as I remember from my dreams. Her eyes are just as beautiful.

The screams of the men are background noise.

*I bet they have never felt unsafe before.* For me, this would be the safest I had felt in a long time.

The power within me flexes and purrs. I would never be one of them. As I rip each of the Order of the Phoenix limb from limb, I am grateful for that.

Marta and I graze and make bloody work of the unholy men on consecrated ground.

Curiously, the one human thought I have left consumes me as I feast on the ravaged flesh before me.

"They really do taste just like chicken."

*END*

# 17

# Don't Drink the Water



2025 KILLER SHORTS SCREENPLAY COMPETITION
SEMIFINALIST

TENISHA'S WORN SNEAKERS SQUEAKED as they rubbed together against the floormats while she adjusted her butt in the passenger seat. She bounced at every bump as the car sailed down the dirt road. The windows were half-mast as the humid Louisiana air whipped around the fullness of Tenisha's cheeks. She bopped to the radio blasting Dirty South Crunk, squinting out the window at the glow of lightning bugs swarming in the high grass along the side of the road.

"Are we there yet?" Fanny urged from the back seat as she leaned out the window behind the passenger side. Her hand floated on the warm breeze in time to the beat. Tenisha tilted her head toward the side view mirror and watched Fanny's coily reddish-brown hair swoosh around her freckled brown face.

"Hush," barked Catina, not turning around as she clucked her teeth from the driver's seat. Fanny leaned back with a *hmpf,* crossing her wayward arms in front of her. Catina was the Jesus who took the wheel of the Oldsmobile as it careened through dust and darkness, the two high beams slicing through the night. The wind barreling through the window didn't faze her.

Catina's jet-black, wavy hair was held back in a tight bun. The baby hairs at the corners of her forehead were swirled and slicked into place with the kind of edge wax that never worked as well on Tenisha's tight curly afro. *I guess that's what it's like to be perfect,* Tenisha mused as she stared at Catina, then returned her attention to the open road.

The closing shift at Far Burger Bar had been like any other night. Catina balanced the registers, carefully bundling the day's receipts to tuck away in the safe. Tenisha and Fanny stacked the chairs, wiped down the tables, and cleaned the grill for the opening team the next day. But this time, instead of walking out to the parking lot and ignoring Tenisha's trek to the bus stop, they...talked to her.

"Hey, T," Fanny said as she cocked her head. "Come here."

Tenisha's eyes widen. *Are THE popular girls talking to me?* She had to admit this was exciting. She tripped over her feet like a carnival clown, her backpack hanging from her shoulder, but she didn't fall. "Hey, Fanny. What's up?" Tenisha asked.

Fanny and Catina looked at each other, whispering between them. Catina seemed to have drawn the short straw because she stepped forward. "So...we're going to a party out by The Wicks down Hwy 57. Wanna come?"

Fanny chimed in, "Yeah! Come on, sis, get your ass in the car." Tenisha did so; the thrill of an invite to a party from the popular clique was as good as it got on a Friday night.

Thirty minutes later, they steered into the gravel driveway of a log cabin. The night sky was thick, and the darkness had a life of its own.

Tenisha looked out the window at the quiet exterior. Anxiousness enveloped her. *They said it was a party. Where is everyone?*

She craned her head out the open window as the other two got out of the car, slamming their doors.

Tenisha desperately wished that she could reverse time and go back to the Far Burger Bar parking lot, where she would have said, "NO thanks!! The Wicks are not for me!"

The sound of Fanny's voice startled Tenisha. "Girl, come on and get out of the car," she commanded with a sly grin and opened the passenger door. Tenisha climbed out, taking in every dark nook and cranny. Fanny took her by the arm as if they were long-lost pals. "Let's see who's here."

The cabin porch creaked as their weight bore down on each step. Catina went ahead of them and swung the heavy wood door open to a dimly lit room.

Derek sat restlessly in the lounge chair near the fireplace. He squirmed his disheveled frame into the leather, legs splayed forward. One foot sported an unlaced tennis shoe, the other just a sock. A letterman jacket lay on the plank floor like a carpet.

Derek would meet Tenisha clandestinely, smuggled into her bedroom. Kisses and conversations made her feel wanted. Tenisha wasn't delusional enough to think Derek's interest was more than skin deep, but she wanted to believe, with time, it could be, so she drank the water. For him.

Her mother had warned her. A sheen of uneasiness always coated her violet and gold-flecked eyes and caused her delicate fingertips to quake when she spoke to Tenisha about "this thing" that they were. But her mother's warning would not be enough. Not even for a rule follower like Tenisha – not when the isolation of her difference, *potential* difference, threatened to eclipse the best years of her teenage life like a black hole swallowing a thousand suns.

*Don't drink the water.*

It was never a guarantee that Tenisha would have the affliction that haunted her ancestors, but it was possible. She always knew this. Every time she started at a new school, it was drilled into her - *don't drink the water*. But Derek's effortless and intoxicating charm stirred doubts and conjured hope.

Chances were taken. Caution was thrown like a kite into the wind.

The star athlete that Tenisha had shared her gifts with every night for a month, until last Wednesday, when she stopped returning his calls, sat fidgeting in front of her.

*You shouldn't have drunk the water. Shouldn't have let Derek get hooked...* but it was too late.

Tenisha took two steps back and then turned to head for the door, but Fanny and Catina swiftly created a human blockade. The glint in their eyes was uncompromising and ruthless. Tenisha stared between the two girls. A fight or flight anxiety rushed through her like a tidal wave.

"Come on, T, don't be like that," Derek's words dripped like the drool that coated his bottom lip.

"Derek told us what you two been up to," Fanny spat out. "We want some too."

Tenisha gasped. The gut punch of those words, the betrayal, left her breath quick and shallow. She screeched, "You got it all wrong!" The words sputtered out of Tenisha like an engine trying to turn over. "Whatever you think you know, it's, it's way more complicated." Her eyes pleaded with Derek, but he was a stone-faced husk of the boy she knew.

"Enough talking," Catina said as she shoved Tenisha against the cabin wall across from the fireplace. Tenisha's elbow slammed into the drywall, leaving a concave dent. A sizzling pain rushed up her arm as she screamed.

Tenisha held her hands forward. "You don't want to do this, I promise you don't," she whispered as she scooted her butt against the wall surrounded by a trio of wild faces. She barely recognized her classmates anymore.

Fanny grabbed Tenisha, then held her down. Catina forced her lips open into a scrunched O and flooded water over Tenisha's face, hair, ears, and into her mouth.

"Drink, bitch, drink!" The chant echoed throughout the room.

Tenisha coughed and choked on the water invading her throat. Immediately, a potent viscous elixir seeped through her pores, covering her body and soaking her clothes.

Derek ripped through Tenisha's T-shirt and yanked her bra strap, the snap of it hitting her in the throat. He sucked on her bare shoulders. Fanny and Catina grabbed each of her ankles like a chicken leg. They slurped and scratched at her slick skin.

Tenisha thrashed, screamed, and cried as they all licked away her salty tears.

The robbers of Tenisha's essence stumbled toward the center of the room, dancing and flailing their arms like a mosh pit made for three. She curled into a ball, shivering, her arms wrapped around her chest. She rocked back and forth as she covered her ears, muffling the erotic groans of their ecstasy.

"I told you," Derek boasted, his head back, eyes darting back and forth across the ceiling. "I told you this was better than any pills." He swung around and around in a circle. When he could no longer keep his footing or balance, Derek flopped to the floor on his back. Fanny and Catina moaned with delight before doing the same.

Tenisha lifted her head as she rolled to her knees. She uncovered her ears. All was quiet. Dust shaped like a chalk outline at a murder scene sullied the hardwood floor. Her skin's secretions caused perfect hallucinations. Her tears caused death. A minor detail Derek didn't know.

Tenisha picked herself up from the floor. The stillness within the cabin was deafening. The absence of sound amplified the memories of the crazed wails that echoed in Tenisha's ears. She would compartmentalize the intensity of the bites from their teeth, the punches from their fists, and the sucking from their lips into a disordered box.

There was nothing else she could do.

Tenisha stumbled to the door and opened it wide. She hitched on a deep breath of moist air. Lightning bugs caught her watery eyes near the trees in the distance. She watched the insects flicker and dim for a while in peaceful silence.

The porch creaked as Tenisha sat down on the first step. She called her mother.

Time to move again.

*END*

# 18

# Extraction

THE SHARP CLICK OF the gold Zippo lighter in Kyle's hand was one of his last anchors to normalcy. A breeze trickled in through the crevices of the single-room cabin, but he did not dare light the twigs in the earthen fireplace for warmth. The chimney smoke it could produce might as well be a neon arrow to his location.

Kyle balanced on his haunches as he rubbed his hands together. The friction generated little warmth. The cold chilled his butt even through his Wrangler jeans. Kyle plopped to the bare wood floor, work boots thumping as he extended his legs, dry mud and bits of Adam flaking off his denim.

He made an internal pinky promise between himself and God that he would make amends, fly straight, and act right. None of these promises had ever come to fruition in his twenty-seven years, but, in his mind, now was a good time to try.

"No more," he grumbled through rattling teeth. For a start in the right direction, he would turn his life around and stop seeing Sheila behind Lorilee's back.

"Okay, don't get stupid," he muttered to himself as he thought briefly about Sheila's double Ds and triple X mind.

He stuffed the lighter in the pocket of his flannel jacket and pulled out fingerless gloves, slipping them on as he flexed his digits.

Kyle grabbed the rucksack to his right and hunted through its contents – an extra T-shirt, blue with a flaking Batterman's logo and *more* faded bits of Adam on the front, a pair of jeans badly in need of a wash. His fingers skimmed over a hard rectangular taped mass in the bottom. Kyle yanked his hand away like he'd touched a hot stove coil. Kyle searched through the front flap pocket, skimming over a dented pack of filter-tipped cigarettes and a passport for the item he sought.

Adam's burner phone.

Kyle pressed the power button and swiped the screen alive. Adam's dried blood crusted on the surface. His hands shook as he stared at the dark ruby smear, remnants of his brother still caked under a few of Kyle's fingernails. The floodgates in his eyes were pushing to their breaking point, but he sucked in a deep breath and exhaled with an audible rush.

*This is not the time to think. Time to do*, Kyle's mind urged.

He couldn't risk keeping the phone powered up for too long. This was his second attempt to send a cellular bread-crumb to his, no Adam's, benefactors. Kyle swiftly tapped Contacts as he had done before. The only saved listing – THE UNITY CORPORATION – came into view. He texted a single word. Simple in its meaning. Slippery in its execution.

EXTRACTION.

Each letter elicited a bop sound as Kyle typed. As soon as the message showed as sent, he turned the phone off and stuffed it in his pocket. Kyle couldn't be sure what exactly he was mixed up with, but he knew the receiver of his message had surveillance capabilities that could pinpoint an ant in the woods.

He assumed the government guys did too.

Kyle patted down his jacket. He couldn't light a fire, but he could light his one remaining joint. The rolled paper spliff felt comforting between his lips. The flame seared the tip as he inhaled.

He let out a mild cough followed by a high-pitched laugh as he spoke into the darkness. "Hello, old friend." He wiped a stray tear from his cheek and wondered how fucked he really might be.

Kyle Batterman drifted through life selling tackle, fishing poles, and bait out of his family's store in the swampy part of NotOnTheMap, Louisiana. Batterman's Tackle Shop regularly catered to stubble-cheeked businessmen more comfortable with a handshake than a fishhook, skull-capped millennials with a performative appreciation for nature, and the locals who hated all of the above. Along with waders, souvenirs, and the standard fishing gear, the store had a very special inventory available to select clientele *by appointment only*.

The flick of the lighter's lid was small, insignificant in the scantily furnished cabin. Kyle fixated on the snap of the metal, thinking through his options in light of the choices made thus far.

Tackle boxes, bladed jigs, and live bait were not Batterman's most lucrative business. The outpost in swampy nowhere had built a reputation for those in the know as purveyors of the finest weed in the South. But it was Adam's craving for more money than weed could produce that would skewer Kyle's reality.

For generations, Batterman's was a fixture in this area. That ended yesterday in a wild explosion that even in this backwater, militia-friendly environment was considered beyond the pale.

"Pigs get fat. Hogs get slaughtered. Ain't that right?" Kyle miffed through a cloud of musky smoke into the cabin's emptiness. It was becoming increasingly clear to him—he needed a

Hail Mary, a miracle in the eleventh hour, his very own *Rudy* moment. What he got was The Unity Corporation, a deal with the devil. *Sinners can't be choosers*, rippled through Kyle's mind, as he breathed in the earthiness around him.

Kyle rubbed his stomach as hunger pangs gripped him hard. The cramps in Kyle's jawline were so intense that his eyes shut, and his cheeks puckered like a lemon tucked between his gums.

"Man, I shouldn't have smoked that joint," he moaned through half-closed eyes. Kyle leaned back against the cabin wall. He ran his hands through his shaggy mop, and then grabbed his rucksack, lumping it between his legs. Two bottles of water and a package of Perky Jerky nestled deep in the bottom. Kyle foraged through to find the salty meat.

His fingers skirted around the edges of the heavily taped brick of bad news.

"Fuck," he whispered.

An image of Adam slumping in the driver's seat blasted into Kyle's mind. He lowered his lids to smother the thought. Kyle couldn't bear holding that memory in his head and wondered how different things would be if he hadn't run out of bullets. He could have erased the memory once and for all. At last, his rummaging fingers found the jerky.

"There you are, you little buggers," he murmured and retrieved the last of his food.

"ALPHA 321, DO YOU copy?" The broad-shouldered man barked, vapor trailing each word. The imposing figure stood erect, his neatly trimmed brown hair just as stiff. He wore a field jacket and matching pants tucked tightly into his tactical boots like a

GI Joe cosplayer gone amok. His outerwear was open, exposing a mossy green thermal shirt that hugged his muscular chest.

The soldiers of fortune he led flanked him in a semi-circle, a visible hammer of authority to be wielded at the commander's discretion. An authority that the townspeople decided to heed when their Jeeps and black-windowed cars rolled into town twenty hours after Batterman's was blown into a pile of tooth-picks.

"Copy." Static punctuated the response to the commander. The voice continued, "Eyes on Weed Wacker. Sheltering in a cabin just southwest of the Copper Swamp. Copy Bravo 1."

The man in charge listened intently to the update. He shook his head as the other sturdy men looked on for cues on how to react to this latest news.

"Alpha 321, hold your position. Out."

"Copy. Out."

The walkie-talkies went silent as the man in charge leaned over the Jeep's hood. He used his index finger to move the 3D satellite image of swampy terrain on the computer screen.

"Okay, listen up, ladies." A muscular fist pounded the metal vehicle. "We are here for a clean, crisp extraction. No frills. Get in. Get out."

The men hovered closely around the stern voice. "No depar-ture from the plan." He paused. "We aren't the only ones looking for him."

He outlined the remainder of the mission with the precision of a scalpel in the same baritone dull roar. The camouflaged mercenaries reacted with the same precision as they moved into their respective positions.

EXTRACTION COULD TAKE 24 to 48 hours, and Kyle wasn't sure he had that long. He scooted into the corner next to the window and lit a cigarette. His hand settled on the bump formed by the drugs in his sack. Kyle knew it was a risk to hold on to the heroin brick, but he had contacts in Picayune, Mississippi. He figured he could make some fast cash, then head to Mexico to lay low with a few Piña coladas and a replacement Sheila.

Kyle closed his eyes. The coolness that shaved the humidity out of the air was the calling card for a good old backyard seafood boil. His mind drifted...a big, metal pot sat sturdy over a wood flame with sausages, new potatoes, and half ears of corn bobbing in the roiling water. He pursed his lips and sucked at the air, slurping the spicy liquid and seasoned meat from a crayfish head in his imaginary feast. Kyle licked his dry lips. Drowsiness was threatening to overtake him.

The snap of a branch outside the cabin jolted Kyle back to wakefulness. His heart hammered his breath right out of his lungs. He stubbed the cigarette into the dusty wood floor, fingers quivering so badly that he singed his index finger pressing on the ember tip. Not that he noticed. Kyle peeked just above the windowsill, his breath shallow with panic.

His eyes adjusted to the tall cypresses on the fringe of the bayou about a half-court distance from the cabin. A sliver of moon hung lazily in the sky, its glimmer shone and winked like it held a secret. The canopy of intertwined foliage was thick like a black cord, but not so thick that Kyle couldn't see a swooping motion winding through the leaves.

He reached for the phone and turned it on. No messages. "That can't be good."

The object disappeared. Trickles of sweat stung Kyle's eyes. The heat of fear swelled in him like a space heater even in the coolness.

The darting object seemed to have vanished as quickly as it appeared. Kyle squinted his eyes.

"It's gotta be a DEA drone. Gotta be." He slapped the side of his face. "Snap out of it, boy."

His muscles relaxed for a fraction of a second until an erratic motion swerved from the periphery into his line of sight. The speed was so fast, Kyle barely had time to scream.

He threw his hands up in a cross-motion and fell backward on his tailbone. Kyle slumped onto his right side. A burst of pain shot through his hip, immobilizing him. He let out a grunt as his left hand tried to press his lower back. He found his butt instead.

Kyle breathed in gulps while his head rested on the wooden floor. He steadily regrouped as the acute pain transitioned to a dull soreness. He stared at the circular pattern of a crack that webbed out across the window above him. He slowly allowed his body to roll on his side.  His eyes focused on the space between the doorframe and the threshold. His stare widened when he realized something was outside the door. A small shadow flopped on the other side.

"For fuck's sake," he groaned. Kyle staggered to his feet and opened the door.

A bat had flown straight for the window.

The drone of his imagination wailed in a high-pitched squeal, almost like a baby's cry, on the porch. Its body lay there, wings extended like a butterfly in a shadow box, its little black eyes motionless as stones. The window had nicked a vital portion of the bat's flesh. A trail of deep brown blood spread from the torso. The belly heaved a few more times, then ceased.

Kyle looked down at the broken creature with sympathy and said, "Last dance for you, buddy," as he closed the door.

He settled back in his corner, wishing he had one more joint left. That bat scared him good, and he needed to calm his nerves. He put his head between his knees and breathed deeply like Sheila did in her yoga class.

Kyle had grown accustomed to the funk that permeated his body. He nuzzled his forehead against his arm without flinching at the musty sweat emanating from his pits. Kyle was nose blind to the barnyard stench and stale urine from his crotch. He hugged his long legs, rocking back and forth, retreating into daydreams of Mexico.

The darkness inside the cabin was static and calm. Kyle grew more restless. He stood and stretched as he peered out the window.

The bat hadn't moved. A scurry of ants had swarmed the blood and disappeared into the fur, excavating its dead eyes. Kyle knew it would only be a matter of time before beetles and flesh-eating flies would join the party to colonize the critter's carcass. The ants came in waves. The feeding frenzy blanketed the soft mound in a well-choreographed danse macabre.

Kyle wondered as he looked down at its lifeless body if there was still a way out of this or if he would be flopping on the same front porch.

The whiz past his right ear as the glass shattered like shredded rain indicated there wasn't.

Shards of window and wood peppered the floor, his hair, and his face courtesy of a bullet from the menace outside. Kyle scrambled into a crouched position. Trying to keep low, he rushed to the other side of the room, dragging his rucksack along the floor. *How low can you go*, whirled maniacally in his mind. A cut on his right hand from the spray of glass bled down his fingertips. Kyle didn't even realize that as he wiped flecks of debris from his blonde hair, he was streaking it a viscous red.

"Dammit!!" He wailed, unashamed of the fear coating his words. "No time to think. Time to do!"

"SHOTS FIRED, SHOTS FIRED," rang into the walkie-talkie.

"Fuck!" The commander muttered. "I'm supposed to get to him first."

### Six Months Earlier

A SAUNA-ESQUE SUMMER HEAT blanketed the air like a moist towel the day that Adam unknowingly, unintentionally, changed Kyle's life.

"Bro, this feels way out there. We ain't done nothin' like this before," Kyle said, sweeping a floppy blonde bang from his forehead.

A few wisps clung to the sweat on his brow. Kyle wiped his soiled hands on his white shirt as he continued to handle containers of fresh worms.

"Do you want to live a little bitty shitty life here in the backwoods forever?" Adam asked, his arms wide like the Fonz in that old TV show.

Kyle rolled his eyes – *Yeah, as a matter of fact, I like my itty bitty shitty life just fine. Me and Lorilee. And riding Sheila on the side.* He waved his brother off with a playful wave of his hand, but his tight-lipped smile told a different story.

"Okay, get to it," Kyle said and then listened as Adam outlined the proposition.

"It's easy. My best weed distributor out of New Orleans laid it out. Real simple. Move some H as a middleman." He took a tobacco pouch from his back pocket, pinched a wad, and stuffed it between his cheeks and gums. "One dude drops it off. I hold it. Then another dude comes and gets it. We are so off the beaten path, ain't nobody gonna snoop out this way." Then he winked and said, "Folks in town know how to mind their own business, so no problem there."

Adam's eyes and hands searched the counter, moving items here and there. "Ah," he said as he turned to the register. He grabbed a red plastic cup and spat a glop of brown juice into it.

"It's perfect," Kyle said with a sarcastic edge from his high stool behind the cash register. "This gig is sooo easy it'll be smooth sailing." He extended his hand in a floating motion.

"Yeah, like I said. Easy," Adam mimicked.

*Easy?* Kyle shook his head, irritated. *Yeah, easy like the check-kiting scheme that Dad had to smooth over for you a few years back. Or easy like when you sold fake moonshine to tourists who didn't know any better until one of them did. Almost fucked up the real weed business with the threat of lawsuits. And that one took a lot of smoothing over from Dad and a visit by local law enforcement to that North Face-wearing motherfucker to remind him who he was dealing with.* Sheriff Knox and his deputized thugs were always up for tourist abatement, but it was one more favor Dad owed because of Adam.

Kyle was not surprised at how loosely his brother interpreted the word 'easy' – achieved without great effort—with the meaning's inherent benefits falling on Adam's side of the ledger. Never mind that his schemes and dealings were the antithesis of 'easy' and made things more difficult for everyone around him. Kyle was glad Dad wasn't around for this mess. Not the weed mess – their father was the enterprising mind who first cultivated it – but for Adam's newest, next-level fuck up.

Exasperated, Kyle responded, "Yeah, man, but—" The bell dinged above the front door. Kyle greeted the customer. "Hey, Mr. Booker."

The elderly black man removed his tattered hat to reveal a silver head of hair that looked almost regal. "Just need some of those fishhooks like I got before. You remember the ones?"

Adam responded, "Sure do."

A few more customers trickled in. Mr. Booker took his items over to Adam, who rang him up as they continued to exchange easygoing pleasantries.

"Hope the fish are bitin' good for ya today, Mr. Booker."

"I sure hope so, too, young man. The Copper Swamp can be as fickle as a woman." He chuckled. "Would you mind double-bagging that for me? Headed to the farmers market over in Calcasieu Parish. Want to keep them in one piece 'til I get home."

"Sure thing, Mr. Booker." Adam wrapped the hooks in a plastic bag and stuffed them in a brown bag.

Mr. Booker tipped his hat and said, "Thanks very much, young man." The doorbell jingled as he left.

Kyle strode to the door and flipped the sign to CLOSED. He turned to Adam, hoping his glare would pierce Adam to the core, but his brother simply raised an eyebrow.

Kyle sighed and asked, "Do you have any idea who these 'dudes,'" using air quotes, "are? Do you?" He paced in front of the counter.

"Kyle, you sure seem to enjoy the cash from the side hustle without getting filthy. Let's keep it that way. I know what I'm doing," he snapped. "Besides, the New Orleans folks have connections. If the Feds or anyone gets too close, I can reach out for help cleaning things up."

Kyle stopped in his tracks and leaned on the counter square with Adam. "Like a get out of jail free card?"

"Something like that." Adam fluffed Kyle's shaggy hair and firmly patted his cheek. "Those folks will always protect their interest. That means protecting me, too." Adam punched keys on the register, and the drawer sprung open. He slipped a few twenties out, folded them, and tucked them in his front pocket. "You worry too much little bro."

By the time the leaves turned brown, and the air prickled the skin, things with the New Orleans folks had gone very wrong.

*Two days ago*

KYLE SAT IN THE shop's backroom with Adam. It was a crisp Saturday evening. Kyle tugged at his flannel jacket, nervous and anxious. "Man, I swear I'm being followed." He slid his rucksack from his shoulder to the floor.

"Don't get hinky." Adam focused intently, almost aggressively, on loading his rifle. "Things are fine." Below his breath, he whispered, "They can't possibly know."

Kyle studied his big brother, his worry building. "Know what?"

Adam lowered his eyes. His chin followed. He loaded the rifle, laying it on the table.

Back when Kyle was in the fifth grade and Adam was in the eighth, he remembered a punk ass kid challenged Adam to a fight after school. Adam was boisterous and confident in his trash talk, but Kyle knew that he saw a glimpse of terror in his eyes right before he successfully beat that boy down. The same terror surfaced in Adam's eyes that evening, but this time it was a sustained, palpable fear, not a fleeting one. This time, Kyle believed Adam knew he was going to lose.

"I might have cheated the...ah...I think I," Adam blustered. "Oh man!" He rested his head in his hands and uttered the dangerous truth. "I skimmed some of the H I was holding. I think they know."

The words hung there like a rope.

Adam never fully suffered any consequences in his almost thirty years of kicking around this earth. If it wasn't their father fixing what Adam had broken, it was dumb luck and arrogant charm that got him the rest of the way.

Kyle slumped against the table, the rifle shifting with his weight. *Oh fuck, oh fuck, oh fuck.* He sucked in his breath, the whistling soft inside the room. As Kyle exhaled, he stood straight, squaring his frame as he crossed his arms.

He stared at Adam. He couldn't find the words. Kyle doubted it mattered anymore. He peered out the window at the thick row of cypress trees just beyond the dirt patch outside. Kyle squinted his eyes. The moon shone, casting shadows in the distance.

Shadows that had grown legs.

A blast engulfed the front of the store, cutting Kyle's silent observation. The roof collapsed on the left side of the building. Tackle, bait, and rods flew in every direction in the backroom. Worms wiggled out of dirt containers. Adam missed the brunt of the debris, unhurt, with his rifle in hand. Kyle collided with the back door but was able to keep his wits about him.

Smoke and flames began licking at the interior. The brothers burst through the backroom door, greeted by four men in camouflage. Guns drawn.

Even under duress, Adam was a good shot. He got three of them in quick succession. The remaining one withdrew to a nearby tree while the brothers ran in the other direction for Adam's truck.

Bullets ricocheted and pinged the vehicle. The truck's body shook as air burst from the front tires. "What the hell?" Kyle screamed, shaking Adam. "Start the car, start the —"

*How did I miss that?* Kyle realized one of the bullets had found Adam's chest. Blood scrolled down the front of his torso and soaked his flannel. Kyle reached over to drag Adam from the car. His shallow breaths gave Kyle hope.

"Come on out!" The voice from the trees yelled. "We can talk!"

The night was still and quiet as the disembodied voice seemingly waited to negotiate. Adam was fading as quickly as the tears that rushed down Kyle's face. "Hang on bro, hang on!" Kyle screeched. Adam's last words would haunt him.

"Dad's gone. I'll be gone soon. You don't have anyone anymore. I'm sorry." Adam's glassy stare and wide-open mouth would be how Kyle would remember his big brother for all of posterity.

"Time to do," Kyle whispered. He could mourn Adam later, but now he needed to stay alive long enough to do that. Kyle clutched the rifle and shakily opened the passenger door, slipping behind it for cover. His bloody fingers slid into the trigger.

Kyle sucked in and decided he had no choice, and one bullet left. He mentally triangulated the distance and location of the voice and used all of his hunting knowledge for the most important shot of his life.

FROM THE PORCH, FLASHLIGHTS swept across the cabin's interior. Kyle huddled in the far back corner behind a plaid gold and orange armchair to escape the glare. He had seconds to move it before whoever was outside made their grand entrance. His fingers feverishly searched the floor for a metal ring fastened to the wood as another bullet came through the front door.

Pulling the sack onto his back, he crouched and tugged at the heavy ring. The square opening led under the cabin. The undercarriage of the shack was a dark crawl space. It smelled of years of damp leaves and swamp critters that had made this dank space its last resting place.

If the goons from the front were also out back, this would be the end of the road. If they didn't notice that the cabin was raised off the ground because flooding was the rule, not the exception, in this area, he had a chance.

Kyle scrambled into the opening, but the strap of his sack caught on the dry, splintering wood. The sound of glass shattering distracted him for a second. The chair obscured his body, but it wouldn't afford him protection for long. Kyle tugged violently as he jolted upright and slipped the bag off.

The normally sturdy wooden front door cracked under the weight of the uninvited guests. The thunderous thump indicated the door had become unhinged by a pressure mightier than Kyle could deal with. He dropped into the hole smoothly and without much effort. Kyle half believed that God was guiding him in the cup of his hand.

A thunderous tremble shook the cabin as the door gave way. At that moment, Kyle knew God had fled the building. *You're on your own, kid*, Kyle imagined as His parting words. He stuffed the bag in the hole and reached for the door cover.

The sound of heavy-footed boots stomping filled the space. Kyle saw lights flashing from side to side as he gently closed the trap door above him.

Firmly on his belly, he inched forward. Kyle winced and spat as his face pushed into spider webs, and fat, juicy tree roaches buzzed around his ears. Kyle's many years in a bait and tackle shop did not increase his tolerance of bugs. As he neared the edge of the cabin, he squinted into the mass of trees that lined the back end of the property.

He listened. To his surprise, the sound of footsteps retreated. Kyle lay still, eyes shifting from side to side like a mouse about to make a break for freedom from a barn cat.

Kyle eased himself from under the house, secured his rucksack over his shoulders, and ran like mad. The branches smacked his face as he scurried headlong into the woods. He got about 100 yards when he heard a booming shout in the night, followed by a light trained on him.

"Adam? That you?"

Kyle heard a low, reverberating voice with weight and power in its tone. He ducked, scrambled to the tree trunk ahead of him, and used the base as a hiding place. Kyle panted as he swiveled his head to gauge the direction and nearness of the voice.

He covered his mouth to tamp down his heavy breathing. He realized a second too late there was a smashed roach stuck to his hand from his adventures under the cabin. His gulps of air sucked the bug into his mouth and down his throat. Kyle swallowed hard and began the journey of mind over matter to avoid throwing up.

The voice spoke again from the darkness. "You called for an extraction?"

The rush of tears came fast and without reservation in a way that Kyle wasn't expecting. He pushed himself up from the ground, holding onto the tree for balance. He peeked from behind the tree trunk. The shadow stood about 20 feet away, parallel to Kyle. The man's figure was imposing, even with the tall cypress trees all around them.

Kyle walked out from his hiding place, wiping his wet face. He looked at the broad-shouldered man, who stood before him shrouded in the dark shadows of nature. Kyle melted with relief. "Yes? Extraction, oh God, yes, extraction!"

The broad man stood with a wide stance, arms crossed. Kyle wasn't sure if it was hunger or adrenaline or a combination of both, but he felt jumpy.

"You're not Adam." The man's tone was quizzical, yet hard like a principal asking for a hall pass but giving you detention anyway because he could.

"Well, no. I'm his brother. Kyle. I'm the one who sent the text."

"Where is Adam?" The tone had turned edgier, a bit more combative.

Kyle strained through the dim mass of trees to see if he could read the man's face. All he could make out was his neatly trimmed hair illuminated by a slice of moonlight. It almost made Kyle laugh with madness to think this guy was as neat as a cucumber sandwich in these backwoods, but he kept his frayed emotions in check.

Kyle had approximately zero choices before him, so he decided this man's fine head of hair was enough to trust him. He answered truthfully. "Adam was killed back at the bait shop." He hesitated. "Yesterday." The weight of the words slayed him inside.

The man nodded. "Hmm. Come on. No time to lose," he commanded. "Keep straight ahead. I'll cover you from the back. Look for headlights up ahead."

Kyle walked unevenly on the terrain. His head bobbed with the giddiness of a man snatched from an alligator's jaws in the nick of time.

"Oh man, am I glad to see you," he half-whispered, mostly wept. "Goons were breaking into the cabin, and guns were going off, and I think I might have shot someone back at the bait shop, and—" Kyle stopped and turned around.

The looming figure stopped as well.

A sinking feeling rushed into Kyle's stomach. He leaned against a nearby tree to steady himself.

"Are you okay? We need to get going." The voice said with a low rumble.

The canopy of the trees shielded most of the light but not all of it. Enough light existed for Kyle to see the truth gripped in the man's hand, a finger snug inside the trigger.

Kyle's body tensed up, and his feet planted into the ground like the gun was Medusa and he had turned to stone. His heart thudded like a wild buck in his chest.

Kyle's isolation was as thick and bleak as the night blanketing him and the gunslinger. The cabin used to be a slice of heaven tucked away off the Copper Swamp where his world was no bigger than one stoplight down the middle of town. The wider world's rules were a true unknown to Kyle outside his *itty, bitty shitty, life* that he wouldn't grasp until someone pointed a gun in his face. Under the moonlight, Kyle would finally admit, even if this was the most inopportune time to admit it...he let himself believe this would all be so easy.

"I didn't *really* have anything to do with the business. That was all Adam." He choked on his words. Kyle stuttered, "You're supposed to help. That's what A-A-Adam said." The tears came again, but these didn't bring a release of relief. They brought understanding.

The figure had stepped forward just a touch, enough for Kyle to see. For his mind to comprehend what his eyes could see.

*Camouflage!* Screamed through Kyle's mind. *The camouflage!* Kyle swayed like he'd been rope-a-doped in the ninth round.

"I swear, I don't know anyth—"

THE LANKY FELLOW WITH floppy blondc hair, known as Kyle Batterman, fell in a heap in front of the commander. The gunshot between Kyle's eyes rang out into the swamp, not that anyone would notice.

The man crouched next to Kyle. Just to be sure. He held his nose and waved away as much of the urine and shit odor as he could. Staring down at Kyle's body, he said, "Well. Greedy is what greedy does, my friend."

He was mildly irritated that this mission even existed. *How could two good old boys in the middle of nowhere cause so much trouble*, was his main question when he was handed the assignment.

His employers out of the Big Easy felt played like fiddles and otherwise pissed, and it was up to him to scrub the problem. The alphabet soup of agencies had been investigating Batterman's for a few months. They were set to come and take their prize, but the commander got there first.

The man stood, got his bearings, and started walking. He could smell the brackish water and the movements of nocturnal creatures up above. He peered through the tree trunks to catch a glimpse of the Copper Swamp and made a mental note to advise the clean-up crew to use the natural surroundings for disposal.

He would personally use the swamp as a teachable moment for the scaredy cat, idiot who took aim at a bat, causing that bat to collide with the target's location's exterior window, nearly giving away their position. He would take great pleasure in that.

As he made his way back to ground zero, he hit the button on his walkie-talkie. The static announced his presence to his team at the other end.

"Extraction complete. Out."

**END**

# 19

# Things Are as They Should Be

2025 HORROR2COMIC SEMIFINALIST / 2024 KILLER SHORTS SCREENPLAY COMPETITION FINALIST

"EENY, MEENY, MINY—"

The planks underneath Max's worn boots squawked but stood firm despite the age of the attic floor. His index finger drifted in a maestro's wave over dented boxes and bins, then stopped at the steamer chest, the kind of vintage mind fuck that would hold moth-bitten blankets and abandoned trinkets in a normal family. Max eyed it with the same enthusiasm he reserved for brussels sprouts and moved on.

The terms of the will were clear. The inheritors would not have the right to "use" and "enjoy" the property as owners, according to the Law Offices of Thibodeaux, Johnson, and Walker, if a series of tasks were not performed in the order listed. *Line the doorsteps with grave dust. Cover the mirrors with a drop cloth. Separate and bundle sprigs of thyme.* Second to last on the list – *find the cameo.*

Through the marching of time and the stealth introduction of latte shops and Birkenstocks, the red line of segregation had disappeared, and now the home on Prentiss Avenue held worth. The prospect of gaining a home that had seen better days but was geographically lucky meant nothing to Max.

He recalled how Lucy had spoken of legacy, of what was once taken from the *gens de couleur libres* — free people of color — who constructed the Reconstruction, with a swipe of a legislative pen. "This inheritance is not ours to give away. It's ours to protect. We are the last ones who can give it a rebirth." Lucy was insistent.

Max was content to let the pile of bricks and melancholy fade into the hands of the State of Louisiana and invite bureaucracy to do the rest. But she had a point.

Persuasion and latent sentiments guided Max to say 'yes' with his mouth but not with his heart.

The sun's brightness spilled into the space, creating a runway of light down the center of the small room. Max strode past the wooden trunk to the boxes labeled *Miscellaneous* next to the arched window. He examined boxes bulging with coffee-stained doilies and homemade quilts with frayed trim. Others contained a graveyard of various vases. He barely caught the blue bud version that slipped from his fingers as he turned it over. Searching. Max confirmed that the item he was hunting for was not tucked away in any of these cardboard time capsules.

He pushed down on the packing paper and soft furnishing to crisscross close the lids. The old dingy chest loomed in his periphery. *Nothing I need is in there,* floated, high and mighty, in his mind. *Nothing.*

The creak of sticky hinges floated to the top of the stairs, followed by the soft bounce of tennis shoes. Lucy came into view on the top step. "Did you find it, or did you get lost up here?" Her white tank was streaked with greyish smudges. Lucy's top confirmed the first item on the list, grave dust lining the doorsteps, was handled.

Max didn't inquire about the dust's origins. He assumed the nearness of St. Louis Cemetery No. 1 proved useful with its ornate mausoleums guarded by stone crosses and weeping angels watching disapprovingly over the good times rolling in the streets of New Orleans.

Max stared, assessing Lucy's toned, brown figure, mess and all. He mentally flogged himself for the thought and shrugged, "I know. I had one job."

"I finished my part of the list," she announced. "Two more to go."

Max nodded and drew in a deep breath, attempting to loosen the tightening in his chest. He patted his upper body and wondered why this morbid scavenger hunt had his nerves on edge like a wild NASCAR race through his veins. He tamped down the growing disillusion that legacy was not a worthwhile pursuit in this case, but didn't want Lucy to see him waver. Max decided to keep those thoughts at bay for now.

Lucy rubbed her bare arms. "I'll look over here." She pivoted in the direction of the wooden chest and halted. She leaned in with her body for a closer look, but her brown eyes did the heavy lifting. She glanced back at Max with a half-smile, then began systematically opening plastic bins stacked along the wall.

She came up snake eyes as well.

They moved about the attic, saying nothing, but thinking everything. The last time Max and Lucy occupied this attic space was meant as a punishment for attracting the attention of a well-meaning guidance counselor with too many meddlesome questions to their front door, the penalty for allowing outsiders in.

For Max, the reprimand, in the quiet and the still of those walls, was an awakening. An unexpected awakening filled with unspeakable delight. He wondered for many years after if Lucy ever dwelled on that night as obsessively as he had. If she did, it was locked in the far reaches of her mind.

After several minutes of hunting, it was clear that the last thing they wanted to do needed to be done. "Are you going to check the chest?" Max asked.

"What?" Lucy questioned, slow and deliberate. "It wouldn't be in there." Max recognized the tone in Lucy's voice immediately. It was the same tone she used when they were kids to prod him into stealing tomatoes from the neighbor's garden or skipping school. Or telling tales to the school counselor.

"For God's sake," Max snapped, then wished he could take it back, hug her. Be with her. *Stop it,* beat in his head.

Max slumped into a cross-legged position. Lucy stood taut behind him as he pushed the lid open. A sliver of sunlight fanned over the knicks and knacks of their childhood.

Comic books stacked neatly to one side, jacks and rubber balls scattered in all corners, an old blues album by a nobody called Josephus Brownstone, whom they were told was kin to them. The only truth they were ever told.

Max rummaged. Lucy reluctantly joined him. One by one, they picked over artifacts, but mostly sat in quiet reverence with their fractured childhood memories.

"What do we have here?" Max held up an old Lipton tea canister. The patinaed and rusted tin was the size of a hardcover book, dented on the left side where the body met the lid.

"I don't remember this," Lucy said. She rubbed her hands with curious anticipation. "Open it."

Max hugged the canister for leverage and pried the cover off. The flat sound of objects knocked the sides.

"Umm, interesting." He thumbed over a dingy Zippo lighter, an amber charm with a gold chain, and a handful of opaque salt crystals. He raised the tin to his nose to smell a small glass jar with a silver lid that contained a thick white substance. "Huh, lavender cream," he commented. The movement caused the jar to slide and reveal a coarse drawstring burlap pouch snuggled underneath the hodgepodge.

Max placed the tin on the floor and fiddled with the bag. He wedged two fingers into the tight opening and promptly received a prick to the pointer finger for his troubles. "Dammit!" A bulb of blood shimmered on the tip. Max sucked the pinprick dry.

"Let me see." Lucy held Max's finger to examine it, blowing gently on the skin. "Does it—" Her words clipped as he unceremoniously removed his hand from her grip.

"I'm sorry," Max uttered, avoiding the hurt circling Lucy's eyes.

"I was just trying to help," Lucy said, faintly.

Max turned his attention to the pouch and tipped it over. A cameo fell, easy as you please, into his palm.

The black background was overlaid with dual figures. At the forefront, an ivory silhouette of a woman wrinkled like a Brothers Grimm crone. A man's face lurked behind the profile of the first, equally as wrinkled, his nose and forehead as off-putting as the woman's.

Max noted the jagged notch on the pendant's filigree edge that caused his injury. His blood still clung to the curves. Etched on the back was a complex highway of lines and symbols screaming out its own ideographic language, encircled by the looping script, *Things are as they should be.*

"Bastards," Max quipped.

"Is that..." Lucy asked.

"Yep," Max answered, "mark it off the list." He raised the carved relief, "Looks expensive." He flipped it in his hand. "Figures those two coots would forge their stupid faces into a fucking piece of—"

"Stop it!" Lucy begged.

Max rubbed her shoulder and said, "Breathe. One thing left on the list. Then we're done." Just as Max leaned closer to Lucy's smooth brown skin, a bang like a bass drum filled the attic. They turned with a jolt.

The door had slammed shut.

A coolness seeped into the small space that now seemed cramped and suffocating to Max. "Let's get on with this. What's the last thing?"

Lucy brushed a chunk of her soft, coiled brown hair behind her ear. She pulled the checklist typed on law office letterhead, in all of its bullet form glory, from her jeans pocket. Lucy unfolded the sheet and bowed her head to read, but gradually lifted her eyes to Max.

"Final item," the smile like an isolated movement that didn't reach any other part of her face, "is our legacy." She pointed with conviction, a conviction that Max did not realize had quietly taken root in his Lucy.

"Whoa!" The cameo trembled in Max's hand as the ivory silhouettes turned a beet red. Lucy backed away from his outstretched hand like she was giving whatever was about to happen room to grow.

"This is not possible!" Max's words hung like a rope in the air.

"It *is* possible because," Lucy sighed, "The vèvè was meant for you. It *NEEDS* you. You're the last piece."

The vèvè. The beacon to invoke spirits rested in his hand.

Max threw the wicked charm to the ground and scrambled to his feet, yanking Lucy up with him. "What the fuck is going on?" He grabbed her by the shoulders as if a good shake would dislodge them both from this completely insane situation. The list in Lucy's hand fluttered and fell languidly to the floor.

Lucy's glassy affect was in sheer contrast to Max's rising manic terror. Her lithe frame swayed like a used car inflatable, lips slightly ajar, ready for an 'oh' or a scream to escape.

Max knew he was losing her.

"I remember when I first learned of what was to come." Lucy exhaled and clasped Max's hand as if to share a tender moment.

He yanked it away.

"I thought you might react this way," Lucy declared, that prodding tone surfacing and coating each syllable. "We all thought you might, that's why we waited until they were gone, and you were ready. And you are." Lucy tried to take Max's hand again, but he recoiled. She didn't seem to notice. "I promise you, it is wonderful what is about to happen. The Man and the Woman chose us because we are the Alpha and the Omega. Please, Max, let go and let it happen."

"We can fight this," he yelled. "They can't control us anymore!" Max's mind swirled.

Lucy laughed, a full robust gaggle of chuckles that caught Max off guard. "Why would I ever want to do that?" She cocked her head. "My eyes were always open to the truth of, of..." She gave Max a cheeky wink as if she were sharing an inside joke. "You had to have known."

Max gasped like a punch had been firmly planted into his stomach. *This messed up, fever dream of a joke is REAL,* slammed through his temples.

"Oh, you didn't know back then, did you?" Lucy shook her head like a disappointed PTA mom, and Max was the disappointment.

"How? How could I have?" Max stuttered.

"Intuition, maybe. What's that Sesame Street song? One of these things is not like the other?" She softened her voice further. "Did we ever feel 'right' except when we were doing something wrong?"

Max pleaded, "Please, Lucy, let's go. We can build a life or something close to it." Now he did take her hand and hoped it would be enough.

"They will never let us go. You have to know that." Lucy paused. "Because things are as they should be. That's why we were brought here from so far away." Her heavy words, followed by a listless smile, chilled Max despite the balmy heat seeping in through the crevices.

They. The Man and the Woman who kidnapped Maxwell Booker and Lucille Brownstone three days and two states apart, sleep still in their little eyes. The coming deceit was unknowable in their young minds, its reverberations felt decades later in a musty attic room.

The house where the lies were conjured on Prentiss Avenue held its own with the other beautiful and strange homes on the block. As the memories before Prentiss were erased, Max and Lucy only knew life as brother and sister. But the kids at school knew. The counselor knew. The way Max and Lucy walked hand in hand down the halls, everyone knew. Something. But they didn't know everything. Neither did Max until the will was read, the theft of their innocence revealed to his horror. And relief.

But it was only the beginning. He could see that now.

Max trembled as a shift occurred in his mind. One he could feel but was stifled from giving voice to it. Max peered at Lucy and recognized the Woman's determined eyes staring at him. He wondered if the Man's intensity shone in his.

Max stumbled backward and into the realization that Lucy had engineered the ritual of the Man and the Woman's last wishes. To a tee. "Restoring the Man and the Woman will be painful but necessary," Lucy advised like a spirited docent from hell. "There was a reason they chose us, but first things first", she whispered.

A wetness slithered across Max's cheek in the form of Lucy's fingertips, if you could call them that at this point in time. His groin ached as his body stiffened. The mix of pleasure and pain made him weep.

"This is evil," choked from Max's throat.

"Evil? As opposed to good?" Lucy's face softened as if a veil of understanding for Max's predicament had been lifted only to fall just as easily. "Such a binary concept." She stood between Max and the drowning sunlight. "What we've been granted is neither good nor evil. It doesn't work that way. It just *IS*."

Lucy bopped Max's forehead with the palm of her hand the way Sunday morning preachers do when filled with the holy spirit. Max fell, flailed really, for what seemed like ages, and landed on the hard floor.

His bones didn't break. Only his mind.

As the sun gave way to incoming fringes of twilight, anyone watching from the outside could see the shadows contorting within the arched window. But it didn't matter. Everyone outside knew what Prentiss Avenue concealed, what manner of beautiful and strange could occur, and knew not to interfere because...

Things are as they should be.

***END***

# About the Author

P.M. Raymond is an award-winning author from New Orleans, Louisiana who knows a thing or two about good gumbo, grits, and café au lait. She is a 2025 Killer Shorts Screenplay and Horror2Comic Semifinalist, the Sisters in Crime 2024 Eleanor Taylor Bland Award Winner, 2024 Claymore Award Finalist, and 2024 Killer Shorts Screenplay Finalist. Her work has appeared in *Ellery Queen Mystery Magazine*, *Writer's Digest*, *Punk Noir*, *Flash Fiction Magazine*, and *Dark Yonder*, among others.

When she isn't thinking up new ways to unsettle her readers, she can be found touching grass and learning French.

Find more about P.M. Raymond at her website: https://www.pmraymond.com/

## Acknowledgements
I published my first short story in 2019, and I never looked back. Through the challenges of finding my voice and finally feeling

comfortable with expressing it, I have had the support of a kind and generous community. Many thanks to:

My critique group – Sue Anger, E Senteio, Beth Walker, and Ashley-Ruth M. Bernier. I am grateful for your guidance through the rejections and the jubilations of every story you reviewed.

Authors whose kindness and generosity made a difference in how I saw myself as a writer – Sara E. Johnson, Karen Pullen, Diane Kelly, Melissa Bourbon, S.T. Schorey, Steph Nelson, and Tamika Thompson.

The professionals who were among the first to choose my stories and made me believe in the value of my work – the editors at Dark Yonder, Eryk Pruitt and Katy Munger, the editor at Writer's Digest – Amy Jones, and Alison Parker at Killer Shorts Screenplay Competition.

And last, my Mom and Dad, my sister Elisia, and my twin Paula. Their love and support mean everything.

Each season writes its own chapter. To all those who have lifted me up during this journey, I look forward to the next chapter with you.

# Also By Uncomfortably Dark Horror

**ANTHOLOGIES**
**Uncomfortably Dark presents The Baker's Dozen**-2021 Dark Dozen anthology & the 2022 Splatterpunk award-winning extreme horror anthology.
**Uncomfortably Dark presents Trapped**-2022 Dark Dozen anthology that explores themes of horror focused on being trapped in an unspeakable situation.
**Uncomfortably Dark presents Dark Disasters**-2023 Dark Dozen anthology that explores horrific situations unfolding during natural disasters.
**Uncomfortably Dark presents Full Throttle**-2025 Dark Dozen Anthology that is a full-blown extreme horror anthology dedicated to survivors of sexual violence.
*This anthology contains no scenes of sexual violence.*
**The Generator**-quad collaboration anthology featuring Candace Nola, Eric Butler, M Ennenbach, and Nikolas P. Robinson.
**Dark Disturbances**- 2024 Uncomfortably Dark Author Sampler Anthology.
**Dark Asylum** – 2025 Uncomfortably Dark Author Sampler Anthology.
**At Midnight, They Feast** – 2025 Mini-Halloween Anthology featuring Cassandra Celia, Candace Nola, and Cat Delani

## **<u>NOVELS & COLLECTIONS</u>**
EPISODES OF VIOLENCE by David Bernstein
DREAMWHISPERS by M Ennenbach
CREMATED REMAINS by M Ennenbach
CUCKOO by M Ennenbach
OLD TOO SOON by Brian Bowyer
BLACKOUT: MICROPOETRY by Brian Bowyer
INNOCENCE ENDS by Nikolas P. Robinson
HAVE A BLAST by Nikolas P. Robinson
COME OUT & PLAY by Patrick Tumblety
ROADS TO RUIN by Brian Bowyer
SUBJECT A by M Ennenbach
OIOS LYKOS by M Ennenbach
STORYSLAVE by Brian Bowyer
VERUM MALUM by Michael R. Collins
SLENDER BONES IN SACRED SOIL by Fredrick Niles
THIS IS HOW A VILLAIN IS MADE by Amanda Headlee
ONE FRIGHT ONLY by Patrick Tumblety
WHITE FLIGHT by Peter O'Keefe
BADLANDS by Jason Nickey

# Note On A.I.

We live in an age of AI. It is all around us. Every day, more ser-
vices arrive, promising revolutionary results that utilize artificial
intelligence. No industry is immune to this.

I want every one of my readers to know that not once did I
employ, nor will I ever employ, the use of AI to craft any part of
my stories. The ability to create is a gift that I will never forfeit
nor set aside to propagate something synthetic and imitative.

Everything you've read by me in this novel, and in my other
works, is 100% authentically created by me, and always will be.
I cherish the gift of creating imaginative work on my own terms
and through the struggle that sometimes comes with this gift.
If you are a writer, may you be incredibly successful, whatever
success looks like to you, utilizing your own mind and abilities.

Sincerely,

P.M. Raymond

## Note from the Author

If you enjoyed this book, a positive review would mean the world to me. Like other indie authors, I rely heavily on word-of-mouth recommendations to reach new readers. I am grateful for every single review. Each one offers an opportunity for me to grow as a writer. If you enjoyed this book, I am incredibly thankful for your support, and I hope you'll continue with me on this journey.

Thank you for reading!

One last thing: If you'd like one more short story to send chills down your spine, sign up for my Substack at pmraymond.subs tack.com. You'll find a little lagniappe with a flash fiction story called Oxygen Rich Tears. https://pmraymond.substack.com/

www.ingramcontent.com/pod-product-compliance
Lightning Source LLC
Chambersburg PA
CBHW021349150726
47989CB00005B/2166